THE SHIMMERING

Reign

ROBIN WITNEY

THE SHIMMERING: Reign

Copyright © 2021 by Robin Witney.

www.robinwitney.com

ISBN:

DEDICATION

Dedicated to everyone fighting life-threatening diseases and those who have fault back to stay with us, and BP4u Solutions for providing brilliant editing, formatting, and publishing services.

PROLOGUE

THE POLICE HAD MADE THE CONFERENCE ROOM a crime scene. Conrad announced that the conference would be continued in the staff canteen on the fourth floor. Stephen added, "Due to what has just happened, you will all be thoroughly searched. If you have any problems with that, I suggest you leave now." None did, and it took about 20 minutes to reassemble the press and a further 35 minutes to finish the press conference. I told them I only had 15 minutes for questions as I had a plane to catch. Conrad was right; all the questions were about the attack and the assignation attempt. I could not give them anything since it was a police matter—as soon as the police had something, it would be shared. I took one more question, about how I felt about the attack and how my family had taken it. I said, "We were all shocked, but with the security that I have, I am confident they will keep us all safe. Please read the press release; there are some significant science facts that your readers will want to know." I left the canteen and made my way to my transport. It would only take 25 minutes to get to Flint, Texas. Stephen was staying with me—he was not letting me out of his sight; he would be my shadow for the foreseeable future. I had mind contact with Sue and told her that our biggest fear was coming true and that I was on my way to Texas. I am fine. The assassination attempt was an occupational hazard, I transmitted to her, downplaying the whole thing. I will see you tonight, and we signed off.

Stephen said, "I am sure I recognise the assassin, but I just can't remember."

"It will all be known in time. We have more pressing things to worry about; our doomsday scenario has just begun."

We exited the verticular and went directly to the lab. Dave Mac and his team were so engrossed in what they were doing, and June, who was the only one to see us arrive, tapped him on the shoulder and pointed. He turned around and got up from his chair, which was immediately filled by someone. The four of us walked back to his house, and June asked whether we wanted some coffee. I asked for a beer, as it was over 42 degrees outside. We went into his study, where the air-con was flat out—the room still seemed warm, though. The last three weeks of his reports showed strange fish movements. The entire Northern Pacific fishing fleets had to travel vast distances to catch fish. Whales were in the wrong place for this time of year—in fact, all activity in the ocean around the Trench had moved as far south-west as they could.

Dave fired up his computer that showed the sensors on the ocean floor. They had started to pick up vibrations that intensified minute by minute now. I asked, "are you sure?" He nodded, "Well, I have some calls to make," I said.

CHAPTER 1

OBLIVION HAD LEFT OUR GALAXY to get stronger. He fed off evil, and Earth—being the only inhabited planet in our galaxy—had prevailed over evil. He knew the convergence would help, in minimising the impact of his super enriched hydrogen magma bubble. He had created it to get rid of both humans and Utopians. Choosing a peaceful existence would only make the convergence stronger, and it would be impossible to defeat Infinity to conjoin with Eternity.

Both races had to go. He had well thought out his plan to destroy Earth. Knowing the weakest points of Earth—the Plains of North America—he knew the convergence would alter and slow the direction of the magma bubble, so it would erupt in the Pacific. The obvious choice had to be the Mariana Trench, the deepest part of the Pacific Ocean. The fact of slowing and redirecting the bubble was part of his plan and was part of a catastrophic trick that they would succumb to the tear in the Trench, where the bubble was now to erupt into. The flow was so slow that it would seal the tear—the cold and pressure at that depth would ensure a complete seal. The magma would start backing up, and before they could do anything about it, the enriched magma bubble would ram the backed-up magma, causing an enormous underground explosion that would completely wipe out Utopia. The explosion would alter the Earth's orbit and put it on a collision course with the moon. Nothing could survive this collision, and it would only be hours after the explosion. Oblivion's problem with Earth was sorted.

CHAPTER 2

THE PRESS WERE INFORMED that the assassin was female, and we were using them to see if they could trace the female or male identities. The only name they had was on the press pass for the conference. Although the pass was bone fide, the details on it were completely fictitious. A photo fit of both profiles was made and circulated via the media.

The news of the assassination attempt had spread around the world quickly. It was headline news in every country that an unknown male had tried—and failed—to kill the head of Earth Corp and was shot at the scene. A leak at Scotland Yard had said that the attacker was female, under the guise of a male. They were trying to get photo fit likeness of both male and female identities and release them to the press; this also went round the world quickly.

Alberto's phone rang at his bedside. Only a select few had this number. Since the last fiasco with the New York police department, he had no fear about phone taps, and his bedroom was scanned several times a day for bugs. On the other end of the call was the president of the Cayman Brac bank. "Have you seen the news? Geflin been shot and killed." He was a little startled as the name meant nothing to him and said so. "This woman sold you Enrico's drug empire." Recognition came immediately.

"Who killed her?" he asked.

"Earth Corp security."

"Damn shame. She was one hell of a woman."

"Why don't you come over to Cayman Brac? I have a deal, and, really, we need to be face-to-face."

"I am too busy just to drop everything at the moment."

"I can give you 700 million reasons why you should make it a priority."

There was a pause. "I will see you tomorrow afternoon."

"Let me know your ETA and we will fly down to my beach house."

Alberto told his consigliere to charter an aircraft to Cayman Brac. "We need to be there tomorrow afternoon." All was arranged, and the President of the bank flew them to his beach house. He showed them to his study, supplied them with drinks, and got down to business. "The $700 million you paid Geflin, most of it still is in my bank.

However, it is not in her account, as we were hacked. The funds that Enrico had at this bank were transferred to Geflin's account. Overnight it was hacked. The full amount went to Earth Corp Swiss bank, I have subsequently found out"

"How did they do it?"

"I have my best people working on it, and so far, they've come up with zilch. To get that money back could take years of legal wrangling and only the lawyers will get rich. It's dead money. The bulk of the money is available for immediate transfer back to you, on one condition; you finish the job that Geflin started, killing those that killed her, all of them. She was the love of my life. My world without her is torturing me so badly I cannot sleep, and they must die, all of them."

Alberto said, "This will not be easy. My people in London supplied her with some very deadly weapons. They didn't fail, but whatever protection they have to stop a rocket attack is awesome. They must have some state-of-the-art military protection, and to get up close and personal to take them out, your Geflin tried and failed. It is a lot of money for a hit, if it was just that simple."

"You now have his drug business, but you did not get how he got his cash here and how I cleaned it up for him, two vital elements that made his cartel successful. Come, I will show you something."

They followed him to his boathouse. Enrico's submarine was where Geflin had left it. "That's how he got his money here, 25 to 30 million dollars a trip. It was specially built for him and virtually undetectable under the water."

"I never would have guessed Enrico for a submariner."

"He wasn't. It is so easy: forward to go forward, back to go back. With the state-of-the-art GPS systems and full automation, the sub does everything. All he had to do was put my co-ordinates in and he's here and similarly to go back, no one knew he had left his island fortress."

They returned to his study, and he explained how the money got clean. "We have over 1500 ATMs on the islands. Most of our tourist trade comes from the States, so we put American dollars instead of Cayman dollars in them all, which suits American tourists. We order American dollars from the Federal Reserve, and they come in special crates— Enrico had them copied. Now, when a consignment of dollars from the Reserve comes in, all I have to do is fill up a copied crate with his drug money and switch the labels, so when the security company comes to collect the cash for the ATMs, it takes Enrico's cash instead. At the height of the season, the ATMs might have to be filled two or three times a day."

Alberto said, "Surely Federal Reserve money would be new notes and the serial numbers would be detailed and easily identifiable."

"You're right. We have two independent auditors. Our main auditors suggested that we do a continuous count of the money held in our vaults. We have 20 bank staff just to count money, overseen by another company's auditors recommended by our main auditors. It takes two weeks to count it all; even the crates with the new money from the reserve are counted, so they get touched, sorted in machines and become used notes."

"It must be a nightmare for your auditors to balance your books."

"Well, you would have thought so, but if you know the amount of the problem and that the financial accounts are just a snap shot of the year-end. you have plenty of time to hide it in the books so they balance. The banking regulations are far more intense, which are overseen by the island's treasury, only the international banking regulations that directly affect the confidence and secrecy of Cayman banking are endorsed by the treasury, all the others are put on a painstakingly slow process to become Cayman law if ever. The other reason is that the bank funds all government borrowings at zero interest, which if they had to go to the money markets for money it would be expensive, so it suits us both well."

"The laundering of money to us is not such a problem. We've been doing it for years. However, the submarine might come in useful," said Alberto. "if I could get one of the other Columbian cartels on board to take over Enrico's production business and start filling the empty containers, we could have a deal. I have no idea how we can knock off those people you want dead, but I promise you I will put my best people on it and it shall be done, somehow!"

"I may be able to help you. Two of the other cartels use my bank; I may be able to broker a deal as both are haemorrhaging vast sums of drugs and cash to the DEA. I am sure they would want in, but I will leave it up to you to decide which one we should approach with a proposition."

"I still can't guarantee that we could liquidate the people you want dead. We are a global organisation, with professional hit men that know the score. I will put a bounty on all their heads and see what happens. Should we be successful, I would expect payment, but not until it's the best I can do."

"That's fair enough. Now the two cartels the bank has dealings with are run by Pedro Aceituno and Raul Cannilias. Do you know any of them?"

"Only Raul. We have been doing business for years."

"That's good. I will invite him over to the island and we can organise everything."

"Make it next week, as I have important meetings. Any time after Thursday will be good."

They returned to the airport and flew back to New York. Back in his secret den, he called all families and told them to, if an opportunity arose, turn the lights out of one or all the people behind Earth Corp and make them hurt. "There is a considerable sum for a successful hit: £10 million a hit at least. Could be a lot more if the hit is one of the principals, but be warned, they have state-of-the-art protection. It appears that the CIA could not knock them off, and one of the most accomplished assassins failed, so be very careful. I have not committed us to deliver on this, but it's out there for you should any of you get the opportunity."

CHAPTER 3

THE NUCLEAR SUBMARINE FLEET of the USA, UK and Russia were all in the Northern Pacific. All had been rearmed with bunker-busting missiles. The commanders of all the subs had been flown to Flint, Texas, a month ago. All were given a thorough briefing on the problem and knew their mission. They were also given bracelets, so communications would be instant, with no time lag in normal encrypted transmissions. Each had been given a section of the Northern Pacific and the dormant volcanoes, which were their targets. For the last month, they had been practising. They had to get less than two minutes from launch to target. Two minutes had been worked out as the safe margin so their vessel would not be affected by the explosion and the volcano. All had fifty missiles and forty submarines on station, giving them enough firepower for the 700 dormant volcanoes that could have needed to be blown.

The biggest problem had been getting this multinational force to operate through Flint, Texas. All Navies wanted to be in control of their own vessels, and it took executive orders from the presidents and Prime Minister to initiate the agreement that Flint was central control, as timing would be crucial. During this period, Tsunami alarms had been quickly established along all Pacific coastlines. All shore-based power stations, nuclear or fuel, were deemed at risk, and vast concrete defences now surrounded them. If the closest dormant volcanoes had to be blown, there would only be a four-hour time frame for the inhabitants to get to higher ground. With several islands, there was not much high ground, so they had to be evacuated. The Navies of the world will now take station in the Northern Pacific under a United Nations mandate. It would be the largest conflagration of Naval power the world had ever seen, whose sole purpose is to save lives.

The world had united politically and militarily, driven by the population of all countries. The world was coming together as one, and their survival depended upon it.

Meanwhile in Flint, the vibrations around the Pacific had intensified but were stabilising. Our people in Utopia said all was well, the existing Utopian defences were under no pressure and coping well now. Looking at the seismograph over the last 24 hours, it was clear when the first seismic occurrence had taken place, but had plateaued over the last hour. "How long will this last?" I asked. None of his team could answer. It was unknown territory—how could anyone possibly know? We were like a fireman trying to put out the fire after it had started. I took the prof over to his desk and told him we needed to be overlooking something: the supreme power that could create this problem would know all about Utopian capabilities and ours. He would know that the convergence would help, knowing they did not have sufficient power to stop the bubble, but could slow it and divert it. We knew this had happened before. If he knew this was what we would do to nullify his threat, why would he not have factored this in? Was the destruction of Earth his aim?

Dave Mac pondered for a moment. "Jesus fucking Christ." He touched his bracelet and connected to his team in Utopia. "What's the level of the magma, not the speed is it rising? I need 15-minute updates on the level." He turned to me. "If I am right, we have a major problem. The magma that is erupting from the Trench is sealing it—the cold and pressure at that depth are working against us. If the tear is completely sealed when the bubble hits with nowhere to go, it's the end of the world." The force of the internal eruption of the magma bubble would be so immense that it would knock us out of our orbit. Two scenarios: we would either collide with our moon or fall into the sun, the ramifications of the latter, a slow burn to complete annihilation, as day by day we edge closer to the scorching star.

"There must be something we can do. It's a setback, that's all. We have both worlds to help us. What do we need to do?"

"It's simple, really. All we need to do is break the seal in the Trench that Oblivion has created."

"Well, let's do it."

He laughed, "You really don't understand the depths we are talking about—nearly 14000 metres. The pressure is so immense nothing I know of can reach that depth."

"So that's the problem. If we could punch enough holes to relieve the pressure, so long as we can get the explosives to the bottom of the Trench, would our explosives work at that depth?"

"Not sure. Not my science."

"Best we find someone that does." I contacted the President and told him of the situation and asked him to get his best weaponry experts to Anders for a meeting. "I cannot stress how important this is. I will be at Anders in 20 minutes. Get your people there soon as." I told the prof to come with me, and we were off to see the President and his best military people. I had summoned my transport, and while in transit, I told the verticular the problem that both the surface world and Utopia faced and asked if they could help, with all their technology—it was all based on protecting. There was nothing they could do. The magnitude of the explosion would be too great even for them to survive. Even if they did, they could not stop the planet colliding with the moon or the sun. It pledged that whatever they were capable of would be available. We arrived at Anders and made our way to the President's pavilion. I showed my pass and said the prof was with me, and I vouched for him. They were about to object, but I changed their minds. The President arrived with his guys, and we got straight down to business. "We need to blow holes at the bottom of the Mariana Trench. It's 14000 metres down...can we do it?" Silence followed. "If we can't, in the next few days, an underground explosion will occur, which will knock us out of our orbit and we will either collide with our moon or eventually, the sun." Disbelief of those assembled was a big problem. They just could not envisage the scale of the planet's plight.

The President said, "You will have to come up with a solution now, and I mean now."

General Dilks was the first to offer his advice; he was in control of America's nuclear arsenal. "I can puncture a hole or crater as wide as you like with any of my atom bombs."

"Will they work at the depth of 14000 metres?"

"Not sure about that."

"Who would know? Get him on the phone now." The General made the call. The simple answer was no, not at that depth; it would explode below 3000 metres

"Could it be made to explode at that depth?"

"Yes."

"How long would you need?"

"Two to three years with no constraints on spending."

"We have hours, not years," I said. "Keep on the line. Do we know the pressure at that depth?"

"It's purely mathematical," Dave Mac said. "If we enclosed the bombs in a case that would withstand the pressure at that depth, the casing could fracture, causing the atom bomb to explode and creating the crater we need."

"How big a casing are we talking about?" the specialist asked.

"The bomb of 100 megatons that would create a crater a mile wide on the surface would need a casing of four square feet."

"How thick would the casing need to be?"

Another specialist was called, and the problem was put to him. After a few minutes, he came back and said, "19 inches thick and of cast iron. Cast iron is a brittle metal and would completely fracture at this depth."

"How soon could you have three casings large enough to put an atom bomb in each?"

"They need four square feet," the specialist said. "Mr President, we do not have the resources in the USA. Our steel industry has moved to producing high-value metals. There are only three or four countries left that make cast iron: Canada, China, India and Russia."

The President asked, "Could they make what we want, money no object."

"Moulds would be made in sand to exact measurements at least one day. The amount of pig iron for the moulds would be also on the go, pouring and cooling at least two days, putting the bombs in and sealing the joints three days, six days minimum."

I turned to Dave Mac. "Do we have that time?"

"I really don't know; I would say not. It needs to be done within the next 24 hours."

"How can you be so sure?"

"The magma level is increasing by two inches every 15 minutes. In 24 hours, we will have filled up all the Utopians defences. At that stage, it would be saturated, before the magma bubble hits, possibly another 12 hours and no more, Utopia would cease to exist at this point, and before the magma bubble hits."

"If we deploy our backup plan and blowholes in the dormant volcanoes in the Pacific, the fleet is on standby now. Could that give us a bit more time? And what would be the ramifications?"

"I imagine there must be an ecology downside, coral, and marine life. In the short-term, should the magma bubble burst through these openings, I believe it would take out all the volcanoes and would be an underwater Krakatoa. It would cause gigantic tsunamis."

"But could we survive them?"

"We are into unknown territory. The entire Pacific rim could be devastated, probably up to a 1000 metres above sea level. We really need the Trench to be our frontline." I turned to the President and said, "In my opinion, we should immediately deploy the submarine fleet and give them the green light to complete the task. The little ecological damage is nothing compared with the doomsday scenario where facing." He nodded. "Prof, deploy your task force now." He touched his bracelet and told the fleet to go and complete their mission.

CHAPTER 4

THE POST-MORTEM OF THE ASSASSIN'S BODY was a surprise to us all. It was female! The head shots had made a mess of the face, but the beauty was plain to see, and the body was perfection. The police were trying to identify her. As soon as Stephen was informed the corpse was female, he knew it had to be Geflin, so the final element of Dark Seven was complete. It only left the children at the temple in Tibet. There was plenty of time to nullify their threat to the world. He was now more relaxed since the final threat to his principal had been removed—she was one hell of an adversary. It was only Utopian technology that had saved them in the desert and in Assington, which pushed Geflin into a fatal error in judgement, losing Messapth, her wealth, her daughters. Even her martial arts skill would never be enough to attempt an upfront assassination, no matter how good she was.

Stephen's men were trained to protect, and with the addition of the Spectre guys, no would-be assassin would get off a shot, but Geflin was unique as she got two shots off before her inevitable death.

CHAPTER 5

STEPHEN SHEFFORD was now somewhat relaxed about the security. Most threats would be isolated to terrorism or nutters, which his company could easily manage—it was their speciality. So reading the report the detective agency in Cayman Blanc had submitted gave him the gravest of concerns.

The detective agency took it on them to bug the **banker's beach house when he was not there. They shut off** the power and intercepted the call from the house and planted bugs in every room, even the boat house.

A transcript of a meeting that took place the previous day between the bank manager and the head of the east coast mafia had been recorded in full. The mafia worldwide had put a hit on all his principals. They would not be so easy to defend against. He put his whole team on red alert, the highest level of security.

He spoke with Earth Corp's banker Herr Hoffman and asked, "How are we getting on in closing down the Cayman Blanc bank?"

"Not very well. It's tied down by bureaucracy."

"I am sending you a transcript of a meeting that was held between the bank manager and the head of the east coast mafia."

"Were the bugs placed there legally?"

"No"

"So none of it could be used in a court of law."

"But we now know how he launders the money and has offered the remaining $700 million of Geflin's money in turn for the killing of all Earth Corp principals. Is it possible to get a European arrest warrant on him should he come to Europe and similarly in the States? Once arrested, we can get him to tell the truth."

"I will contact the head of Interpol and show him the transcript and let you know the outcome." They signed off.

Stephen would confront Alberto at his home. He is, after all, a businessman, dealing in everything illegal. They are no longer gangsters of old but well-educated villains and have the finest brains looking after their illegal interests, removal of problems or obstacles that affect their organisation are removed should it be necessary. They are still ruthless in their resolve to nullify any opposition to their business.

Stephen pulled me to one side. "There is a mafia hit on people connected to Earth Corp. They had been told there is a bounty on all the principals' heads, $10 million."

"Best we pay him a visit," I said. I turned to the prof and the President. "We need to see someone urgently. Prof., keep me updated. It seems the mafia has put a hit on all of us, and we need to stop this immediately. We are off to see Alberto and change his mind."

We knew where Alberto's house was, and the verticular took us directly into his garden. The alarms didn't sound until we exited, then all hell broke loose. Stephen told us to put our hands up to show we were no threat, his bodyguards' guns drawn. We froze them in their stride; they were conscious but could not move. We went into the house and turned the alarm system off and then searched room by room apart from the staff...still no sign of Alberto. Stephen reckoned he would be taken somewhere safe at the sound of the alarm. "He must have a secret passage, and we need to find it quickly." It wasn't too hard to find in the master bedroom. The bookcase quickly opened, and we descended the steps. We were spoilt for choice on which corridor to follow, so Stephen removed an infrared heat monitor from his pocket and pointed it down each corridor. Only one showed a heat signal, so we chose it. As we advanced, the signal intensified at a door. Stephen said, "Four to five people behind that door. And if we go through, they will shoot first"

"How can you be so sure?"

"Because that's what I would do." Stephen then shouted,

"Open the door! We are not armed. No harm has come to any of your men. We just want to talk to Alberto about the $700 million promised to him from the bank of Cayman Blanc." There was a small pause, and the door opened. We walked in with our hands up and found Alberto sitting at his desk. We could see the surprise on his face as we introduced ourselves.

The guards had their guns drawn. I said to Alberto that was not very friendly, and he told them to put the guns away. We sat down, and he asked if we would like a drink. We both declined. "To business. We have a complete transcript of your meeting in Cayman Blanc, and you have been offered Geflin's $700 million if you kill all the principal people at Earth Corp. Stephen and I are here to dissuade you from doing so." I went into his mind and quickly got his most secretive stuff. "I now know how Enrico's drug empire works in its entirety—the distribution is remarkable—where Geflin's laptop is, all the passwords you use, and the combinations to your safe here."

"Impossible! Only I know," he said.

"Give me a piece of paper, and I will write them all down as you don't want anyone else here to know your most secret information." It took a couple of minutes, and I handed the piece of paper to him. The shock on his face was plain to see.

"How?" he asked.

"I can read minds, and a bit more."

"If I shoot you, the information would be safe." He was a ruthless bugger; he told his men to shoot us, and they tried, in vain, to get their guns out of their holsters as I had frozen them. Alberto went for his gun in his desk, and I froze him too. Stephen got up and gathered all the firearms. They were helpless but fully conscious.

I faced Alberto and said, "That's the bit more I can do." The anguish on his face was plain to see. "Now that I have your full attention, I could easily close your whole east coast operation down with what I know, but is not in my interest to do so. I want you to rescind the global hit you have put on all of us. If you do this, it's business as normal, but if any person in Earth Corp is intentionally harmed, you will be held responsible. Put it another way, you will be our second line of security. Your eyes and ears will be part of Earth Corp security. You are a global organisation. You need to talk with all the godfathers and bring them on board; I do not have the time to do it myself—I have some real problems to resolve. Do you agree?"

"We are global, but each family makes its own decisions."

"I see. Who is your most loyal guard?"

"Giovanni," he said and nodded towards a six-foot-eight guy.

I took a gun and handed it to Giovanni. I entered his mind and told him to point the gun at Alberto as if he were to kill him. But put a bullet over his head into the bookcase behind, I told him, and he did so. Alberto nearly had a fit. "Now, do we agree? I could have easily wiped out your whole organisation, but I choose not to, and that is the same for the whole organisation. I am going to need your drug distribution to ensure that those addicted have a supply of quality controlled drugs. You must ensure that your dealers do not cut the drug and add toxic chemicals—you will enforce this ruthlessly. I do have a problem with extortion, prostitution, robbery and sanctioned hits, but currently, I shall ignore them but would seriously suggest you divest them in the future and concentrate on a legalised drug culture similar to tobacco and alcohol and position yourself to be in the forefront of a worldwide legal drug culture. If the $700 million comes back to you, use it for this. It would be the best investment you will ever make."

He nodded in agreement. I continued, "You can tell the Cayman Blanc bank president anything to get the funds promised. You can also tell him there is an international arrest warrant on him, and so he will be confined to the island. We know about the submarine, but you do not have to tell him we know. If he asks you for a new identity, oblige him, but let us know. Are we clear?" Another nod. "We will see are selves out. You've got a lot of phone calls to make."

We left the way we came. As we entered the verticular, I removed the paralysis from their minds. Stephen said, "How can you be certain that the illegal drug industry will be legalised?"

"If we save the Earth, there will be a new understanding, a United Nations with clout elected by the world's population. The best people will sit on the security panel, not countries who have only self-interest at heart as it is no. The world is coming together. It is now beyond politics and party rivalry. We are entering a new age."

CHAPTER 6

COMMANDER Rob Free of HMS Nautilus was on station in the Northern Pacific. His submarine would be the first to go into action. He was totally confident that he and his crew could deliver the missiles when asked to do so. They had been practising for the best part of a month and nothing was left to chance. They would deliver. Similarly, all the other submarines on station were all prepared to the same level.

We arrived back at Anders. We had been gone a couple of hours, and Prof bought us up to date. A third of the volcanoes had been vented. "Levels are increasing every 20 minutes, so it is making a difference. How big a difference, we will not know until the last volcano has been vented."

I turned to General Dilks. "Where is your nearest base to the Trench?"

"Guam."

"Have your nuclear devices there?"

He looked at the President for sanction. "Yes."

"Will they do the job?"

"No, they need to be modified."

"Have you the materials and resources to modify them there?"

"We have everything apart from the personal."

"How long to get them there?"

"Just under 18 hours."

"That's too long. I can do better than that. Phone them and have them ready immediately." He did so. After 12 minutes, we were in Fort Worth, and 45 minutes later, in Guam.

CHAPTER 7

THE UTOPIANS WERE AWARE of the problem we now faced. They met us in the technical area, and we showed the droids the blueprints for a casket to house the nuclear devices. The importance of the casket failing at 11500 metres deep, not before, was paramount. We asked them to make four. I believed we only had one chance at this; the magma bubble could burst through at any time. Making things that fail was an anathema to the droids. My sign language was not so good, so I got Robert to sign for me. He explained the reason for failure was so the nuclear device would detonate at the bottom of the Trench, making a crater a mile wide and lengthening the tear that the magma had sealed. This, with the venting of all the underwater active volcanoes, would reduce the pressure enough to nullify the bubble. If this did not work, the surface and Utopia would perish.

The droids took to their task, and the caskets were made within an hour. The only problem was that they would not fit the verticular portal—easily remedied. A ray emitted from the craft made them disappear. We entered the verticular. It took a few hops to get to the military base at Guam in just over 30 minutes. All sorts of alarms sounded as we exited the craft. The General was there first with his team and quickly quelled the security alert. The verticular re-materialised the caskets. The General was surprised to see four, and I told him we would use one as a test to see if it would fail before we deploy the bombs. The prof checked where the nearest submarine was and instructed them to get to Guam at full speed. He ordered two further submarines to take up positions at the Mariana's islands and gave them the co-ordinates before telling them to await further orders.

The prof told the General that we would put a sonar receiver inside the test casket and fill with sand to make it the same weight as the bombs. It would take about half an hour to reach the bottom of the Trench. We would receive a sonar signal while it descended to the point of the casket's failure. However, we would know the depth at which it would shatter. Should the depth be correct, all submarines would discharge their devices simultaneously. All would explode within minutes of each other.

I asked, "How far from the explosions will the

submarines have to be for them to be safe?"

The General said, "There will be 300 megaton explosions about 1500 miles apart. The shock waves will bounce off the sides of the Trench if most of the wave is forced downwards by the intense pressure at that depth. But when it hits the bottom, it will oscillate upwards. It would strengthen towards the top of the Trench and then enter the ocean with a substantial force but would dissipate relatively quickly due to the vastness of the ocean. However, if I were the commander of the submarine, I would want to be at least 100 miles from the explosion."

"How far can a sub travel in half an hour?"

"About 20 to 25 miles."

"It's a possible suicide mission."

"Well, we are going to have to ask for volunteers to deploy the devices. We can't order them. contact the commanders"

Prof. Dave Mac touched his communicator and was instantly in touch with all the commanders so everyone was kept in the loop. "It appears that deploying the nuclear devices has an element of extreme risk to your vessels. Our best guess is that you need to be 100 nautical miles from the detonation area. At full speed after deployment, the maximum distance you will have travelled will be no more than thirty-two nautical miles, which will put you in harm's way. We have no idea as this will be the first time a nuclear bomb has exploded at this depth. We are of the opinion that the pressure at this level will work in our favour and any shock wave will be forced down in to the Earth's crust. But if it's not totally absorbed, it will oscillate upwards with tremendous magnitude leaving the Trench before dissipating in the ocean. The chances of the shock wave travelling in your direction from your deployment is quite small still an unacceptable risk, so we are looking for volunteers to deploy the bombs."

Commander Rob Free was the first to reply, volunteering himself and his officers and a few essential hands to carry out the task. The rest would be evacuated to the surface fleet until the mission is completed. Similarly, all the other commanders concurred.

The bombs fitted like a glove inside the casket. The sonar receiver was installed into the test casket, and the makers of the receiver have said it should work at that depth and had been worked out mathematically. However, to their knowledge, none had gone to this depth. We would soon see. General Dilks had said that bombs would not be armed until put on the submarines as two of the caskets had to be flown to the Marianna's islands. the Lancers would take just under an hour to get to the islands and helicopter to the submarines, a further 90 minutes to be on station at the Trench. The bombs would be held on my explosive magnetic bolts and blown remotely at that exact time, and fall to the bottom of the Trench under their own weight.

The prof checked with his guys in Utopia. The magma level was increasing, although slower—the venting of the underwater volcanoes was helping. Had we gained some precious time? Time would tell.

"I think it is time to evacuate the low-lying island in the

Pacific," I said. "We do not know what will happen when the bombs go off. The Secretary-General of the United Nations will have to give the order for evacuation as the flotilla is under his mandate. I will see him on my way back to Anders. General, I would advise you to get as high above sea level as you can—certainly the civilians at the base and non-essential personnel too." I turned to the prof. "It seems that it's now all under control here. Are you staying with me or going back to Flint?"

"It would be better if I were in Flint; it's the command centre. I certainly will get a better picture after the explosions," he said.

I dropped him off at Flint and got to the United Nations where I saw the Secretary-General who would speak everyone affected by all means possible. He said, "No one will be forced to leave; it is a precaution. But if people would rather sit it out, that would be up to them. We would not go back for them if it put lives in jeopardy."

I returned to Anders and got the President up to speed. In just over an hour, I would be responsible for putting three enormous holes in the Earth's crust. The consequences were unknown, but without this decision, the Earth would perish. Let history be the judge.

CHAPTER 8

THE TEST CASKET WAS RELEASED, the sonar working perfectly. Commander Rob Free tracked the depth as it descended, and the rate of fall was around 1000 metres every two minutes, just under half an hour to the bottom of the Trench. Flint HQ were relaying it to Anders. It seemed like an eternity. The casket had settled on the Trench floor at 13900 metres, the sonar reading was still coming through. Had the casket shattered as was supposed to do? Another couple of minute went by…silence. Prof. said, "Sonar reading now 13800. It's ascending casket has failed at the prescribed depth. We're good to go."

All three devices had been deployed. The submarines

were now heading away from the blast area at full speed. While we waited for information, I realised I had not been home for over 24 hours. I told the President I would be at home and left for Assington. In the verticular, I noticed the silver and white telltale sign that Infinity was present, and I was now travelling to meet with Eternity. No sooner had I noticed its presence, I was there. They had turned the magma bubble into a sausage shape. It now would not displace the magma in front of it. It would travel something like a javelin, slicing through the magma, rather than pushing it forward. The downside was that it would take significantly longer.

Time was not the problem, but had we made enough holes so it would pass through? The convergence thought that what they had done was enough and had taken out the risk of explosion that would knock Earth out of orbit, but a small continent of magma would still break through both in the ocean and on land. It would try to find the path of least resistance—the eruption could last for months until spent.

I arrived back in Assington. Apart from security, everybody else was in the communication centre, watching relayed pictures from Flint, Texas, and it was minutes from the detonation of the nuclear devices. I went over to Sue who was so intent on the pictures coming from Flint. She gave me just a quick acknowledgement, then returned her attention to the TV.

Watching the seismograph displayed as a world atlas, all eyes were on Flint cameras on the Northern Pacific, then suddenly, 1, 2, 3 nuclear devices detonated. Vast shock waves formed in the Trench, but we could not tell which direction they were travelling. Each explosion measured 10.4 on the Richter scale, as if a massive underwater earthquake had taken place. With this amount of water displacement, inevitably, we had created at least three tsunamis. I contacted the prof. "Too early to tell," he told me. I told him what the convergence had done to the bubble. "That's fantastic."

"The downside is it could go on for months."

"Everything else is manageable. knocking us out of orbit was my greatest fear. There was no other way out of that predicament"

I told Sue the same and sensed the relief—her whole being seemed to relax. I updated the President, Prime Minister and the rest of the Star Chamber. Time, at last, was possibly on our side. I suddenly felt exhausted. It was 19:00 UK time. I started to yawn and Sue said, "You have not slept for two days. If we are out of imminent danger, go to bed," and I did so. I fell asleep before my head hit the pillow. I slept soundly for six hours and woke up just after 1. I showered and changed and headed to Flint, Texas. It was tea time in Texas. I could feel a sense of calm. The prof bought me up to date—the magma level had dropped significantly since the detonation. "It has virtually disappeared. We now have far more room to disperse the bubble, and there is no sign of unusual activity. The downside is one of our submarines are missing. We lost contact about five and a half hours ago. The bombs have created three tidal waves. We believe one of them took out our submarine. We have over 300 aircraft searching the area for debris and survivors, nothing yet."

"Which submarine was it?"

"HMS Nautilus, Commander Rob Free and forty-six crew."

CHAPTER 9

ON HMS NAUTILUS, the deployment had gone well. They were now full speed away from the detonation area. What they had not realised took them into the direct path of a shock wave from one of the other detonations. The first notification on their instrumentation was too late. They hit the shock wave at full speed. The coning tower was ripped off like a twig. The vessel turned broadside in the shockwave and instantly moved along with the shock wave at over 130 miles per hour. All aboard were helpless. With no communications, they were just like an enormous surf board at the will of the shock wave. All were safe aboard; they just had to ride it out.

It took 4 hours for the shock wave to dissipate. The Commander gave the order to send a remote drone to check the vessel for damage. The camera relayed pictures of the top surface of the vessel. There was nothing left of the top superstructure—all had gone to the exit hatch where the conning tower should have been. He asked the operator to zoom in on the hatch. The damage to it was extensive. They would not be leaving through that. He told the operator to check all the other emergency exits since these were all damaged. They were trapped inside the submarine. He gave the order to surface. Once surfaced, they would be seen by any of the rescue ships. Now on the surface, air would not be a problem, and a nuclear sub could stay submerged for a year, and with only a third of the crew, supplies will last indefinitely.

His first officer advised that they did not know where they were or where the wave had taken them. "Good point. We need to get on top of the sub. From the camera, all missile launch tubes have been affected the same as the emergency exits, so the only way out is through the torpedo tubes. We need a volunteer. First officer, who is our best diver, the boson." The boson was six-foot-eight and weighed eighteen stone of solid muscle. "What size are you across the shoulders?"

"Do not know, sir."

A measure was quickly found, 44 inches. "Tubes are 36 inches. We do not want you stuck in one, so thank you, but we need someone a lot smaller."

All submariners can dive. It's a safety measure in case of

emergency evacuation at depth. All have to pass the test before being allowed to become submariners. Some take to it like a duck to water, while others do enough to pass, and some do it but hate the water in the face mask but suffer in silence, as they only have to do it in a controlled manor, it's never done at sea. Evacuation is really the last resort. Not to do so would be certain death, which focuses acutely on the mind. The smallest of the Nautilus crew was leading cook James Baker. He hated diving. He was in the galley when summoned to the bridge; he knew the submarine was in difficulties but had no idea he would be the key to unlock the situation the sub was in.

Arriving at the bridge, the Commander explained the problem and asked him to volunteer to go to the surface via the torpedo tube. The blood completely drained from his face. He felt his knees go weak and thought he would fall, but he got a grip of himself. The Commander explained what he had to do. His shoulder measurement was taken at 32 inches. "What we need you to do is to put on the emergency escape equipment. There is enough air for 20 minutes. We are on the surface but cannot open the conning tower or any of the emergency hatches or missile silo, the force of shock wave must have destroyed the top of the sub, so the only way to the surface is via the torpedo tube. You will be put into the tube, and it will be flooded. This will take no more than 15 seconds. Once flooded, we will open the tube door and you will swim to the surface and get on top of the submarine using the steps near the conning tower. The communications officer showed him how to assemble the satellite dish and the laptop. He will need to take to the surface to communicate their position, as they were over 500 miles from the search area."

James was helped into the torpedo tube. Not only did he hate diving, he was a bit claustrophobic. And when the door was shut, panic started to build up. The outer door opened slowly, and the water started to fill the tube. He crawled along the tube and got closer to the exit of the tube; the water started to enter his mask, which he dreaded, and the feeling of claustrophobia was eaten into his psyche. The door opened fully, and he launched himself out into the ocean. He hadn't even taken a breath before he was on the surface, a deep sigh of relief, swam round to where the conning tower should have been and climbed the steps to the top of the submarine, where he set up the satellite and laptop and contacted Flint headquarters to give them their position. He told them all was fine with the crew, and he would stay on deck, but there was no shade as the whole of the surface had been sliced away with the power of the wave, and cutting gear would be required to free the crew. Flint informed him that a helicopter was despatched to pick him up, and a destroyer was on the way to release the crew. "It will be 3 hours before it would get to you. Will you be ok in the heat?"

"Yes, I have plenty of water and will try to rig something up for shade with what I can find and keep cool in the sea if necessary."

He went to where the conning tower should have been and tried to find what the commanding officer had asked him to look for, but there was nothing. He went to the hatch and used Morse code to tell the Commander what was happening.

He now set about to make himself safe while waiting for rescue. His wet suit would give him some protection. Although he felt himself cooking inside it, the biggest problem was the heat of the sub superstructure; his flippers were sticking to the metal flooring. The sub had now been on the surface for over an hour. How much hotter could it get? He tapped a Morse message and asked the commander to submerge so the sea would cool down the superstructure. Slowly, the sub started to submerge. When the deck was awash with about a foot of water, he tapped and told them to stop. He now just had to wait.

Flint control centre notified all concerned that the submarine had been found and all crew accounted for. They were receiving reports from the Northern Pacific rim of the destruction our bombs had caused. The tidal waves had caused massive damage, no casualties, although some people were missing. *So far, so good,* I thought. The magma levels in Utopia still had not risen for 2 hours. How long had we got? I was now confident we would survive the magma bubble, but what destruction to the surface population when it erupts? No one had the faintest idea. The active surface volcanoes were pumping ash into the atmosphere, and flights were being diverted.

It was more of a hindrance than stopping air travel at the moment. The ash was not in the main flight paths and levelling out around 20000 feet, and most aircraft would be well above it. Should it drift into the main flight paths, it would not pose a problem until it reaches any land mass with airports. Aircraft would not be able to fly through it to land. Otherwise, all was looking good.

It **really didn't matter where** I was. As soon as something happened, I would be first to know, so I made my way back to Assington. It was about four in the morning, and I slept for a solid 8 hours. Sue brought me a cup of tea. She could see that I was more relaxed, and I told all that I knew and how confident I was that the planet would no longer perish, and no one had any idea about the level of destruction once it erupts. Everyone in the northern hemisphere should be quite safe—we would probably be the last to be affected.

The President had mobilised the National Guard, who had taken up strategic positions along their Pacific coast. All the countries on the northwest Pacific rim had done the same. There were hundreds of thousands of troops being deployed and on standby for any eventuality.

CHAPTER 10

HOW LONG DID I HAVE before the eruption? As they say, every minute counts, so I took this precious time in catching up on the programmes I had instigated. The carbon neutral fossil fuel leasing scheme had been taken up by every major polluter. It was initially expensive for Earth Corp in the first two years, but we would see a positive cash flow from then on. We did have the funds, and the benefits for the planet would be enormous.

Alec's report said that he had committed £3.75 billion, most of which was on tidal schemes of some sort or another. As I started to read through the report, I was astounded that when the Thames barrier was built to protect the city from floods, no one had thought that the tidal surge of about 7 miles per hour could not be harnessed to produce electricity for the city. The University of East Anglia had come up with plans to do so; it could create over 2500 megawatts of clean power, enough to power the city and still protect it from floods. Earth Corp committed to the design and development work. Construction was to be funded by the city and government—our costs or investments would be paid as percentage electricity generated. Currently, Alec had negotiated a 23% return over 20 years, which would make Earth Corp an enormous profit on our initial investment. There were 170 cities that had a tidal flow similar to London, so if we did the same for each, that money after our costs could go to the United Nations and would ensure the independence they needed to ensure worldwide peace, a sustainable planet and elimination of starvation.

Herr Hoffman report showed that 17.8 billion had been donated to the United Nations so far. Being the liquid assets of Messapth, the antiquities were between six to seven thousand years old, and some were unique. Placing them on the market would devalue their intrinsic worth, as the collectors of this type of artefact were few. Most would be purchased by museums that have strict budgets and to enhance their exhibits. Hopefully, time was now on our side. We could wait and take our time to maximise the profit opportunity for these items.

The scrolls found at the site that looked like the Dead Sea scrolls turned out to be only the accounts of all the houses of Messapth. The accounts were so detailed, showing the financial gain and where the victims were from, to ensure that some traders always got through to keep the trade going. Had they killed them all, the trade would soon dry up as there would be no profit for the merchants. Losing half only made the prices higher, and so the trade flourished. The significant part was the detail from where the caravans started and finished—even those killed at their origins were known, allowing a detailed trade map of the whole middle east to be drawn. As each scroll was deciphered, more and more detail was entered to the map. When all the scrolls had been deciphered, we would have a detailed map of all the inhabitants of the middle east. This would be extremely useful in disputed areas of the middle east, which had caused so much conflict over the centuries and would help in establishing independent homelands for the dispossessed that had claimed sovereignty of parts of countries which were still being fought over until we brokered a peace.

I picked up the latest report from the United Nations. No consensus had been reached. There was still no trust—there were walk-outs, and even fights had broken out, but they were still talking, and the fragile truce remained in place. I spoke to Herr Hoffman. "Could we not speed up the translation of the scrolls?"

"More people." He explained that we had all the Vatican interpreters with the unique abilities this language required.

"Surely the Vatican are not the only guys that can do this. What about the universities? They must have people that specialise in ancient languages," I said.

"They probably do, but it will upset the Vatican, and they might pull out, and we will be back to where we started."

"Don't care. The talks at the United Nations seem to be bogged down, and the detailed trade map would really help to establish the who's who of the middle east several thousand years ago. Let's get some original text that has already been deciphered and send the original to every university. Ask for a translation and see what comes back and check it against the decrypted text, then invite all those that can to Zurich to help."

"What if the Vatican find out?" he asked.

"Call their bluff. The closer we get anno domini, they won't want to be far away, just in case some disciples turn up."

"Ok, I will let you know."

Conrad had reminded me that the elections in the UK and USA were 2 weeks away and told me it was most unlikely that the honourable Stephen Halstead, British Prime minister, and Rodbridge, American President, would not run a campaign that held my views of one world run by a truly independent United Nations. He said, "They hold the sovereignty of their countries as being the most important aspect of nationhood. Relinquishing any power to an outside organisation would not happen under any circumstances. In interviews with Media Corp, they have intimated just that. I know you are seeing them on a daily basis with the crises we face, but you have not had meaningful conversations with them; you have acted on your own with the funds taken from Messapth, for example. I am not insular in my thinking; I just want to do the right thing for everybody, and I mean everybody, as everyone matters. I am a great advocate for democracy, so I will let the people decide. I have one political broadcast in both countries, which will express my views of a united planet and let the electorate decide. If they decide that sovereignty is more important than the principles I believe in, I can live with that."

I needed to make my views clear regarding the United Nations and the establishing a truly independent organisation. The funds that supported their independence had no strings attached. Although Earth Corp instigated the funds to them through their Swiss bankers, we had no say in how they'd use it. The meetings I had with the General Secretary over the current crisis we faced, both of us had the same ideals for everyone on Earth, and we would produce a People's Charter of fundamental rights enshrined into the United Nations Charter and will form part of all countries' legislations.

"I appreciate Conrad's concerns with the British Prime minister and the American President, and which must include the rest of the Star Chamber. I can see the need to meet, hopefully to get unanimous approval of the actions I have taken regarding the Messapth fortune." I asked them to meet at Anders Airfield in two days so I could see them personally—nodding tacit agreement online or bracelet, I could not see what they really felt, but face-to-face, I could read their concerns and put their minds at rest.

I needed to record my political broadcast. I had read through the script that Conrad and his political writers had put together, and it was a fine speech but just was not me. I told him I would be at Media Corp, and I had made some changes. It would not be a live broadcast. As a new party, we were only given one slot, as we had no history.

After makeup, I went to the studio and told the director that I was not using the prepared script but had my own. "My speech will last no more than 3 minutes. The other 7 minutes will be a documentary on what's happening in the Northern Pacific and around the world. I want to show the collaboration between all the countries in the world which I now feel has saved the planet. To my knowledge, although there are several hundred missing, no bodies have been found, so the whole of the Northern Pacific could have been devastated. I appreciate that the problem was created, but I now believe it has saved the world."

My speech was all that I believe in, that the Earth and all its people would be governed by the United Nations Human Rights Charter. The sovereignty of every country would be respected. For those choosing not to bring into their sovereign law, the charter would be excluded until every article is enshrined into their law. No country would be allowed to veto any part of the charter.

I proceeded to say, "In the next ten years, our dependence on fossil fuels will be minimal. My companies are working on a free power source by fusing three of the most abundant chemicals found everywhere in the world.

We have produced this energy, but to date we have not been able to make use of it. Believe me, we will find the link that is missing, then all electrical appliances will have to change—a colossal change. It will be gradual, whole new industries will be created, existing industries will make the change... Who's going to pay for this? As always, we are. Governments only have our money; they have no money of their own. What they get from us allows them to borrow huge sums of our money saved in annuities and private pensions at ridiculous rates, setting a tremendous balance of payments deficit. My company could pay off the national debt, and similarly, I could give you all £1000 for your vote, but I will do neither. We will work off these debts, as a new dawn is coming. Prosperity belongs to everyone."

I went to see the final edit before its release and left the studio

CHAPTER 11

THE ASH FROM THE NOW-ACTIVE VOLCANOES continued into the atmosphere and would soon cause concern to aircraft, according to our meteorologists, because of the sheer volume and its gaining altitude. The holes we made in the Trench seemed to be working. The levels underground were approaching critical levels but remained contained. Everything we planned seemed to be working. It could only be the enormity of the magma bubble. All seismic information showed that the dormant subterranean volcanoes we vented were discharging magma, so I wondered what needed to be done about the ash.

"How long, at the current rate, will this ash cloud cause

a problem?" I asked Flint.

The response was, "It's only an annoyance to aircraft at the moment. Should it continue at its current level, it would take about 3 months to circumnavigate the globe and block out sunlight, causing a premature winter in those places effected."

"Will it cover the whole planet, causing an ice age?"

"That's doubtful. It's more likely be a nuisance to the planet."

"Just suppose these ash clouds stayed over the main growing areas of the world and starved of sunshine, nothing would grow. Would we be able to feed everyone on Earth? ...as we can't do that at the moment."

"The best we can do is get some meteorologists to work out the prevailing winds and where the ash clouds will settle."

"What we have done in the Northern Pacific may have altered the prevailing winds." "Good point. I will get them to factor it in"

"Have we any intel on the holes in the Trench? Have we sent any submarines back in to have a look?"

"No, I have had them stand down for 48 hrs."

"Do you think there will be any risk?"

"Robin, we are really in unknown territory. We have only two left of the submarines that deployed the bombs. HMS Nautilus had its whole conning tower removed by the blast shock wave. We have just only cut through the bulkhead to rescue the crew."

"Would the other two subs volunteer to go back and

have a look? There are the only eyes we have to see what's going on down there."

"I agree. I will send them back to reconnoitre the whole area and report back."

"How long before they get back to us?" I asked.

"2 hours at full speed."

"Do we know what's happening above sea level?"

"We have satellite data but only infrared because of the dust. Commercial flights are giving it a wide berth. Helicopters can't operate at the altitude and neither can any of our Naval jets."

"Surely, a piston-driven aircraft would not be affected as much. We have had dust clouds before, not at this magnitude, but they must have been mapped at some point. Check it out and let me know."

The prof returned in less than 15 minutes and said, "The Icelandic government uses an Austrian turbo prop aircraft, a diamond DC08, which can fly in and around the dust cloud safely."

"Where is the closest?" I asked.

"6000 miles," he replied.

"Any based in UK?"

"Yes. They have a subsidiary in the UK."

I called the CEO of the company, and his receptionist said he was out. Bless her heart, she was protecting him, and no matter what I said, I was not going to talk to him today. "Please let him know I called," I concluded.

I collected Stephen and took the verticular to the CEO's office—we were there in minutes. We walked through into the reception hall and found the receptionist—who was also the secretary. I jumped into her mind and found out the CEO was playing golf at his local club, in a competition his company had sponsored. I learned that a brand-new aircraft was ready for delivery to Iceland and one new aircraft arriving later today from Austria. *Spoilt for choice,* I thought.

I asked if we could have a look at one, and she showed us to the hangar where one was being serviced. With my limited knowledge about aircraft, other than being a passenger, it had only four seats, including the pilot's.

"Is there anyone that can give some technical information about the aircraft?" I asked.

"I may be female, but I have been flying these kites for 12 years. I know everything about them, so ask away."

Well, that put me in my place. I told her what I wanted and why. She knew all about the Northern Pacific as it had been headline news. To get the aircraft to the Pacific would take 27 hours. She explained, "Once there, one plane would not be sufficient to fly you between the explosion sites. You would need three equipped with the technical kit to map the cloud and atmosphere surrounding it."

"I will hire, lease or buy three aircraft," I said.

"Fine," she said. "There is a 9-month lead time."

"Not good enough. I want them now."

"Impossible," she said.

"Why so? You have one awaiting delivery, one being delivered to you today, and I am looking at one."

"These are all sold and paid for, and the one you're

looking at does not have the tech kit on it. Plus, who do you have to operate the tech kit? It's really specialised kit."

I had to think. I contacted the prof and told him what I was trying to do. He concurred with her and suggested that we talk to the scientist who developed the kit and pick him up on the way to the Pacific. He felt the scientist would be pleased to see first-hand of his handiwork in the Northern Pacific. I asked her for the scientist's name and contacted him.

Lars Erickson oversaw the whole Icelandic scientific survey group. He volunteered his team to analyse the Northern Pacific and made his aircraft available to us. I told him to stand by and have his team ready to go in an hour.

"How long before the arrival of the plane from Austria?" I asked. She phoned and found out it had not left. "Tell them we will pick it up on the way." She did so, thinking it would be safer there as she did not have the authority for us to have it—only the CEO could do that.

"No problem. I will go and have a word with him," I said. The look of horror on her face...disturbing his golf day would be catastrophic! I reassured her that I would not spoil his day and left. We at the clubhouse in 3 minutes. I checked the scoreboard and realised our man was on the twelfth green. Stephen got us a buggy and drove it to the tee of the thirteenth hole, where four men approached the tee. I recognised my man and asked him if I could have a word. I quickly altered his mindset from being outraged to compliant, and I quickly got his agreement, providing £1.1 million was lodged as a deposit and £1200 every flight hour would be deducted from the deposit. He used our phone to call his secretary and gave the ok.

We returned to the airdrome. We had our three planes, assuming Lars had a pilot—Stephen was an accomplished pilot and could fly anything, but we were one short. I turned to her and asked if she would join the team.

She replied, "You will need more than that."

CHAPTER 12

WE NOW HAD UP TO THE MINUTE weather forecasting in and around the Mariana Islands. Data from the submarines and aircraft was backing up satellite and space station data. Although just 2 days of information was at hand, the meteorological stations of many nations seemed to be coming up with the same prognosis. The climate around the blast areas had significantly altered the climate—we had rain in dry seasons; the Pacific winds had changed direction completely; the rain was torrential in some places and flooding was on a grand scale. However, the rain was washing the volcanic ash away. According to the first photographs of the Northern Pacific rim, the ash—brought down by the rain—covered vast areas of tropical forests and turned the greenery to a reddish brown. The latest photos showed green again. The consensus now was: if it kept raining, the ash would not present a problem other than the clean-up and some dredging, as the ash in some places was over a foot deep.

The data was being sent to the University of East Anglia. With some modifications to their weather forecasting computer, they could predict the weather to 95% accuracy, certainly for the UK; Northern Pacific could be different. They made the first map and forecast prediction, which showed the globe with vast rain clouds, now covering the entire Northern Pacific. Using the data, assuming the conditions remained the same, showed a seven-day prediction of the rain continuing and moving toward Australasia, Africa, middle east, eastern Europe, and the east coast of North America. Predicting further, it showed that the whole of the globe would be covered in rain clouds within 3 weeks, and it would rain potentially everywhere. The computer model would be updated automatically as the data was received with free access to anybody that had an interest in it.

What were the ramifications of continuous rainfall? Flooding but what else...we should find out, so I put the question out to all my scientists on the payroll, and all advised that I gather a specialist team of climate change, agriculture, flood drainage consultants, hydroponics, and water treatment experts.

I contacted the General Secretary of the United Nations and told him what we were doing for the UK and advised that all counties do the same. He agreed. If all the counties shared their information, we could build up a map where the greatest problem existed and then we could target resources directly to those places.

I then spoke to David and asked him to find the scientists required. He had a tremendous amount of information on scientists from when we first set up the team to help the Utopians and keep me posted. It took a couple of days to get the team together. Weather trends had remained the same, and the magma flows were still at critical, but our defences were holding with no sign of easing. The team chairman, Michael Blowers, produced his preliminary report. A month's rain, depending on its severity, would not cause much harm to the ecology and economy of the UK. In fact, it could be a bonus for agriculture, certainly root crops. But if the ground becomes saturated, it would start to become a problem. The water would have filled all the natural aquifers and its only route would be the river systems, which would cause widespread flooding and commercial damage to properties built on the floodplains. Vast areas of rural east Anglia, a major source of our food production, would be submerged. Having 2 months of rainfall would ruin all our cereal crops, only be fit for fodder.

The toll daily rain would have on society raining also needed to be considered, especially if it caused cold atmospheric conditions as well. Homes and workplaces as the only dry areas would affect productivity, and cause serious transportation problems. If the rain would last 3 months, the problem would increase tenfold, a year of starvation and homelessness. A year of rain was quite frankly unimaginable. Now, these were assumptions based on experience.

"We shall meet next week and try to substantiate our assumptions with fact."

I took the report to the Prime Minister, and we both went to see the environment secretary. He explained that with successive cuts in his budget for the last 10 years, flood defences had been cut back drastically. He added, "This year's budget is committed. It would need new money for us to do anything, and the costs would be enormous £25 billion-plus. We just do not have the resources to do anything. All the properties should be insured, and the insurance companies will have to pay."

I reminded the Prime Minister: "When you gave planning permission to build on flood plains, mortgage and insurance companies were given assurances that the government would help in a major disaster. If you reigned on that pledge apart from the litigation they would bring, it could send the financial markets into turmoil, and the last time that happened, you had to find billions to bail out the banks. So £25 billion-plus seems the cheaper option and makes sense, plus its infrastructure, a once-only payment with just maintenance, which could be covered in the annual budget."

I knew exactly what the Prime Minister was about to say, and I told him we would not finance the project, as I would be obliged to fund everybody's flood problems, and these issues should have been addressed years ago. He told his minister to get the ball rolling and would speak to the Chancellor to organise the funds. Back at Number 10, the Prime Minister went through to Number 11, where the Chancellor was having a treasury subcommittee meeting. The Prime Minister put his head round the door, apologised for the interruption and told the Chancellor to get £25 billion over to the environment immediately for important flood relief projects, which had now become a priority. It took about an hour before the Chancellor was in Number 10, saying that it was impossible to fulfil what the Prime Minister had asked. "All the funds are committed," the Chancellor added.

The Prime Minister replied, "Well, you will just have to uncommitted £25 billion," and explained why the urgency. "It's going to start raining, possibly in a week's time and could last months, maybe years. We have 6 weeks before the land gets waterlogged. The river systems will be our only drainage of the land. I shall broadcast to the nation and put in special measures for houses and factories that are on the floodplains. You have seen the plight of Asia on the news and its coming our way, and its inevitable—we will be effected. Divert funds from infrastructure projects as their will be no point if the UK is under water."

The early evening weather forecast was now showing the enormous rain cloud directly from satellite data. The ash cloud was reducing and being washed into the ocean. They were pinpointing the Mariana Trench as the epicentre and cause of the problem. The map showed the cloud expanding over an 8-hour period and then went live, showing where the cloud currently was—it had moved. They estimated 1000 miles in every direction and concluded that if the volcanic eruptions did not dissipate, the rain cloud would reach us in 7 days. There would be an extended news bulletin at 21:00, covering the possibility of widespread flooding. One of the Prime Minister aides came in and told him about the extended news bulletin. "Damn, tell all the broadcasters I will be speaking to the nation before the 9 o'clock news. They will have to alter their schedule to accommodate me."

I was relaxing at home, and Sue told me the Prime Minister would be addressing the nation about the current situation in the Northern Pacific. We watched the broadcast together. He put the problems facing the UK and the world succinctly, asking viewers for their understanding in this manmade climatic condition. He reiterated the reason behind the explosions; for the venting of the subterranean volcanoes; the surface volcanoes that started the ash clouds. He explained that the venting of the Trench was to relieve massive underground pressure, which would have destroyed Earth. We were entering unknown territory. "We have our best minds working on the aftermath of our actions, and we will keep you informed. To this end, my latest report on the magma flow is still critical but under control, with no sign of easing. So, the weather system you're watching will get larger and eventually cover the globe, my people tell me. This will result in flooding on a grand scale, and today, I have set aside £25 billion for flood protection. Those homes and factories at risk should now take all steps to prevent and minimise the flood risk and should contact their council flood protection officer. I have asked all the councils to put in a dedicated hot line monitored 24/7. Excluding factories, we estimate 750,000 homes are at serious risk. We will be relying on rivers and streams, and to this end, please report to your local water authority any blockages in natural watercourses. I have put our military on standby, and we will be ready for the oncoming deluge. Thank you and goodnight."

"The general election is 3 weeks away...should it not be postponed?" Sue asked.

"I think you're right. I will talk with the PM," I replied.

I called the Prime Minister and said, "I had watched the broadcast, and that should quell any concerns that the people have, certainly in the early stages. The election is 3 weeks away—if it's pouring with rain, the turnout will be low. Can we not postpone it until we are over this crisis?"

"I really don't know. Parliament has been dissolved, and in theory, I am caretaking as the unelected PM, although I have my party's full support. I will have a word with the leader of the house and the other political leaders. If there is a consensus to postpone, I think we should."

"Ok, let me know."

Day 1: Indonesia; Japan

Mike Blowers and team analysed one day's data of rainfall. At the epicentre on the Mariana Islands, the rainfall for the one day was 65 inches per day. From the epicentre, with a map of the globe on the computer, he started to put

500-mile radius rings until all the current rain clouds were encompassed. He then superimposed all the weather stations close to his perimeter lines; it was not until he got to 2000-mile perimeter that weather stations started to appear. The rainfall was similar at each weather station, but a lot less. They were all reporting between 38/39 inches, a further 500 miles, and the rain was 32/33 inches and so on until it reached the end of the rain cloud. All this information was put in, and the computer started to predict rainfall. As more stations came on line, the more accurate would be the predictions. One thing was quite clear: the further you were from the epicentre, the rain would not be so intense.

The computer was now asked to predict global rainfall on the actual data, and it showed that we would have about 2 inches of rain in the UK. With this information, he put the data into the Met office computer, and a daily picture of the UK, going further 2 inches daily, confirmed his original assumptions. If we couldn't get rid of the water, we would have massive flood problems. However, if the rain was constant, but not unduly heavy, our natural water source could cope, providing they were free flowing, but would be at an extremely high level. If our moorlands decided to drain naturally instead of absorbing, our reservoirs and water treatment would start to unload excess water, and could put us in a perilous situation. The real problem was our moorlands discharging excess water.

He asked his specialist, "Do we know how much water moorlands can hold, and is there any way of measuring it and anticipating the discharge?"

"It will take some time, but I will get on it straight away."

Weather stations across Japan were showing 15 inches against a computer prediction of 24 inches. The computer model was updating every time new data arrived. The next weather stations were in the Philippines, and the prediction for them was 13 inches.

Day 2: Philippines; Papua New Guinea; Taiwan

Actual rainfall from all weather stations measured 11 inches; the rain was not torrential but heavy, and the flood defences were coping. Twice now the predictions were wrong; we needed top get it right this time or confidence would be lost. The team put in many scenarios, using existing data to see whether the computer would get close to the actual measured rainfall. One scenario fitted the last two actual rainfalls. "Run with it," said Mike, and the computer predicted rainfall at 9 inches

Day 3: China, Shanghai; North Korea; Russia, Vladivostok; Australia, Darwin, Cairns

The cloud now approached the northern part of Australasia, still some way from India, and would reach the east coast of America by the end of Day 3. The computer was updated, and 80% of the rain was still falling into the ocean. The data from the islands was now replaced by an automatic weather station and was controlled remotely. The aircraft on station had done a remarkable job flying in torrential rain, but now the runways were breaking up and washing away; landing and taking off was becoming hazardous. The airborne data had not significantly changed in the 3 days. The scientists set up the automatic weather station that had arrived 2 days before, but their planes were grounded because of the state of the runways, and the pilots and scientists were now stranded. The ambient temperature was 30 degrees, but the relentless torrential rain was, for the team, like living in a power shower. It would be another week before they could be extracted from the islands. The flotilla that had been assembled were now helping the coastal countries with their flooding problems. The helicopters were now well out of safe range for extraction.

I got the updates and noticed the predicament the team were in. I had got them to the islands, so I told Stephen I would go back to get them. I had wiped their minds when we left them there—as far as they were all concerned, they had flown to the islands—and I would have to do the same for their return. We left Assington just before dark and got to the first island, beamed up the plane and left the verticular to get the crew. The portal opened, and the rain was as intense as when we left them. A force field emanated from the verticular to the accommodation and we collected them. We repeated the process on the other two islands, and the next stop was Iceland. We dropped off Lars and his team first; they asked the same questions about the transport they were on as they did on the way out. Stephen felt it so amusing, but they were scientists, and I answered their questions, knowing that their memories would be wiped clean yet again when they left.

When we got her back to the UK airfield, we put the

secretary-turned-guest-pilot in one of her aircraft and Stephen in the other. She thought she had flown both aircraft back. We said our goodbye, and she went into her office. As she looked round, we left for Assington.

For Mike Blowers, his assumptions and predictions on the rainfall were based on 20% of rain cloud over land. The countries in the southern hemisphere were now in their winter months; warm air from the rain cloud would meet up with the cold air fed from the Antarctica. It would be a tremendous battle, but who would win? He spoke with the Australian Met office, who had been monitoring the rain cloud too. Their synopsis was: "should the warm air win, we will have an extremely wet and barmy winter. We have the land mass to soak up the rainfall and believe it could be a bonus for us, since we have seven desserts, which could do with a sustained soaking, but it would make travelling across them hazardous—a small price to pay. We have had serious drought problems for the past two decades; being awash with fresh water would be a blessing. If the cold air wins, the rainfall will be snow.

Our guys say it could cause a 2-degree difference in our winter average temperature, which would cause us problems. Looking at your computer predictions, our north-east coast 9 inches of rain converts to about a foot of snow every day; that's chaos for our main towns and cities. Inland not such a problem would isolate lots of people, but we're used to travelling by air. Our military has been put on standby."

Mike said, "Queensland is going to be the first to be

affected, and it's going to be the first the rain cloud to encounter a mountain range of any significance. If it's possible, I would like hourly updates on the temperature, wind, rain, snow and air pressure. Do you have a weather station on the highest mountain?"

"Yes"

"Can I access it remotely?"

"Yes. These are the codes."

Mike wrote them down. "The reason I ask is the cloud, in 2 days, will confront the Himalayas. Everest, at over 27,000 feet, is a real obstacle, but it's summer; warm air meets more warm saturated air."

"You have an interesting problem there, mate. Keep in touch." He turned to check the monitor that showed the cloud in real time, inching its way across the globe. He hadn't slept for 36 hours, and it was time for rest. He couldn't see that much changing over the next 8 hours. He handed over to a colleague who had just come on. Would he be able to sleep with all that coffee he had drank?

He had slept soundly albeit 6 hours, but he felt refreshed and eager to see what was happening in Australia. He re-ran the tapes to before he went to sleep until the current time. In fast forward mode, he saw that the raincloud had gone around the Bellenden Ker range instead of dropping the rain to allow it to travel over it. It was a phenomenon he had never witnessed; even the computer was perplexed. The computer was still extrapolating the data but did not produce answers to what had happened. None of the team, who had spent most of their lives studying the weather, had seen anything quite like it.

Mike said to the team, "It seems like our raincloud does not want to go above its canopy of 22,000 feet. Mount Bartle Frere is over 5,600, which would have pushed it out of its comfort zone. What we have now from Australia is a raincloud that does not like heights." He emphasised the need to find out why. "Go back over all the data. The cloud must have encountered other mountain ranges. We need to know what happened then." The data from the top of the mountain and the other weather stations showed a drop in temperature. It was now snowing all over south-east Australia but only about four inches in steady snowfall; central and the northern territories were experiencing rain only 1.5 inches, much less than was expected. Most of the rain fell into the ocean, causing localised flooding in Cairns. So far, the raincloud had not caused much of a problem, depending on how long it would last. The next day, the rainclouds would hit India and Nepal.

Day 4: India; Nepal

Using Australian data, the computer prediction had changed to 3 inches of rainfall. The cloud was now in the foothills of the Himalayas and was separating again to find a route that prevented it from increasing its overall height. We were now getting gaps in the raincloud, as a deluge was now falling over arid India. However, the whole of India was experiencing rain and coping. The raincloud regrouped over the Indian Ocean. From satellite pictures, we could see that Tibet, Mongolia, the Gobi Desert, eastern Russia, and Siberia were now affected by rain. It was hard to tell how much, as they kept their data close to their chest. What was interesting from the satellite pictures was that the Himalayas were surrounded by the raincloud, and we are peaking through the cloud as it remained under 22,000 feet.

It was clear to Mike and his team that the computer predictions were far from accurate about the rainfall. None of the team had any answers to why the weather patterns were so different. In another 21 days, the whole of Earth would be covered by the raincloud.

Mike asked, "What do we actually know?! Fact the epicentre is still pushing billions of litres into the air, fact the cloud is still travelling at 1000 miles every 24 hours, fact the rainfall on land is far less than predictions, rainfall at sea is about what has been predicted, now that is an interesting fact, anybody have an opinion on that?"

"It's more interesting than that. It rains harder over arid and desert terrain than in overpopulated areas," said Casey Grey, the UK's top climatologist. "All the data so far collaborates this scenario." She continued, "Mike, nothing of the raincloud makes any sense. We are using the data against historical and known data, and it's giving us the wrong predictions. We should produce a new computer model based only on the raincloud itself. We have 4 days now of factual weather data to use and to see if there is a pattern."

"Ok," Mike said. "How long will it take?"

"4 to 6 hours."

Day 5: North Pole

The Earth was covered by 70% of water. From world

shipping, they sent in reports of weather conditions in all the oceans, with over 50,000 cargo ships on the sea or in ports ready to sail. Their basic reports supplied the new computer model with the data. The first 4 days of all data showed that rainfall at sea was 75% greater than on land. This figure correlated back to Day 1 and was correct to a quarter of an inch.

"I have an idea," Casey said. "The raincloud is travelling at 42 miles per hour or thirty-six knots; what if we asked some cargo ships to sail with the raincloud on all it fronts and measured rainfall? We could then advise the nearest landmass what could be the expected rainfall."

"Let's do it," Mike said.

They enlisted 750 cargo ships, which were now reporting rainfall while sailing at the edge of the raincloud. Despite being at their maximum speed of twenty-eight knots, they could not keep up with the cloud and passed the baton to the next ship the cloud was approaching. Only this data was used, and the 75/25 split appeared to be accurate.

The weather stations from the North Pole reported heavy snow and below average temperatures. It was the height of its summer, and at these temperatures, the ice would stop melting and begin to reform in a summer position, so the winter ice would double the total volume of the ice cap. On one day's data, it would be hard to convince anyone of the repercussions of such an event, but the cloud would be in Antarctica in 2 days with temperatures of minus 60 degrees. It would have a devastating effect on the continent; a colossal amount of ice would melt, glaciers would start to recede and a catastrophic increase in sea levels would ensue. All eyes were in Antarctica.

Day 6: USA; Iran; Moscow

I had been getting reports from Mike's team regularly, and I noticed they were experiencing difficulties with some countries. I told him I could help, and he gave me a list of countries that were not cooperating. I spoke to the General Secretary of the United Nations, and within a couple of hours, all countries now complied. The extra data confirmed the 75/25 split but not in all places; arid areas were getting far more than the populated areas.

It just does not make any sense, Mike thought.

Casey was perplexed, too. In all the years of data she had in front of her, nothing came close. This weather system was unique, a one off, manmade. It appeared to be under some control. *Is it an entity in its own right, choosing when and where to rain? Impossible,* she thought. She would need a lot more data before she put this hypothesis to Mike.

The raincloud was a thousand miles from Antarctica and was now confronting freezing air. Great chunks of ice were now falling into the Antarctic ocean. Three cargo ships that followed the cloud reported this and had to withdraw for safety reasons. Some of the ice lumps were estimated to be over 4 tonne, and the ships had sustained damage from the ice. Photos of the sea showed the ice floating, as if an ice breaker had just gone through, and it looked like a slush puppy. We still had a few submarines at our disposal; it would be safer for them to monitor the Antarctic ocean. It was a vast area, and with a possible thousand miles extra of

Antarctica, 100 submarines were given parts of the ocean to gather data. It would take for some 3 or 4 days to get into position.

Day 7: UK; Europe

The weather information today was from all European weather stations. The cargo ships in and around the Mediterranean, the north Atlantic approaches, North and Irish seas, and the English Channel were registering about 3 inches. That would mean a far more manageable amount of rain for the UK. We would know for sure by day 8.

It had drizzled the whole of the day. All weather stations reported ¾ inch of rain. No problems at all were reported across Northern Europe, but Southern Europe was reporting double that amount. They had rain whereas we were having drizzle. It was good for Southern Europe as they had been near drought conditions for several years, but they relied on tourism to help their economies and this could suffer because of the rain. However, if it rained everywhere, which it would be in few days, sunshine could be found above 22,000 feet but a lot colder. Holidays to the Andes and Himalayas might take off. Only time would tell.

Day 8: It was now raining or snowing over 2/3 of the Earth's land mass. Satellite data showed the North Pole expanding when it should have been retracting as it was summer. The Antarctic showed an ice floe had been created from the raincloud surrounding Antarctica, give or take a mile. The ice ring was a thousand miles from the contours of Antarctica, and travelling towards the land and ice mass, the ring was over 24 miles wide. Reports from the few submarines on station showed the thickness of the ice at the outer edge a foot thick, and the inner edge: 4 feet thick.

The UK team were asked for answers, but no one had a clue. The new computer model was working and proving that the model was accurate in forecasting the rainfall, and that was it. Why the weather was acting this way was a mystery. Mike had been in contact with his colleagues across the world, and no one had a worthwhile explanation on the weather phenomenon, which did not please their political masters. All Mike could tell them was a completely new weather system had affected the world and would remain for the foreseeable future if the eruptions continued.

Day 12: It was now raining everywhere. Actual figures and predictions were the same. In the UK, it had drizzled now for 5 days, and Wimbledon had to be postponed. The rain affected all sporting venues around the world. Earth's population was getting somewhat annoyed at the constant rainfall. They soon forgot the rain was a direct consequence of saving the planet.

The Prime Minister had said that the election would still take place in now just over two weeks. The opposition leader felt he had a better chance because of the weather. His supporters were activists, and he felt Earth Corp and my party would get the blame for the rain.

My one and only political broadcast had gone out before the rain had started and had been received well, according to the pollsters, and had put me just behind the incumbent party, pushing the opposition party into third place. What a difference a week makes; we were now pushed back to fourth place. I spoke with Conrad. For weeks now, he had been plugging Earth Corp, not only in our press, but all Media Corps papers and journals. The message was out there but not coming home to rest in the public's conscience.

"What to do?" I asked. "How to you fancy a live debate, with all the parties, broadcast live, no rehearsals and not knowing any of the questions you will be asked?"

"I have no problems with that. Let us do it."

"I will try to organise it the day before the election. I will get back to you."

Conrad spoke to press agents for all party leaders and told them I had challenged them to a live debate the day before the election, with no prior knowledge of the questions. Hours later they came back with a unanimous no; they would have to know the questions before even considering it.

"Not acceptable," Conrad told them. "Media Corps' current affairs programme attracts 23 million viewers on a Wednesday evening. I will devote the whole of the show to him. The audience will be invited across the whole spectrum of the public, and he will not know the questions; the audience will be asked to write their questions down, a week before the broadcast and email or post them to the show. An independent panel will select the questions to be asked, so if you want an hour listening to Earth Corp just before the election with no interference from your leaders, so be it. Those are the conditions; it's a take or leave it proposition."

Day 15: All the submarines were now on station, and the Antarctic was now surrounded by an ice ring over 200 miles wide. The outer rim was still only a foot thick, but the inner rim was now over 10 foot thick. All the ice was heading southwards, towards Antarctica, as if magnetised. No ice was moving northwards to warmer waters, which would naturally happen; sea currents and wind would influence the ice. Every Met office throughout the world shared data. The best brains were as perplexed as the UK team. Nothing made sense.

It had now drizzled in the UK for eight days, but everything was coping well. Alan MacMillan, who had been tasked with monitoring the moors and flood plains, had already told the team the amount of water the moors could take. "They are a sponge. It's the level of rainfall that really matters." He advised the team that all the moors, after 8 days of drizzle, were coping well naturally although saturated. The rivers and streams were high and fast-flowing back to the sea. The Fens would normally be dry during the summer. From Wicken fen to Welney, all was flooded in a controlled manner as if it was winter. The flood plains had started to build up with water, but still under control, as everyone had been prepared. Casey asked Alan if he would like to go to the canteen for a coffee. "I would like to run something by you before I talk with Mike."

Over a coffee, Casey told Alan: "I know this may seem weird. The raincloud, I believe, is not a threat to us. We must start thinking outside the box. There has never been such a vast weather pattern. It is controlling all the traditional weather patterns, ocean currents... it is creating a significant amount of ice around the poles. I ask myself why. We know the reason this weather pattern was formed— nuclear explosion in the Trench to vent the Earth's crust to stop it being knocked out of orbit. No one had given any thought to the repercussions and consequences of these actions, and anything had to be better than annihilation. What if this weather phenomenon is the final part of a grand scenario to rectify all the ills that have beset the planet since industrialisation? It is raining mostly at sea. Over land, the amounts of rain seem to vary to where it is needed. I have checked over the last week high tides in the last week, since the poles have expanded, are not as high as forecast. It's too early to tell, but this ice is going to lower sea levels, which will allow saturated land to drain into the sea and not be pushed back by high tides, causing widespread flooding. This whole event seems to be orchestrated, for our good, I believe. The only downside could be if the rain continues, cereal crops will deteriorate through water-logging, no sunshine will not ripen the crops, root crops will tolerate the conditions, but it's getting them out of the ground will be a major problem."

"Well," Alan said, "I would not take this theory to Mike. He wants facts. My advice is to wait until you can substantiate it with facts."

"Ok, I will sit it on it for few more days."

Day 16: The president of the Cayman Brac Bank picked up the phone; the call was from his eyes in the island's treasury department. "There is tremendous pressure from the US Federal Reserve, FBI and Interpol. I think the island government is going to buckle to this pressure, and you will be audited by a task force of very clever auditors who will not miss a thing, so unless your books are squeaky clean, they will find it. I don't know if you know, but there is an arrest warrant on you if you travel to the States or Europe," they told him.

"How long have I got?" he asked.

"No more than 3 days."

"OK, thanks for that."

He had close on to one billion of toxic money in special accounts, most of which was Enrico's. It had been 12 weeks since the last shipment of drug money from Columbia, and all had been laundered; only Federal Reserve money was in the vaults. It was the special accounts which would cause him a major problem. He decided to send it all back to Alberto through the banks he used to fund the purchase of Enrico's drug empire. The money came from a consortium of American Las Vegas Casino who wanted to open a branch on the island. Gambling was illegal on the Caymans, but there was a free vote every 2 to 3 years on whether to legalise it. The Cayman tourist industry wanted it, and the bank said it was holding a billion dollars for the immediate construction of a casino complex that would be the envy of the Caribbean. The vote went against gambling again by one vote, the closest it had ever been, and therefore, the return of the funds to the consortium would be seen to be the direct outcome of the island's vote. He was now confident the bank would pass the closest security checks, but it would still put up a defensive posture, arguing the island's rules on banking.

Day 17: Alberto's consigliere came to the house and told him that the money was back in their bank accounts. Since the visit of the CEO of Earth Corp, Alberto had no intention of carrying out a hit on all the principals and had advised all the other mafia bosses to stay well clear of Earth Corp, as the threat from them was very real. It left Alberto with no intention of hurting Earth Corp and the money back. Plus, the President of the bank would be looking for him to complete on the contract. He told his consigliere that it would be best if a fatal accident befell the bank manager. "As long as he is alive, he poses a threat to them, and with his hatred of all at Earth Corp and his financial muscle, he could get any crank to finish them off and get the blame. I have seen first-hand what that guy can do and believe he can carry out his threats. The DEA, FBI, CIA, and NSA I can deal with; they're predictable, and we have leverage in all those agencies. But what that guy did to my closest bodyguards, who would rather die than see me harmed, frit the life out of me. We are not going to do anything that will have him knocking on my door again, so see to it."

Annabella Pucci was in her solarium. It had not stopped raining for days, and the ultraviolet lights were no match for the sun, but at least her tan would stay. Her phone tinged with a new message, which she acknowledged. She got up from her sun lounge and went into her study, where her laptop was. There was an encoded and encrypted message for a new contract—the hit was a bank manager in the Cayman Islands, and it needed to look like an accident. It was always a problem to make the hit look like an accident; you needed to get up and be personal to the target, rather than just blowing them away. She thought there maybe sunshine there but was disappointed when she googled the weather. The flight she booked would take her from Nepal to Rome, then London to Miami; she would stay over one night in Miami and fly the following day on to Cayman Brac.

In the message was a photograph of the hit and several photos of a woman. Looking at the woman, there was not one of her face. It was as if she knew she was being photographed and knew how to avoid the cameras as she did. The only clear feature was that she was undoubtedly beautiful and had a great figure and long blonde hair. She could easily imitate her and get the guy's attention. She sent an encrypted message back, accepting the contract, and asked who the woman in the photo was. The answer came back dead. Good, that will make it easier. She packed several clothes and wigs, including the long blonde one. She would travel to Rome as herself, the rest of the journey would be one of her many aliases. The flight time from Rome was 2 hours 35 minutes. Her connecting BA flight to Miami gave her a couple of hours at Heathrow. The 10-hour flight to Miami would give her lots of time to plan the hit's 'accidental' demise.

After travelling for over 16 hours, she took a cab to the Four Seasons Hotel and checked in. It had been raining for days in the sunshine state and everybody looked miserable. She did not care. All she wanted was a shower and bed. In the morning, she checked out and got a cab to the airport. The flight to Cayman Brac was only an hour and a half. She had already booked Le Solei d'Or from Naples, a small but impressive hotel, expensive but exclusive. The hotel collected her from the airport and took her directly to the hotel. All her luggage had followed her—a bit of a miracle, after four flights—until to her room. Everything was now in place. It would take a couple of days to get acquainted with her hit. She would follow him discreetly and observe. The hotel hired a car for her, and she went about her business. After two days, she knew his routine and decided that the best opportunity for an accidental meeting was at the bank. It was now Friday—too late for anything to happen today, so she planned it for Monday.

Days 18 - 25: The weather pattern across the world remained unchanged. On the 25th day, magma levels in Utopia were decreasing rapidly and normalising. The eruptions from the Trench and vented volcanoes stopped. The land-based volcanoes, which caused the ash cloud, fell dormant. The raincloud was no longer increasing and decreasing rapidly in the northern hemisphere where the summer sun was at its highest and soon got to work on the raincloud. The pictures from the orbiting space station for the first time in 25 days showed the raincloud grip on the Earth dissipating. All the pictures showed the raincloud over the last ten days was cloud, with holes around the poles and mountains over 22,000 feet. Now, the cloud had started to break up over the middle east, and gaps had started to appear working northwards from the Equator.

85

CHAPTER 13

IT WAS THE EVE OF THE GENERAL ELECTION, and I made my way to the Media Corps television centre. The other major parties had insisted on knowing the questions, and as that would not happen, they would send representatives of all the parties to be part of the audience. I had to take part to give a chance for all the Earth Corp potential MPs as we were flagging badly in the polls because of the blame for the rain. The incumbent party were also doing badly, as the opposition party had accused them of working with us to make it rain. But as the opposition was doing so well, they still did not want a face-to-face confrontation with me.

After makeup, I was introduced to the presenter of the

show, television political legend Jon Henderson. He had ruined careers of politicians who tried to duck questions. I had admired him for years and held him in great respect, and I hoped he had mutual respect for me. He ran through the opening part and would call the parties cowards for their no show stance and then introduce me.

The audience whose question was chosen would ask it. He said, "There will be five questions, and we will allocate 12 minutes for your answer and subsequent questions arising from the question. I will select from those in the audience to ask the subsequent question."

I said I had no problem with that. I was deposited in the blue room for him to open the show, and 5 minutes later, I was walking towards him. We shook hands, and he showed me to the chair. He turned to the audience and asked for the first question. A very hesitant 14-year-old girl got up, gave her name and asked, "Why do you want to be Prime Minister?"

"Oh!" I said. "That's easy to answer. I don't want to be Prime Minister. Should Earth Corp win the election, those elected will form their own cabinet."

The opposition delegate raised his hand, and Jon pointed to him. "You will not have any influence and have the last say on who becomes leader of this country?"

"Certainly not. The only influence that I may have is that they all agree to the United Nations Charter on human rights and will be the fundamental part of UK law for which I believe in. That being said, they have been elected, not I, so however they make the transition will be their own time table."

The second question was from a former treasury civil servant. He asked, "Your manifesto on taxation and the simplification of it...has it been costed out?"

"No," I replied. "My belief is that the simplification will work to the benefit of everyone."

"Surely, getting rid of VAT as we know it will cause a tremendous loss of jobs."

"Only if they want to. Depending on age, some might retire under the exist sting pension arrangements, but I want them to ensure that the lower taxes are collected from every business and any person who buys and sells in the UK."

"Your sale tax of 10% on everything will increase inflation."

"Possibly, if everyone pays this tax. With no loopholes, I think it's right and believe it's fair."

Another spokesperson raised his hand and said, "So this 10% tax will be on everything?"

"Correct."

"Children's clothes, food, utility bills all will have this tax. There will be no exemptions?"

"Yes. It's a sales tax on everything that is sold."

Someone from the audience asked, "Will this be enough to fund government expenditure?"

"Now that's a difficult question—I would hope so. Bringing the black economy into taxation should have a significant effect. I really don't know. What I can tell you is that should we fail in bringing the country into surplus at the end of our term in office, I will personally underwrite the cost of their policies that my elected members have embarked on."

Someone shouted from the audience, "Have you enough money to do that?"

"Ample with a few quid left over," I said and smiled.

The next question came from a single working mother. "Will I be better off if I vote for your party?"

"Yes. Although everything you buy will be taxed at 10%, your income will only be taxed if you earn over £20,000 a year. You will have to pay 10% on whatever you earn as a contribution of 5% to the NHS, and the other 5% will be locked away for your retirement. You will not have to pay for child minding as we will fund it. All the things you need will be provided. I personally believe that you will benefit from electing an Earth Corp MP."

Next question, a man introduced himself as an NHS consultant surgeon and asked, "Will the NHS be safe in your hands; will we receive the necessary resources we so desperately need?"

"Yes, but it will be funded differently. Quite simply, the tobacco and drinks industries will foot most of the bill as excise duty will be abolished from day one."

"Supposing that's not enough," came from the opposition spokesman. "I can tell you have been a career politician, as it's a simple matter of putting the price up." Laughter erupted from the audience. He was wounded and said, "But you could price it out of the market."

"Now that hasn't worked either, and would that be a bad thing?" I said. "In my view, the NHS is like a sponge—no matter how much cash goes in, it's absorbed. We need the best kit money can buy and the very best people that will not have to look outside the NHS to supplement their income. The NHS is the envy of the world. It's possibly a little bruised, but it's in great shape to move forward and I believe could be managed better. The current budget of £120 billion did not prove to be a stumbling block to the tobacco and drinks industries at preliminary talks. My team feels that with the removal of excise duty and the general reduction in overall business tax makes the scheme doable."

The consultant retorted, "We have had these would-be finance and efficiency bods in what seems like every month. They are only interested in saving and not funding the equipment we need to do our jobs better."

"Can you give me an example?"

He thought for a moment. "A second MRI scanner would reduce waiting times to days instead of weeks."

"Have you got the space and team to operate it?"

"Yes."

"Well, sir, you have just got yourself a second scanner. My team will be in touch with your hospital tomorrow." A round of applause bubbled from the audience.

From the front row, one of the party spokesman said, "That was just a cheap PR exercise." I supposed it ruffled my feathers. I asked the consultant about the cost of running the second scanner for a year. "About £8 million for the very best Tessler."

I turned and directly faced the camera and said, "If there are any other NHS hospitals where a second scanner would reduce waiting times to a week or less, contact the show and I will personally pay for the machine. Cheap PR trick, I do not think so." Everybody got to their feet and applauded except the opposition party. The other parties also got on their feet.

Next question: "I am a financial advisor and intrigued about your tax simplification. Will it meet the government spending needs?"

"I believe so. The top rate of tax will be 30% and will start at £100,000. The threshold for paying income tax is £20,000 at 10%, then £50,000 at 20%, not forgetting the 10% national insurance which starts from the first pound earned. I have an example: 2018 minimum wage is £7.83, a 40-hour week making total earnings of £16,286.40 or £1,357.20 a month; after deductions, £1221.48. Under the new scheme, to spend his deduction of £135.72 against the current taxation of £169.77, he will be better off by £34.05."

"That's all very well but he or she will have to pay an extra 10% on food and utilities."

"They will be saving on fuel, tobacco, alcohol and any commodity that had excise duty."

A big smile formed on her face. "So what you are saying is if it's cheaper, the consumption of tobacco and alcohol will increase and the general health of the nation will get worse?"

"Possibly, but one who used to smoke 60 a day. I know how hard it is to stop when you are addicted, and I have found that it's the poorest of society that pays the cost. In my mind, there are two sorts of people: the haves and the have-nots. The audience was chosen at random, other than the people whose questions were selected. Would everyone in the audience stand up? Those that own their house, sit down." About 60% of the audience sat down. "Now, everyone that lives in rented accommodation sit down." It left about 15%. "Remain standing if you smoke." One or two sat down. "Remain standing if you drink alcohol every day." All remained standing. "Finally, sit down if you have a job greater than 16 hours a week." All remained standing.

I picked on one guy and asked, "If you have no work, why do you smoke and drink?"

"Boredom. Nothing else to do."

"Would you work for minimum wage if you could?"

"Yes"

"Would you move to find work elsewhere?"

"No. My home is where I was born. There was plenty of work for my granddad and father. I even had an apprenticeship, but at the end of it, the government of the day closed it down, putting thousands of us on the dole. We have been long-term unemployed and no chance of rewarding work."

"Thank you," I said, turning to the others standing. "Is this gentleman's plight the same as yours?" All nodded. "Sit down, and thank you." I continued, "This audience was picked at random to represent the population in general. There were over 700 invited, and if truly representative shows that only about 2/3% of the working population are really the have-nots"—Everyone shot their arm up to ask a question—"Please allow me to finish. With only a small percentage, I do not feel that it is an enormous problem to reverse the situation for them. I am well aware that owning or renting your own home does not make you a have, but the new taxation programmes that we would introduce would give you more money in your pocket to do with as you wish."

The final question came from a senior fellow of Cambridge Universities: "Would you abolish tuition fees?"

"Yes...and cancel all student debt. I want our finest minds to enhance our society, not worry about debt, but we will also want highly skilled engineers in all sciences and proper 5-year apprenticeships will be available with tax concessions on corporation tax. There will be 100% offset allowed to cover the true cost of the apprenticeship."

The opposition spokesman butted in, "More tax breaks for businesses? You are all tarred with the same brush."

I looked at him incredulously. "You mean that your party would not look to apprenticeships as solving the unemployment problem that faces this country and the world?"

A big smug grin appeared on his face. "It's all in our manifesto."

"Has it been costed out?"

An even bigger smile. "£11 billion a year," he said.

"And where is that money coming from?"

His smile started to wane. "The Treasury."

"Will this be from taxation, or are you going to borrow it, as your party has done in the past?" I asked.

"No taxation," the incumbent government spokesman

said.

"We have costed out your manifesto and all your pledges will cost this country a further £300 billion or 5% increase in income tax." I said.

A bit on the defensive, he replied, "We have costed out much lower. It's under £200 billion, and we will raise this tax from industry."

I said, "How do you know my company will pay it?"

"It will be law," he said proudly.

"And where am I going to find this money?"

"From your profits."

"What are you going to do to ensure that I make sufficient profit to pay this tax?"

Silence. I read his mind—he was desperately trying to answer, and he started to hyperventilate. I entered the presenter's mind to close the show and get the opposition spokesman away so he could be treated. The stage manager came through and took the opposition spokesman away.

Jon then turned to the audience. "Has anyone a question to ask?" Several hands shot up. Jon pointed to a guy who asked, "Does your party believe in the death penalty?"

"No, we have hanged too many innocent people, but life means life."

Another question: "What's your policy on immigration?"

"I suppose we have no real policy. We need to attract the finest minds from around the world if we are unable to fill these roles from within our borders. But I suppose your real intent to the question was the refugee problem created in the middle east and all over the third world. The United Kingdom is a great place to live, no wonder every displaced person wants to come here for all the things we take for granted. Most of us have a good life here; what we need to address is the problems in their own country, which in some cases we caused and have a moral responsibility in putting right. The United Nations are trying to bring peace into the middle east. It has been hard getting factions since their ideology is so far apart to even sit down at a table to even discuss any conciliation. On the table is self-determination for every individual, free and fair election, and the lands they have been fighting over for centuries being returned to the legal historic owners, with fair compensation to the displaced. The peace has held now for over 4 months, and everyone is still talking. When consensus is reached and new countries and boundaries are formed, the United Nations will police. Earth Corp will build the factories and hospitals to support their economy, while the west will pay for the damage to the country's infrastructure mainly caused by them in the first place. It will take a long time to get everything back together but the threat to the displaced people's reason for leaving will no longer exist, and the gradual voluntary repatriation to their homes will take place. We, that is the UK and Europe, will spend whatever it takes to make the refugees' life better in the camps they are in, but we will say no; we no longer have the room and infrastructure to cope with non-essential welfare refugees."

I looked at my watch—we were running out of time, but

so many hands were held up to ask a question. Jon came over and said that the programme could end now if I wanted to. "But we can reschedule all the next programmes if you want to continue."

I said, "Ask the audience if they would like to continue." Unanimously, they wanted to continue, so the programme would now overrun.

Jon took another question. A prison officer asked, "In your manifesto, you will decriminalise the sale of illegal drugs."

"Yes, there is so much criminality surrounding the illegal drug industry. For over 200 years, we have tried to stop it. Recreational drugs are available illegally more than ever. We would treat illegal drugs the same as tobacco and alcohol, and any person that has a drug-related prison sentence, where violence was not involved, will be released the day after Earth Corp forms a government."

He retorted, "So you will be soft on crime?"

"I don't think so. My view is that the minimum prison sentence will be 3 years without parole until 29 months. The Judiciary will have to think seriously on their judgements, but one thing will be totally clear to them: tax evasion or avoidance will be tolerated twice; third time, it's a custodial sentence of 3 years, and nobody will be exempt. All criminality will be treated the same: you will be given two chances, third offence: 3 years mandatory, no matter what crime, and will not be entitled to any remission of sentence until the last month of their sentence. If they have shown that their life has now changed, they will be released earlier. Any re-offending of any crime will put them into a 6 year prison term. Should they, after release, offend again, it's life. Those people that think that prison is an occupational habit will have to think again. Prison will not be a soft option; every luxury will have to be earned."

He then asked, "What about the privatisation of prisons?"

"All prisons will be the sole responsibility of the home secretary. We will compensate those private companies at an equitable sum, but all prisons will be controlled by government. None will be operated in the private sector."

Next question: "Were you responsible for this rain?"

"Yes, it was my people that put together a plan to prevent the underground explosion that would have certainly knocked the Earth out of orbit and would certainly have destroyed the Earth—no one would have survived, so venting the pressure was our only solution. We did not look enough into the repercussions of our actions in the Pacific, but I do not feel guilty about that. The world is now safe but a little damp." A wave of laughter emanated from the audience.

Another question came: "How can you be so sure that full employment will ensue once Earth Corp is elected?"

"That's quite a complicated question. Earth Corp and Leiston Semiconductors are on the verge of bringing a new source of energy to the world. We have fused three of the most common elements found in the world—salt, sand, and hydrogen to form a completely new power. It's more like Wi-Fi than it is to electricity. It's not harmful and will be free to everyone. This white energy will be integrated into the fabric of our homes and factories. All new builds will have courses of interlocking bricks, similar to Lego and machines and household appliances will tap into this energy and work as they would with electricity. Everything would have to change to use this energy—every washing machine and cooker and anything that needs electricity—to make it work. To replace every electrical item on Earth will take decades. The electrical appliances will be recycled, creating a whole new industry throughout the world. Plus, the new factories to build or convert existing factories will take an incredible amount of human resources to accomplish, so that is why I am confident that full employment will be a reality."

"When will these new appliances be ready?" he asked.

"I currently, as of yesterday, have no idea, but with the best brains and unlimited funds at their disposal, a breakthrough could happen tomorrow, next month, or next year, but I can assure everyone that Court Leiston and I will make it happen."

Next question: "How do you feel about the consumption of animal flesh?"

"I have a fondness for all animals. I do eat their flesh, but I reconcile this, they are bred for the table and therefore would not exist at all if we stopped eating animal flesh. To me, it is similar to growing vegetables. One thing that is fundamental is that all creatures will be slaughtered humanely with no exceptions. Sacrificial and religious slaughter will be a criminal act if not done humanely. There will come a time when the food we want will come from machines; you tap in what you want, and the machine will make it for you. Its source will be synthetic, but you would not know the difference. If you ask for a steak, it will look like a steak, taste like one and have the same protein content as a steak. How do I know this? It is an extrapolation of what some of our companies are striving towards now. Currently we are a long way off."

Next question: "Why do you hold so much faith in the United Nations?"

"The whole world is interconnected, and we need a truly independent organisation to look after everybody's interest. I have given the United Nations the fiscal ability to be totally independent. The General Secretary has told me that the rules for membership will alter in line with the new independence. All countries of the world will be eligible to join. There will be two types of membership: those counties that have enshrined the UN charter on human rights into their own law, and those that have not. The security and all other councils will be made up from those that have adopted the charter, and only these have a vote. The delegation size of each member country will be its total population divided into its land mass or a similar formula that recognises the density of population and the size of the country."

I answered several more questions but had to point out that these were my views and not necessary the views of Earth Corp's candidates. I saw the studio manager waving his hand in the familiar manner to start winding the show up. We had overrun by an hour. Finally, I said, "We are a truly right wing party, but our right is doing the right thing for everybody. All will benefit from electing an Earth Corp MP. Thank you for listening."

Jon took over and ended the show. He thanked me for being honest, then thanked the audience for their participation. He then turned to face the camera. "Tomorrow is the day you all can make a difference, so please vote. Voting starts at 07:00 to 22:00 hours. Join me tomorrow night. My election show starts at 22:30, and we will start getting the exit polls from constituencies that have predicted quite accurately the result of the election. Thank you, and goodnight." A round of applause came in response and some audience members even stood. I was pretty sure they were voting for Earth Corp.

We walked off together, with the applause still sounding. Conrad met us and gave a thumbs up. "That has put a lot of pressure on all the other parties and really cannot counter it before the election," he said. "They made a tactical mistake not coming, and I personally believe they will rue this day and Earth Corp will win tomorrow."

I took off the makeup. I could not take my preferred transport, which would have got me home in minutes. A convoy of cars got me to City Airport, and I took Stephen's helicopter to Assington. It took just over an hour, and as we flew in outside the Priory main gates, a small army of the press had gathered. I read Stephen's mind, and he was not at all pleased, something more for him to worry about. We exited the helicopter, and he went directly to see his guy in charge of security. I went straight in, and Sue was waiting. She had heard the helicopter arrive.

She asked, "Do you want something to eat?"

"No. I had something at the studio. What did you think of the broadcast?"

"I think you will have made more people want to vote what you propose is extremely radical and maybe too radical for a lot of folk, but you came over as sincere, and if Earth Corp get elected, you will be the difference from the other parties. We will know in 36 hours."

I went into my office and waded through loads of mail and reports. The bank of TV monitors showed real-time pictures of the Earth. For days, it had been cloud, although lights were now visible during the night in the northern hemisphere and where the cloud had broken up. Despite the rain, there had not been any reports of major loss of life. I supposed it would take some time before we knew what harm this rain had caused.

CHAPTER 14

ANNABELLA ASKED THE OWNER where the best Italian restaurant on Cayman Brac was. The owner advised that the best was on Cayman; however, the Cayman Brac Beach Resort had just employed a first-class Italian chef.

"I will have a word with the hotel to see whether they could do something special for you," he said.

An hour later, the chef called, saying he would be pleased to do something special and asked if there was anything she had in mind. She suggested some of her favourite food, some of which needed marinating for 24 hours, but the chef said it was fine.

"What time will you be dining?" he asked.

"About 8 pm."

"I look forward to seeing you then."

The rain had stopped, and the sun was out. With the sun shining, this island was magical; the beach was marvellous. As far as she had so far seen, there were no negatives, and although she was using the ploy of buying property to meet her mark, why not make Cayman an additional base as most of her contracts were in the States? Miami was only an hour and a half away; it would make sense.

She asked the manager to contact an estate agent so she could view some holiday homes and spent the rest of the Friday looking at properties. She saw five properties but none fitted the bill exactly. The agent had several more places to show her as she had given him what she was looking for and would pick her up at 10:30 the next day.

On Saturday, she viewed eight more properties, and three looked promising. She picked a favourite and put an offer of 500K less than its asking price as she would have to spend that sum on renovations. A French couple owned the property, and the agent would email them the offer but would not hear from them until Monday, as he only had the business email. He dropped her off at the hotel, where she was now going to transform herself from the Plain-Jane to her normal beauty.

She looked stunning when the taxi came to pick her up. The red dress and long blonde hair left nothing to the imagination. The taxi driver rushed to open the cab for her, and 20 minutes later, she entered the hotel and walked to the restaurant. The maître showed her to her table, but she asked if she could sit at another table and pointed to one against the wall, with no view of the ocean but with a panoramic view of the restaurant. She ordered a bottle of Chianti, but before it arrived, the Italian chef came to her table with a menu of what he had prepared for her. Had this been her last meal ever, she would have chosen it, hoping that the taste of it lived up to her expectations. Her first course arrived—it was as good as she had ever tasted—possibly the best. So engrossed into the starter, she had not noticed the arrival of three men who were being shown to a table. After finishing her first course, she looked around the restaurant and realised that one of the men was her mark. Perhaps she would get this contract over sooner.

Her second course arrived, and it was sublime. She noticed that her mark had not taken his eyes off her. Their eyes met, and she did not look away. He rose from his chair, walked over to her and asked what she was eating as it looked so nice and he could not find it on the menu.

"It's being done especially for me. The chef is Italian, and I adore Italian food," she said.

"May I join you?" he asked.

"What about your friends?"

"They are colleagues and will understand."

"I don't know whether chef has made enough for two."

"Don't worry. I will go and find out," he said before he walked directly to the kitchen. He returned moments later and said there was enough for the both if them. He introduced himself as the President of Cayman Brac bank, and she replied with her cover story and added: "I have spent yesterday and most of today looking at properties to buy as most of my work is in the States. I have made an offer on one that I like buts it's ½ a million short of the asking price. Won't know till Monday."

He asked where it was and she told him. He replied, "You were right. I know the place and it is overpriced. Why don't you let me show you around the island? My bank has several properties that are not on the market, and some could be real bargains as we only need our loan money back."

She agreed. The third course came—steak Lorenzo. The chef bought it out and said he had used the best and most expensive Argentinean fillet but have added a touch of ginger and caramelised shallots, so it was a Lorenzo with a Luigi twist enjoy. After he returned to the kitchen, they both started the meal—it was sublime, and on that they agreed. The second bottle of Chianti opened, and he started to open his heart out to her. He had been married but divorced for the love of his life who was brutally slain by thugs employed by Earth Corp. "They are thieves. They have stolen money from my bank, and it will take years of litigation to get it back."

His soft expression had really hardened; he realised he was ranting and apologised. She said it was ok, and they continued eating. They finished, and he charged the bill to the bank.

They were the last people to leave the restaurant. It was a warm night outside. He insisted he took her back to her hotel and summoned Charles, his chauffeur. Shortly, the Rolls Royce arrived at the front of the hotel. Charles leapt out and opened the door for Annabella to get in.

Her date walked round and got in the other side. He turned to her and said, "The night is still young. Do you really want to go back to the hotel?"

"What do you have in mind?"

"I could take you to the best night club on the island."

"Sounds good to me," she said.

They arrived at the coral club. He was well known and was shown to a table close to the dance floor. Primarily, the bands played Reggae, but there was a DJ tonight.

He asked, "What music do you like?"

"Strange as it may seem, I like 60s and 70s music, mostly. But all good music."

The waiter came over for their drinks order; the speciality was Caribbean Punch. "I must warn you, though," the waiter said, "it really packs a punch. But it really is nice and very drinkable."

"I will try one," she said, and they both had one. "It's gorgeous," she said. "It doesn't taste of alcohol at all."

"That's the problem with it. It's so moreish," the waiter said. They ordered a second, before her companion went over to the DJ and asked him to play some 60/70 music.

She started to tell him her cover story, and the third punch arrived. Her mood was mellowing, and she was becoming quite attracted to her mark. Although at least 20 years older, he did not look it; he was a very handsome man, incredibly wealthy, and she knew he was lusting for her. The record stopped and next was Chris de Burgh's Lady in Red. He asked if she would like to dance, and both got on to the dance floor. He held her really close—he was an accomplished dancer—and she was enjoying every moment. They continued dancing for several more tunes, and eventually they sat down and he said, "I have a beach house not far from here. Would you like to come for coffee, and then Charles will take you to your hotel?"

"Ok, let's go." She was feeling sexy. Knowing it was wrong getting so intimate with her mark was against all her reasoning. It must have been the punch. They arrived at the beach house, and even in the dark, it looked impressive. He opened the door and turned on the lights. They walked into the massive, ultra-modern kitchen. "How do you like your coffee?"

"Black but not too strong. No sugar."

He took some beans from one jar then a similar amount from another. "It is my own special blend," he said as he put the beans into the grinder. He put equal amounts into the expresso machine and two small cups and then pressed a button, before the coffee flowed into both cups.

She sat at the breakfast bar as he brought the coffee over; it was piping hot. If it tasted as good as the aroma it was giving off, it would be wonderful. It cooled to drinking temperature, and she took her first sip. It was divine. She was a coffee connoisseur, yet she had never tasted anything quite like it. He could see from her face she was really enjoying it.

"You must tell me the coffee beans you are using. The coffee is incredible!"

"I am glad you like it."

"I love it!" she said.

"Well, you will have to marry me for it." They both laughed, and he went back to make another cup to show it was no fluke. The second cup tasted even better, if that was possible.

"Could I have a look around the rest of the house?"

He agreed and gave her a guided tour of the house.

"How much is this worth?"

"About £37 million—nearly as much as my Yacht moored at the boathouse."

"So it is a bit out of my league," she commented.

"Not really," he said. "If we were married, it would be ours."

"That is the second time you have mentioned marriage. Do you ask every girl you meet?"

"No. The moment I walked into the restaurant and saw you, it was love at first sight. It has only happened to me twice. My first wife was more of a friend. We had met at college, and after graduating, we just got married. I was 21, and I started working for the bank I now own—it was quite small then, and I built it up to where it is today. After many trips to America, I met the girl of my dreams. We had a torrid affair for about 5 years, and it cost me my marriage, but it was for the best as she is so happy with her second husband. I pleaded for her to marry me many times but after 5 years, she just vanished and left me heartbroken and turned up out of the blue last year with a tribe of beautiful young women. I tried to start where we left off; we made love several times, but it was not the same—her eyes were cold; she had an overwhelming sense of hatred, and the fire in her had gone out. Do not get me wrong, I again asked her to marry me, and she said she would after she had finished a vendetta against Earth Corp. I have told you she was killed by Earth Corp, and hopefully, I will finish off what she started."

He looked quite sad after confessing his other love. She reached for his hand and pulled him close to her. Their lips met first gently. He pulled her closer into his body, and the kiss became more passionate, and a sense of urgency overcome them both. He swept her off her feet and carried her up the stairs to the master bedroom, where they tore off each other's clothes and fell onto the bed. Now both naked, he was so gentle, caressing and kissing her all over. They made slow, passionate love, which she enjoyed. She headed into the shower, and several minutes later, he joined her, and they made love again. During this, he asked her to marry him again, and she screamed yes, mid-pleasure. They dried each other and headed to bed. Not another word was said until the morning.

He bought her coffee and sat on the bed and asked, "Did you mean it that you would marry me?"

"Yes," she said, "but it's only to get the secrets of your coffee." They both laughed. She had fallen in love with this man. Everything he did was gracious, and the age difference did not matter. In fact, he was fitter than most of her previous lovers. With all his money, she would be set up for life, but there was just one problem: she was supposed to knock him off accidently. Since that wasn't going to happen, she would seriously piss off Alberto and put herself on his hitlist and both of them would perish. However, with the connections her new love had, it would not be difficult to protect him, but as she eliminates the first hit man, tactics would change. She would need to see Alberto in person and tell him that her husband no longer posed a threat and did not want to pursue his vendetta against Earth Corp. It would be a big ask getting her fiancé to stop the hate he had for Earth Corp. She would deliver it as a condition of their marriage, as if he pursued the vengeance of an old flame, he must still love her more than her. She would not marry him if he continued in his quest for vengeance against Earth Corp. Simple. Should she find out that he had continued his pursuit, she would be on the next plane out of Cayman. He agreed and contacted Alberto, telling him the Earth Corp principals were not to be harmed and that he could keep the funds for the extermination of the principals of Earth Corp.

It would normally take 7 days for a marriage licence for the Cayman Islands. The posting of the 7 days' notice was waived, and a special licence was prepared. They married Sunday afternoon, with two bank officials witnessing. The honeymoon was at the beach house. It was the same as the night before: sex until exhaustion took over. Staff had been summoned to ensure that all they needed was provided; breakfast was served to them on the bedroom terrace, which looked over the bay. She could see the magnificent Yacht moored.

"I will take you to our main home," he said.

Charles arrived and took them back to the capital. His main home was possibly better than his beach house, but without the views. She was introduced to the staff that made the house work, and he took her round the whole house and ended up in the garage—not a garage, more like a showroom of the most beautiful and expensive cars ever made, and they were in pristine condition. There were over 40 classic cars. There must have been over £200 million of cars: Bugatti, Lamborghini, Ferrari, Porsche... but the one that she saw was a red Alfa Romeo spider, circa 1972, in immaculate condition.

"Can I use it?" she asked, excited.

He said, "I promised to show you the whole island, and we will do that tomorrow. I need to pop into the bank and do some work then I can put all meetings on hold and devote the rest of the day to you. The following day will be different. I must spend time at the bank. That way, I can make room in my diary so we can have the honeymoon of a lifetime."

After a light breakfast, the following morning, they went down to the garage. The Alfa with its top down looked stunning. They climbed in, and he started the car. That oh-so-familiar sound of an Alfa! The electric garage doors opened, and they were off. The bank was just 10 minutes away. He parked in his spot, and they both left and entered the bank. Everyone in the bank was waiting to greet the presidents new wife, and she felt a warmth towards when she met the staff.

He led her into his office and asked his secretary to

cancel all his appointments and rearrange them for the following day. "By the end of the week, I want the whole month off with no disturbance at all. I am not contactable; everyone will have to hold the fort until I return. We will be using the company plane to go where my wife wants to go."

Twenty minutes later, the Alfa was purring away. Every time he changed gear, that telltale throaty purr vibrated through to the cockpit. He had not stopped talking from the moment they left the bank. She was so excited about what was to come and just laid back to listen to her new husband who had only one objective to make the rest of her life pleasurable.

He was so excited talking about the honeymoon and wasn't paying too much attention to the road. He indicated left too early, having not noticed the vehicle trying to enter the road he was on. The other driver saw the Alfa indicating left and started to pull out in front of the Alfa. It was the next left he wanted to take, but it was too late—the truck had pulled out. She saw what was about to happen, and her survival mode kicked in. He started to brake but was too late. She flung herself from the car and heard the car crash as she hit the kerb and felt her collar bone break. Her momentum kept her going forward, and the second crash happened—a wall stopped her momentum but her head was the break and she fell into unconsciousness.

She woke up a few hours later. Her shoulder had been pinned and was in a sort of plaster. She couldn't move her arm. There were several people in the room. She asked how her husband was but was greeted with silence. A police officer moved forward and told her that he had died at the scene." The car had got trapped in the side of the truck, and as it finished its manoeuvre, it left the car at a right angle to the approaching traffic and was hit by another truck which tee-boned your husband car. We are not sure which crash killed your husband, but even a modern car with air bags and all the safety features would not have saved him. It is a tragic accident. The indicator on your car was still blinking at the scene, which supports what the lorry driver said. He thought you were turning left and felt safe to pull out. The best we can do to the driver is driving without due care and attention. I am so sorry for you."

She was gutted, angry and in a lot of pain. A nurse gave her an injection that eased the pain eased, and she drifted off to sleep. She was kept in the hospital for 24 hours because of the concussion. Afterwards, Charles came and picked her up.

"Where would you like to go?" he asked.

"The beach house." She went to his study, where she found photos of her husband sailing, playing golf, horse riding... he was a very active man. There were not many photos of any females and none of his first love, which was strange as the affair lasted for 5 years. Were there any photos of them together? She hadn't taken any during the 36 hours of marriage. She asked Charles to find them should they exist.

The death of the president of the bank and major shareholder meant an extraordinary general meeting had to be held, and a date was set for the following Thursday.

CHAPTER 15

THE POLLING STATION AT ASSINGTON VILLAGE HALL also had the press and TV crews to see us vote. We had elected for postal votes—and already voted—so camping outside the Priory and village hall would a waste of time for them. The pub was doing a roaring trade. Villagers were being interviewed for their views. The pub landlord, who I had met a few times, said I and all the people from the Priory were nice people.

It appeared that the voter turnout was large. Exit polls showed the incumbent party and Earth Corp being neck and neck, but the opposition were doing poorly. In the past, exit polls had been a surprisingly good barometer of the outcome but time would tell. Polling was scheduled to finish at 22:00, with the first result round about midnight. I had the whole day and evening at home. It was the first time in a while I had time to relax. I needed my wellies to take the dogs for a walk since the whole of my estate was sodden. My boots sank at each foot fall. I made my way to the higher part of the estate, but it made no difference—it was well and truly soaked. The dogs seemed to be impervious to the conditions and were playing as normal. On my return, my calf muscles ached. We really needed some hot weather to dry out the land.

I spent the rest of the day in my office, catching up on all mail and reports. Wading through, I stumbled upon one from Conrad, which he had received via Reuters, that Bruce Kennett had been murdered on death row. The murderer was pissed off with him moaning it was all a mistake and claiming he was innocent. The whole of death row was similarly annoyed, and when the guy stuck a prison knife through his heart to shut him up, no one blinked an eyelid. His arrogance was the death of him. He was by far the most ruthless businessman I had ever met and had people eliminated if they got in his way, so I was not sorry. Even his ex-wife had not claimed the body, so he would be interred in the prison cemetery.

The space station link showed an growing reduction of cloud. About 36 hours had passed since the rain had stopped, and it looked like the middle east had lakes instead of sand while the Sahara Desert looked like a sea. I contacted the Met office and asked Mike Blowers his views. He insisted it was too early to make a judgement; as always, he wanted facts. He added, "One of my staff, Casey Gray, has a hypothesis with no basis in fact, but extremely interesting, and if she is anywhere close the world as we know it today, will be totally different. I will put you through to her."

There was about a 30-second delay before she came on the phone. "How can I help you?"

"Mike tells me you have a scenario based on no facts, but your intuition. Could you tell me what you think and when you first became aware of it?"

"It was about a week into the rain, had the rain been the same over the ocean as over the land, mass flooding, deaths would have been in the millions for those who couldn't get to higher ground. This got me thinking: the land mass is getting water logged but natural drainage and flood plains around the world have coped. The poles ice cover has increased phenomenally. Antarctic has increased its ice mass by 1000 miles. The arctic is already greater than normal for this time of year, and when winter comes, it will connect the two continents with ice. All this ice will reduce sea temperatures and change the currents, that is a fact. My personal slant on that is the currents will go back to their original positions prior to global industrialisation. The currents are well documented since Vasco de Gamma's circumnavigation of the globe. Only time will prove me wrong. The lower water temperatures in the Pacific and Atlantic will mean that cyclones and hurricanes would not be so intense and will cause less destruction. It will take some time for the water to cool, but it will happen I am sure.

The hole in the ozone layer was measurably getting smaller; I believe it will close and this cloud will make the ozone stronger, keeping the planet cooler. I believe that the rain will be beneficial for the globe; I see no downsides at all."

I thanked her and hoped she was right. Time would tell.

I went in search of Sue and asked if she fancied some lunch.

"Yes," she said. "Where?"

"How about the Red House? It is been such a long time."

"Fine," she said.

"I will get Trevor to get the car." I told Trev we were going to our old local pub, and he reminded me to inform security. I fetched Sue and our dogs and led them to the massive Hummer purring outside with three security vehicles surrounding it. I thought it was a bit over the top. The security at the gate made way for the convoy, and the press snapped pictures as the vehicles sped away. When we hit the main road, the police stopped the oncoming traffic for us to join the main road and stopped any following press. The convoy was speeding now and bumper to bumper. I turned and looked at Sue—big smile on her face.

"Now you know why I don't go shopping," I said.

Police waved us through at every junction, and 25 minutes later, we were at the Red House. The police had created road blocks at either end of the village. Everyone in the pub had been searched, and Pauline, the new landlady, of the pub had to vouch for everyone present. I apologised to Pauline and Sue, and I sat down.

"This level of security is way over the top. I will talk to

Stephen. We're more likely to die in a convoy accident."

"The cost must be enormous," Sue said.

"I have used the helicopter, but the security is the same. We really do not have enemies anymore; it would only be cranks."

We had lunch and spoke to those villagers that went through the search. I asked if they had voted yet and all said they had. Good. We left the same way we came. The front vehicle radioed through, and the gates were open, allowing us to sail passed the paparazzi.

The 6 o'clock news featured on the turnout—it appeared that all that could vote had voted. It was unpresented, it would be an interesting night, so many new voters had Earth Corp galvanised the disenfranchised to vote at last. If we do not win, at least the result will reflect the whole will of the people. In 24 hours, we will know for sure.

In every general election, there is a constituency that wants to declare first; it's normally a race for about three small constituencies. It was just after 11 o'clock when the first recount had to take place, soon followed by two more recounts. The sitting MPs of these three constituencies always had a large majority, never had there been a recount. Jon Henderson, the TV anchor, went directly to the first constituency. The reporter advised that the turnout had been 98.7%. On the first count Earth Corp were in front by eleven votes. Overturning a majority 7500 in favour of Earth Corp, the other recounts were showing a single figure majority in favour of the sitting MP, but both had Earth

Corp second, and both turnouts were above 96%. During the day across the country, people queuing to vote were asked why they were voting, and all came with the same reason: they now had something to vote for. The TV camera came back to the studio to the assembled political pundits to comment. They were amazed at the level of turnout. They said it was due to the Earth Corp phenomenon. "It's rewriting the political agenda. If they don't win by a majority, they will have won the most votes."

Jon Henderson turned to his statistical guru, and she entered the first count results into her laptop. A map of the UK appeared with a forecast based on the results. It showed the opposition party wiped off the political map with just twenty-six seats, the incumbent party 330, others 19, and Earth Corp with a staggering 275 seats and 67% of the popular vote.

At four in the morning, with ¾ quarters of the results in, the computer predicted that Earth Corp would end up with 291 seats; 314 for the incumbent party would not be a majority, and they would have to rely on the other parties to form government. However, Earth Corp had over 69 percent of the popular vote, but not the seats to show for it.

The Leicester East result came, and the programme diverted to hear the result. The returning officer announced that a total of 87,529 votes had been cast, and the results showed the Earth Corp candidate receiving 83,118 votes. The room erupted. The sitting MP's shock was very apparent. The returning officer waited until the noise stopped and carried on announcing the remaining results and declared that our candidate, Sinah Patel, was duly elected the member of parliament for Leicester East. They all shook her hand; I could see she was troubled—it was written in her face.

She was a fourth generation Kenyan Asian. She had been outstanding in the induction at Cheltenham. It had taken a great deal of persuasion to get her to agree to becoming an MP, as she really wanted to go back to her ancestral home in India for humanitarian work. Earth Corp had given her this opportunity, and now she was an MP. She had a first-class degree in Economics, Politics and International Law. It was natural for her to become leader of Earth's Corp Political party.

All the elected Earth Corp MPs would travel to Media Corp in London and use the conference facilities there. The election had been a resounding success for Earth Corp—we had won the peoples vote in the towns and cities, though the rural areas stayed with the incumbent party, who would try to form a minority government. They were doomed to fail as what's left of the opposition would never countenance any deal with their arch-enemies no matter what cabinet positions were offered. There were not enough others to form a government, so they would have to talk to Sinah Patel, and if an acceptable deal could be struck, they could govern with a majority unprecedented in British politics.

The honourable Stephen Halstead had spoken to the opposition, and they said no—if the others would come on board, he would technically have a majority of three. What they were asking for this coalition was totally unacceptable to his party. Having failed, he asked Sinah Patel to try to form a government, and she agreed to do so.

I arrived at the conference room and walked to the lectern, applauding all the new MPs. Sinah Patel joined me at the lectern. I turned to all of them and said, "Well done. None of you have any experience of government but you are all clever enough to excel as ministers and MPs. As I have already said, I want no part of government, and our manifesto will now be enacted. Let us be the first country to fully embrace every article in the United Nations Charter and be the first member of that organisation and be the first low-tax capitalist country in the world, and make that happen immediately."

I spoke to Sinah: "the incumbent Prime Minister and Chancellor are the best we have had in an exceptionally long time. Form a coalition with them and leave them in place providing they embrace our manifesto totally. If you make yourself foreign secretary, it will give you a big advantage in India and place you in charge of the overseas budget. You could make a serious change in the format of that country. I am only advising you; it is up to you. You are now the official leader of the party. I am off to see Conrad about some other issues I need to catch up on. I will look forward to your first broadcast to the nation this evening."

Sinah spoke to her MPs and put forward the proposals for a coalition. There was some discussion about the Prime Minister and Chancellor remaining the same. All assembled could see that there really was not an alternative. None had held positions in government and would need the experience of members who had. Later, she held a meeting with the incumbent PM and told him of her wish to form a coalition between both parties, he and the Chancellor would remain in situ, while all the other cabinet positions would be split equally by both parties, and she would become foreign secretary. All the Earth Corp manifesto would start from midnight tonight.

"Impossible," the Chancellor said, "we can't go from a high tax economy to low tax economy overnight."

Sinah said, "We can and will make it possible. All excise duty and VAT will be abolished from midnight. The new sales tax of 10% will be introduced at midnight on all goods with no exceptions. The new salary tax and allowances will start on Sunday for weekly paid employees and the first of the month for salaried personnel. Any shortfall will be adjusted in following months' salary. We will both address the nation at ten this evening, advising the population of the coalition and the adoption of all Earth Corp policies that will start from midnight."

There was no use in arguing with Sinah as it was the main part of their outstanding electoral victory. People wanted change and quickly, so the Chancellor would take on this challenge with vigour. His outstanding mind was working on the problem. There would be chaos in the ranks of the civil service, but the problems arising from it would all be sorted in time.

The Chancellor left to see the governor of the Bank of England and told him about the midnight deadline.

Although shocked at the speed it would happen, he knew that it was on the cards with the election result—there would be enough funds to insure the smooth change—and advised the CEOs of all banks of the change and the Bank of England would cover all extended borrowings from businesses until everything is sorted.

The governor said, "There is going to be a lot of winners but also a fair number of losers. the new government are not out to make losers so those cases will be taken on board and an equitable result will be found, the whole concept of this new government is fairness, and everyone should pay 10%."

He went to the Treasury and told all heads of departments of the immediate policy decision and that it would not be a problem if they needed extra staff. "All budgets are suspended until the transition of the new low-tax economy and the true cost of change is known. It will probably take 6 months to resolve." He went back to eleven Downing Street and told his private secretary to notify all businesses of the change and put an embargo on notifying all but those that needed to know to make the transition as smooth as possible.

"There will be a broadcast tonight at 10 pm which will advise the public of the changes. Can you set me up a conference call with the CEOs of petrol companies, tobacco and all companies that have excise duty on their products? Let me know when there all on conference."

It took about an hour to get them all on line. He told them that custom and excise duty was being abolished at midnight. "You would be picking up the bill for the NHS and the road and rail network. £250 billion needs to be raised and your products must reflect this in your retail price. You need to collaborate to make the transition successful. The Bank of England has told all banks that it will underwrite the extra costs in the short-term if it effects your cash flow, but it will be left to you to insure you raise sufficient monies to fund both organisations. The removal of excise duty on all your products the public believe that the costs will come down and we don't really want to disappoint them. You will have to factor in the changes in corporation tax, which are reductions, and these will come in to effect at midnight. The new taxation system will put more money in the pockets of the public, and they will spend this money. Interest rates are still low and the Bank of England has no intention of raising them in the short and medium term as price and tax reductions will have a dramatic effect on the retail price index. The Prime Minister will address the nation at ten this evening and would like some examples on the reductions. You have 5 hours to come up with the new price of petrol, a pint of beer, a bottle of wine, a packet of cigarettes and a London to Birmingham season ticket."

There were no questions from all the CEOs. They would have their work cut out as it was a big ask, but the Chancellor was certain they would come up with the prices before the Prime Minister went live to the nation.

CHAPTER 16

I WAS BACK IN ASSINGTON, talking to Court Leiston. We were no further forward in using Utopian white energy to replace electricity, which was a major factor in bringing back full employment to the whole world as every electrical appliance would need to be changed.

I said, "Perhaps we are looking at the problem the wrong way; we are trying to make it adapt to our usage when its development was based on Utopian usage. We need to send some of your team to live with ordinary Utopians, to see how they go about their normal life. They must cook, wash, iron, and watch TV and find out how they work. You will probably need help from the drones—it is that technology we need."

"Ok," Court replied. "I will get a team down there."

Sue and I listened to the 10-minute political broadcast, ending with what the public's expectations on the reduction of retail prices: 34 pence off a litre of fuel, £1.10 off a pint of beer, £2.50 off a bottle of wine and £1500 off a seasonal London to Birmingham rail ticket and £3 off a packet of cigarettes, and this would take place from midnight tonight, along with the whole of Earth Corp's policies.

Businesses would be affected by this, and the Bank of England had told all banks to extend their borrowings if required until everything was sorted. It could take 6 months to resolve. The sales tax would come into force at the same time on everything. It meant that all 'vatable' items would reduce by 10%; conversely, all 'non-vatable' items would increase by 10%. The whole basis of this government was fairness and if some people or business felt the tax effected them adversely, they could petition to a committee who would waive it for them. A new era of prosperity for all would start from midnight. Those weekly paid would see the difference in their pay packets the next week and the following month for salaried employees, but everyone would notice the price reductions the next day.

When the broadcast ended, I turned to Sue and asked what she thought of it. She felt that there was fairness at last and the Prime Minister and new foreign secretary came across as caring and sincere. "And I believe in what they said," she added. "I still think it won't really help the poorest in our society, which are mainly the unemployed. They haven't mentioned how unemployment is going to be resolved."

"True, but if people start spending their extra income, the knock-on effect should improve the employment prospect of the unemployed."

The news followed the broadcast. Opening financial and currency markets in Australia and the Far East had jettisoned the pound and shares knocking 30% off the value of the pound and UK shares. I immediately instructed Herr Hoffman to buy all that they were selling. It should bring about some sense and balance into the markets. I could not understand why the markets were reacting this way when I would underwrite the UK debt if it was caused by our policies. I then spoke with Conrad and told him to get that point across and use all Media Corps sources by midnight. The message had reached the Far East markets, and the pound started to rally similarly. UK shares got back to close to their starting prices.

The following morning, businesses that were open 24/7 would have the biggest problem balancing their stock. Manufactures would be reinvoicing and crediting—it would all take time, but there was a general feel from those questioned in the news bulletins that everything would be resolved fairly. The biggest complaints came from the building industry who were exempt on new build and now were going to have to pay the sales tax. Similarly, estate agents. They would be first to seek the newly formed committee to get a ruling on the tax and try for an exemption.

CHAPTER 17

THERE HAD BEEN A BREAKTHROUGH in Utopia—white energy was not an electrical source; it was a chemical catalyst that reacts with other chemicals to produce heat or cold. The fusion of these chemicals was the key and Court had now involved the absolute best chemical engineers to see if we could replicate the process. Utopia was a zero-waste society for self-preservation; they had no way to dump it so, aeons ago, recycling took hold. Their waste was broken down to their chemical elements and reconstituted into whatever was required.

Kingdom Clouche was the thirty-seventh richest man in the world according to Forbes. The previous year, he was the seventeenth richest, but his industry that employed over three hundred and thirty thousand people in forty-nine counties, was the largest single-use plastic manufacturer in the world, taking a market share close to eighty per cent. Why did he want to see me? He did not want to say much over the phone and wanted a face-to-face meeting; he reminded me that I had a fifteen per cent share in his business, which made me the largest shareholder apart from him. I could tell from his voice that he was anxious, so I told him to come to Assington, and I gave him the co-ordinates.

He asked, "Is there a helicopter landing pad?"

"Indeed, there is."

"I will see you in thirty minutes."

I told security about the visit, but they were not too happy about the helicopter. Nonetheless, they took the utmost precaution on its decent and landing. I went out to meet my guest. He ducked under the rotors and we shook hands, and I welcomed him to Assington Priory. As I showed him to our conference room, I read his mind and felt his anxiety, so I told him our conversation was for our ears only.

"So what is on your mind?" I asked.

"As you know, my business is in single-use plastics, which currently is not recyclable. We are getting bad press on what it is doing to the oceans and landfills. I have personally given 500 million euros to clean up the oceans, invested heavily into incinerators to produce electricity and burn the plastic as a fuel source with zero carbon emissions. The take up on my offer has been slow—no one wants a rubbish dump at the bottom of their garden. The success we are having is sighting them near hospitals for the free electricity and the balance is sold off to the grid. This is time-consuming. My company is trying to find a biodegradable plastic, and we have an open cheque book to come up with an answer. We are getting close, but they have told me it will be at least another couple of years before we have something we can go to the market with," he explained.

"So what's the problem? You seem to have all avenues covered. Most things take time."

"We don't have that much time. Last year, my share price was £12.70 a few of the large pension funds that have an eco-ethic sold, which dropped the share price £9.10. We were still paying a dividend of 8.5%, and I increased it to 9% this year, and its kept things on hold. With interest rates still at an all-time low, the fund managers saw the share price as a blip and it would bounce back. Since the rains around the world, a new philosophy by the public at large, they are staying away from anything that is not recyclable. Our order books around the world have collapsed—if I can't get orders, then my company will go into receivership—leaving big holes in peoples pension and over 330,000 jobs gone. As you are by far my largest investor, I have come here to buy your shareholding at today's price."

"Would you like to stay for dinner? It's not often we have guests... because I have an idea, if you are up for it. I will just tell my wife one extra for dinner, if that is ok, and you can stay the night. We have plenty of room."

He nodded. I went in search of Sue delivered my

message, and then I contacted Monk to meet me in Utopia. I told Kingdom that what he was about to see was highly classified, I summoned a verticular and 20 minutes later, we were in Utopia City. I introduced Monk to Kingdom and said, "We have come to do some shopping in your mall, the food hall mainly."

The expression on Kingdom's face was the same as everyone that visited Utopia for the first time. We took the transport from the city to the mall, which was not too dissimilar from the surface shopping malls.

I asked Kingdom where his research facilities were, "Seattle, Cambridge, and Beijing."

"How good are they?"

"All three are managed by my research and development director, and he has equal confidence in all of them—he handpicked them all. He is within the industry the best scientific brain in the business."

"Ok, let's do some shopping."

On our way round, I told Kingdom that everything in Utopia was recycled, "...so all the goods you see, if packaged, the material used is recycled. I don't have a clue about plastics but you select all that interest you and take enough for all your research teams." He did so.

I told him we would drop the packaging off on our way back to Assington. Little did he realise that Beijing was the first stop, followed by Seattle, and lastly, Cambridge. This was all done in less than 2 hours. The time difference meant that it was either early or late so at each drop, he phoned the head of department and told them that there was some important packaging that had to be analysed very quickly as it was all recyclable and could be what we have been looking for. It is very doubtful that the packaging is from oil-based polymers.

I knew he had so many questions, and over dinner, I explained just enough about Utopia, their part in saving Earth, and why we had to stop the acid rain caused by fossil fuels. I skirted round the magma bubble and what caused it, but to say that the engineering skills of the Utopians developed a tunnel to vent the bubble and the detonation of dormant volcanoes saved Earth, the resultant month of torrential rain was a small price to pay.

After dinner, he declined staying the night, opting to get back to his office. He would get there at 23:30. While on the helicopter, Kingdom had spoken to his research director from and told him this packaging could be what they had been researching for.

"Where did you get it?" he asked.

"I am not at liberty to say, but there are no patents to worry about. If we are able to replicate it, it will be us that patents the packaging. I have left samples at all our research facilities, and I want round-the-clock research on the packaging. I will go to the Cambridge facility now and start. I hope Beijing has started already; I will phone them and get back to you when we have something."

Kingdom decided that he needed to accompany the scientists and got his helicopter to take him to Cambridge, where he arrived at 01:30, and went straight to the laboratory. The whole team had been summoned, and all were at their stations. Beijing had reported that the packaging was soluble in water but was not dissolving in the water. Instead, it was reverting to its molecular state and was suspended in the water. So far Beijing had identified fourteen different molecules; ten had been recognised, leaving four that they were working on, and of course, there could have been more molecules still to be found.

Kingdom asked, "What could hold us up?"

"Our ability to identify the molecules and atoms that make up the packaging. Our electron microscopes are excellent for our current work but are not going to be good enough. Beijing is still looking, but I fear with the equipment we have, neither research facility will be able to find all the elements we need to replicate the packaging."

"Can we not buy better scopes?"

"We have the best that are commercially available. Seattle have just started, and I have told them to concentrate on the four elements not yet identified. All the elements so far found are organic, and if the remaining ones are similar, we have a remarkable product, providing we can manufacture it."

"This is top priority. Drop everything else. I want all the teams working on this 24/7 until we have cracked the problem. If you need more specialist staff, hire them. You have an open cheque book to resolve this quickly. I am returning home. Any breakthrough, I want to know."

A week had passed, and three more elements had been found, still organic, but the one element was elusive for now. Over 4 days, all three teams had been working on identifying the last piece of the jigsaw. They needed a better electron microscope. The most powerful was in the Lawrence Berkeley laboratories in the States, but there was a year-and-a-half waiting list for time on the microscope. Kingdom spoke to the CEO that funded the scope. The amount of money he offered would get him immediate access to the scope. The office in Seattle had a contact in the Lawrence Berkeley lab and asked for the names of the companies and universities that were ahead in the queue. One by one, they were contacted to see whether they would give up their place in the queue, but no one would. Kingdom, in desperation, contacted me to see whether I could do anything, and I told him I would try.

The US elections had taken place, and although not an emphatic victory as the UK, Congress and the Senate were now reliant on Earth Corp as we had achieved nearly a third of all votes cast and were the balance of power in both chambers. The President-Elect was the son of the outgoing President Rodbridge Anders the third, Carlton Anders. He had run as an independent candidate, much to the annoyance of the Republican Party. I contacted Court Leiston first, as the scope had to be filled with his semiconductors and maybe he could put some weight behind the request for Kingdom. He got the same answer.

I asked him, "Can we not just tap into it as we did the Cayman Bank and Cheltenham GHCQ?"

"We can get into their computers, no problem, but would not be able to use the microscope. Only the team that built it would have the skills to do it. I suggest you talk to the President; the only way you will jump the queue is by presidential order. I am not sure that he will issue it on your behalf, as it is a commercial venture. You would have to put a very ethical case for him to use that power."

I thanked him for trying and contacted Rodbridge—I asked him if I could meet him in the evening at Anders Airfield as the White House security was so intense. I emphasised the importance of the meeting, and he agreed. The President said he would organise dinner, and I told him I would be bringing a guest. "Get to my pavilion about 8 o'clock, OK?" he said.

I contacted Kingdom and told him I would pick him up around 23:00 for a meeting and dinner with the President of the United States.

"Don't eat too much beforehand, as you would not want to upset the President if what I am hoping for is to get a presidential order to get you first in the queue."

"What do you think of the chances of him issuing an order?"

"I honestly don't know. He was a businessman before he became President, and with his son as President-Elect, it is not going to be easy. He would not do anything that would harm his son's presidency. We must play it straight, and somewhere, it has to help America in the long-term, even better if a benefit can be found in the short-term."

We arrived at Anders Airfield around 19:45 EST. The portal opened, and we exited the verticular. I told Kingdom to put his hands up as the security surrounded us. Once they recognised me, I told them we were expected. The lovely Rachel arrived and told the security she would escort us to the President, but we still had to go through a frisk search before taking the lift to the President's home.

The President met us at the lift, and I introduced him to Kingdom. They shook hands, and he showed us to his lounge. He went over to his bar and asked what we would like to drink. Kingdom and I asked for a beer each, and two beers arrived in bottles with two glasses.

"Dinner will not be long," he said. "Now what is so important you need my help."

Kingdom told him the plight of his industry now that people had boycotted single-use plastic since the rains. He explained, "Robin took me to Utopia, and we took samples of all their packaging, as they recycle everything—it is quite remarkable; it just dissolves in water. But in such a way that the chemicals do not actually dissolve in the water; they revert back to their single element and are just suspended in the water, making them easily recyclable. My science teams have identified thirteen of the elements, leaving just one element to identify, which is causing the problem, and we need the use of the Lawrence Berkeley microscope. The problem is that there's an 18-month waiting list to use it. I have tried offering a fortune to them to jump the waiting list, but it was declined. I even offered to buy someone's time but they would not budge and sell their place in the queue. So, I asked Robin if he could help. I contacted Court Leiston to see whether we could back-door, as we have done in the past, and he agreed that the computers were easy to get at but the science to operate the scope was so specialist, the people that built it would be the only ones able to use it. I think the only way to jump the queue is by presidential order."

The President replied, "That is a big ask for a commercial company."

"I have no interest in keeping this in-house all that we find will be published worldwide for any company anywhere to use or reproduce. We will have an advantage as it is the industry we are in. However, the elements so far detected are not used in the plastic industry currently, and we would all be starting from scratch. I have nine factories in the US employing 80000 people; their future relies on us coming up with a solution for the toxic plastic waste and the first step would be to make all packaging 100% recyclable and then deal with the existing plastic problem."

The President asked, "Will your companies in the US make this new material and safeguard their jobs?"

"Of course," Kingdom replied. "I think I would need to double the workforce and build more factories here once we are able to replicate it commercially. I promise you that I will make the US the biggest supplier of this new product. My American competitors will be given all the information so they too can take advantage of the product."

The President contacted his son Carlton, President-Elect, and got him up to speed. His son said it was his decision and would back with whatever he would decide. "I will, if necessary, give a presidential order but I will talk to the CEO first and see if I can persuade him." He then told his aide to get him on the phone, and 3 minutes later, he was talking to the director in charge of the laboratory.

"Hi, Mike. Rodbridge Anders," he said.

After a slight pause, he heard, "Yes, Mr President, what can I do for you?"

"I want to save 80,000 American jobs, and to do this, I need some time on your microscope."

"And when would you like to use it?"

"Now would be a good time."

"Its offline at the moment, having some upgrades applied to it to make even more powerful."

"When's it back online?"

"In 2 to 3 hours."

"Can we be the first to use it? I will come myself with the team and will work on it until we have identified what we need."

"Mr President, the waiting list is over 18 months."

"I am aware of that. It's why I am phoning you. If it's easier for you, I will issue a presidential order, that's how important it is."

"How long will you need it?"

The President looked at Kingdom for a response. "Could be an hour or a week," Kingdom replied. "I need to get my science team there; they will be able to give a better timescale."

"I am sending my science team now. They should be with you before the scope goes back on line."

"I look forward to seeing you, Mr President."

Kingdom contacted his science director and told them to pack a bag—they were going to the Lawrence Berkeley lab in California to identify the last component in the jigsaw. "We will be at the Seattle office in an hour and a half and special transport will take you directly there," he said.

I asked, "How many people are we talking about?"

"Eleven in total."

"We will need two verticular," I concluded and then asked Monk to organise.

"Enjoy your meal," Monk said. Did I note a bit of envy in his voice? As a Utopian, he had found our food so much superior to his own, and missing out on a meal with the President... worse still, not being invited—he will get over it. The meal was not fancy but delicious, washed down with an American red wine that was rather good.

We left for Seattle from Anders Airfield. The President had not told them that he was going to California via Seattle, and for all they knew, he was retiring to bed. We entered my transport, and 20 minutes later, we were in the grounds of the research laboratory. Kingdom led the way and gathered up his staff. By the time we got back to my transport, Monk had arrived in his verticular with Stephen Shefford, and before I could say anything, he told me that I was not wandering around America without his protection; I knew that it was pointless to argue.

The microscope was in a terribly busy area. Stephen had a large office 20 minutes from the Berkeley laboratory, and we would arrive there and do the remainder of the journey by car. It was just after 8 pm California time when we arrived. The five vehicles were ushered through security and were met by the director and his team. The President introduced us to the director and his team, and his team and Kingdom's went off to the microscope while the director took us to his office. At 20:00 all the offices should be empty, instead it was like nine in the morning; everybody was at their desks to get a glimpse of the most powerful person in the world. Rodbridge had always been a reluctant President, but he did enjoy the adulation shown by the population everywhere he went, and true to form, he mingled with the people, signed autographs, and spoke to some of them on his way to the director's office.

He would never have been given this freedom if his secret service had organised it. In the director's office, Kingdom thanked him for allowing him to jump the queue. Nobody knew how long the scope would be required for, but the director said it was at Kingdom's disposal for as long as it would take. The President asked to be shown around the whole complex, at the end of the visit. I told Kingdom we were leaving; he was going to stay with his team. We dropped off the President on our way back to Assington.

The President's visit had been well documented by members of staff at the Lawrence Berkeley lab. He had been Facebooked and Twittered. Every social media site had been used to show selfies with the President. The downside to this was when he arrived back at Anders around three in the morning. His secret service team were frantic, so when he casually walked to his home, all he could hear was "POTUS is safe. Repeat: POTUS is safe." The head of the security team approached the President. "Mr President, the internet is going wild. Have you been to California this evening?"

"No, how could I get to California and back in under 3 hours? It is at least a 10-hour trip."

"That's fine. Of course you couldn't."

As President, he didn't need to say anything apart from "goodnight."

At the security debrief, all the agents sifted through the footage and media material appertaining to the alleged visit to California. It all seemed so genuine; nearly all were about the President. There were some faces in the background.

"Let us get names to those faces."

It did not take long. "Robin Witney, Kingdom Clouche, Stephen Shefford and another guy—as yet, there is no name, but he had been ID'ed many times and is always in the company of the CEO of Earth Corp."

One of the security agents said, "The first two guys had dinner with the President this evening. They arrived about 19:45, and I did not see them go. To that matter, I did not see them arrive. They appeared at the President's pavilion, and I was told that they were expected for a private dinner with the President. I can confirm they are no longer here, so they must have left the same way as they came."

Scouring the CCTV footage, they found absolutely nothing. Something was highly suspicious, but the President was safe at home. He could not have got to California, had a meeting, and returned in 3 hours—it was impossible. He closed the debrief and would investigate further. He felt the need to identify the guy with no name was the key to the event. He, as head of security for POTUS, had security clearance to the highest level—he could access anything. Back in his office, he started digging. The guy with no name must work for Earth Corp. He pulled their file but found nothing. Maybe the guy was one of Stephen Shefford security guys. He pulled their personnel files - another blank.

He tried a different approach. Looking at the earliest photographs, the guy seemed to appear exactly at the same time Earth Corp became a leading player in the world's economy. The CIA had, at first, viewed Earth Corp as a possible threat; similarly, the National Security Agency had some serious concerns. Reading minutes from both agencies, the feeling of both had mellowed when Earth Corp had ended a Russian general's operation Phoenix, which would have plunged the world into a recession. The General's sleepers who were strategically placed to cause maximum harm to the world's economy had all been arrested with the help of Earth Corp. It was not until they had publicly agreed to meet directly with the world's terrorist organisations that attitudes had changed in Washington.

He pulled the file on Operation Wipeout; it had been reconstituted after the jailed National Security Advisor had destroyed the complete file. He had not destroyed the compilers original plan, and Robert Saxham, the compiler, used it as evidence in the NSA advisor trial. He knew Robert Saxham was to be eliminated to rid any trace of Operation Wipeout after the suicide of the American President. He was now looking at CCTV footage of the park where Robert

Saxham disappeared. He could be seen clearly, and three people confronted him—the same three people that were with the President this evening.

There were four people in one frame and nothing in the next—four people had just disappeared. This had collaborated by NSA agents sent to bring him in. One minute they were there and next, gone. He bought up another computer program which could seek heat sources, infrared and ultraviolet, no success with the first two but ultraviolet showed something. Slowing the film down, he saw exactly what had happened and where the four people had disappeared. It looked like a door had opened, and they stepped through before vanishing. There was nothing the US had that could do this, so it had to be foreign.

Alarm bells started to ring in his mind. Has the President been turned? Is there a security problem at the highest level? His son will be taking over in February; where can he take his concerns? He decided to go to the President and ask for an off-the-record meeting at once. The President had not been in bed. He told his head of security to come straight over if the meeting was that important. He came straight to the point—he told him what he had found on the film and asked what the machine they disappeared into was.

The President said, "I do know what that machine is. I have been on it many times; it is a special transport system. How it works, I do not know but I can tell you that it can get you round the world in 45 minutes."

"Have you been compromised in any way? Will it affect

your duties as President?"

The President laughed. "This and other technology have bought us to peace in our lifetime. Earth Corp is a positive influence for prosperity and peace, and I and all of America will embrace it. You have nothing to worry about. In the morning, I will show you that your concern is unjustified, but you will have to keep it a secret. This information is for your ears only."

The President looked at his watch and realised it was too early to contact me in our normal way, so he emailed me and told me of the dilemma his head of security had and the need bring him up to speed on all that had passed as he was worried the POTUS had been compromised. I picked up the email in the morning, and for the same reason, emailed him back and told him I would be at Anders at 13:00. We were escorted to the POTUS, having again appeared from nowhere. We met with the President and his head of security. He knew us but not Monk, and so I introduced them. I told the head of security that Monk was my left and right hand. "His knowledge and power has had been immensely useful to get us where we are today. The world owes him a great deal, but he normally settles for a good lunch or dinner." Everyone laughed. "If you are up to it, I would like to show you something of our achievements." I turned to the President. "Are you coming?"

"I am afraid I have meetings all afternoon at the White House."

"Can you spare your head of security?"

"Of course."

We entered the verticular and shortly arrived at Leiston Semiconductors in California. We found Court Leiston in his research centre, having bypassed all the security on our way in. I had earlier told Court we were on our way, so he met us with the necessary security passes. I told Court to explain what we were trying to do here, and he turned to the head of security. "Twenty minutes ago, you were in Anders, New York state; you are now in California. Check your phone." He did so. "You have travelled over 3000 miles in 20 minutes. None of us here, even the very clever Monk, know how it works. It just does, and we use it to get round the world and to circumnavigate the world in under 50 minutes. My company, Earth Corp, and the President are no longer hampered by distance, so we effectively have a 24-hour day to work with. This technology is not ours but Monk's; he is part of a secret civilisation that has lived underground for 4.5 billion years. They can read minds."

He handed Monk a piece of paper and told him to write down all his security passwords. He did and handed them to him. You could see the shock on his face.

"So, no one can tell us lies. We know what everybody thinking, should we wish to. My part of the puzzle is to work out how to use their energy source—we call it white energy. We have managed to fuse the elements that make it but have not been able to go further and get something to run on it. We know things work on it as you will see on your next stop."

Court came with us to Utopia City and continued his briefing. He took us to the technical area—I had not been down to Utopia for some time and the technical and industrial areas were less busy. There were still plenty of droids about.

Court continued, "These droids made the tunnel that vented the magma into the Marianna Trench. It was over 3000 miles long and completed within a month. You know about the additional venting, you were privy to the nuclear strikes by the Navies of the world, but without this tunnel Earth would now be history. The tunnel and nuclear strikes combined, saved their civilisation and ours. The Utopians are not only able to read minds, but they can also control them. They have no sickness, no hostility, no crime... it is a wonderful existence. We are going to adapt their technology to rid our world of carbon. Well, at least, that is the plan—it is proving a lot harder. Yet, we are unable to take technology from here to the surface; the transport will not allow its transportation. It happened aeons ago that both civilisations should not interface. It was not until our acid rain reached their crops and started to destroy their civilisation that they needed help. They chose Robin, and he started Earth Corp using the vast wealth amassed by them, via Swiss banks. Since Earth Corp's inauguration, everything is well documented for you to check. The mergers of the ten largest companies into Earth Corp was amicable and under the protected financial umbrella of Earth Corp, as in some way, all were dependent on fossil fuels, which were to be eradicated long-term, short-term reducing emissions by half. The Anders Corporation, the President's company, are equal in every respect. It is the friendship between them and utmost respect for each other that makes them a formidable twosome—the richest man in the world and the most powerful man in the world get things done quickly."

I asked the head of security, "Have we answered your concerns?"

He said, "Yes."

I added, "What you have seen must remain secret. Do you have a problem with that? We can wipe your mind of all that you have seen. It's painless, and we will put you back at Anders Airfield, and all you will know is that 2 hours of your life have disappeared.

"I don't think that will be necessary. After all, I am head of the President's security."

"Very well. Are there in other questions or concerns you have about Earth Corp and the President?"

"No, I'm fine."

"Well, we will get you back to Anders. Monk, can you take him back? I want to go to California to see if there is any headway at Lawrence Berkeley. It's not been 24 hours but there may be results. Court, can you tear yourself away and come with me? Another technical brain may help."

At Lawrence Berkeley, I contacted Kingdom. He and his team had been there since we left. Kingdom and the director came with passes, and we went directly to the microscope. There were banks of monitors with photos of the elusive element; it still had not been identified. Court went over to an operator and asked if she could change the aspect of the element through 360 degrees. Slowly it revolved. Court asked her to freeze it a few times, looked closely until it had completed its complete cycle, and then asked her to do it again. This second time, he nodded it all the way round.

"Gentlemen, your missing element is actually three fused elements—silicone, sodium and hydrogen. Robin, it's white energy. I have been working with this for the last 18 months, so I should know."

"That would make sense," I said. "White energy would be used in the production of the material, and we know it is not aggressive like electrical current and would revert when immersed in water."

This prompted perplexed looks from Kingdom's team and the microscope team. Court asked the operator to split the picture into three separate sections apart from the fused joins. "You could see the individual elements distinctly when fused; however, subtle changes take place and make it one element that emits what we call white energy."

He said that the making of it was relatively easy for us to produce and took extraordinarily little time. "...however, trying to make it into a motive force like electricity has been a complete failure so far. Our approach has completely changed."

Court took Kingdom aside and whispered to him, "We know white energy drives everything in Utopia. You have been there and seen it in action for yourself, so we know it works. We are now looking in a totally different direction. We believe it is a chemical reaction that creates a force similar to a motive force, but we are just at the beginning and getting chemical engineers into the team."

Kingdom said that most of his team were from a chemical engineering background. Court and I had a telepathic communication and agreed that Kingdom's team could join Court's in Utopia, and both teams would concentrate on the packaging. With both teams focused on just one problem, we may get a breakthrough. Court advised Kingdom that they would join forces until they were successful and all would be working in Utopia. It would be a big surprise for Kingdom's team.

Kingdom said he would stay with his team, so I got a bracelet from Monk and said to Kingdom, "You will need one of these," and I put it on his wrist. It snapped shut as always. "This is your communication device. All you have to do is think of the person or persons you need to contact and you're in touch. It has some rather good side effects— it super enhances your immune system, which has the effect of rejuvenating your body, and in 24 hours, you will look 20 years younger. You had better tell your guys they will be working away for some time. Do you need any guys from your other Labs?"

The science director rattled off ten names—six from Cambridge and four from Hong Kong.

"Monk, you pick up the four from Hong Kong, and I will pick up and deliver the others."

We thanked all at the Lawrence Berkeley laboratory, got back to Court's factory and took them down to Utopia where introduced them to his underground team. My Cambridge lot said they would be ready in 2 hours. I popped back to Assington and advised Sue I would be home for breakfast. She reminded me it would be dinner. "You have not slept for 24 hours," she said. I did not feel that tired until I realised I had been following the sun. I had a power nap for 2 hours, picked up Kingdom's guys—it all took 20 minutes. Monk arrived at the same time with his guys. We let Court and Kingdom fill in the new people, and Monk and I left for Assington—the invitation for dinner is never declined.

CHAPTER 18

ANNABELLA PUCCI WAS AT THE BEACH HOUSE. It was coming up to year since her husband's tragic accident, a day after they married and only four days after knowing each other personally. Her late husband's first wife was a board member of his bank and was the principal shareholder. The board had tried to stop Annabella from inheriting the shares but the highest court in Cayman had ruled in her favour, and an offer of 2.3 billion dollars for her shares was put to her at the following board meeting. It was just too much money. Had it been 50 to 60 million dollars, she would have taken it and left the island for Naples. She would not decide yet, as she wanted time to think.

It was during this time that she became friends with her late husband's ex-wife and together ran the bank as she did with her ex-husband. Annabella was now looking through a dossier that the first wife had given her about why they divorced. Her then husband had fallen in love with a bank customer and spent a great deal of time in the States. She had hired a detective agency to follow his movements while in the States. Two detectives had just disappeared with no trace and the third detective was a lot more careful and had produced the dossier. She had confronted her husband about the affair, and he had admitted it. He vowed never to see that woman again, and she forgave him. It only lasted a week—he was besotted by this woman and resumed his affair. She could not forgive his infidelity a second time and they divorced, and that is how she got the shares in the bank.

Looking through the photos, there was not a full picture of the woman's face, but she was beautiful. She had field-craft, you could tell. CCTV would never see a full-on face. Who was this woman that came into her husband's life and just disappeared after seven years, only to reappear some 14 years later in Cayman Brac, in a submarine owned by a drug dealer that his whole organisation wiped out? She had now disappeared again, and as hard as she tried, she could not pick up her trail.

Three women had used the company aircraft to fly to New York, but the trail went cold. Unless she could access the NYPD or FBI files, it would be impossible. She could not use her normal source—the mafia. Alberto would find out and wonder why. She was intrigued that there was a worldwide directive to leave Earth Corp alone as all were under a mafia protection protocol. She googled Earth Corp and got masses of information. It would take ages, but she went on to the Media Corp website and searched Earth Corp news. Scrolling down, she found a second assassination attempt on the CEO at Media Corps headquarters. The assassin had been shot dead at the scene, and a security personnel took the bullets meant for the CEO. The interesting fact was that the assassin, presumed male, was in fact female. The photos of the assassin were mainly taken from mobile phones. She copied and pasted them and superimposed them onto the photos she had and bingo! one of the same. Her late husband was infatuated with a killer. She wanted to continue what her husband wanted to do, but considering what she had found out, she would concentrate on running the bank.

CHAPTER 19

IT WAS OVER A YEAR SINCE THE RAINS. The newly formed ice caps at both poles had remained, and worldwide sea temperatures had lowered by two degrees on average, resulting in hurricanes and cyclones being less of a force—strongest winds were under 120 mph, which still caused destruction but nowhere near as much as the previous years. Local weather had really changed; all the deserts had become enormous freshwater seas. Freshwater was in abundance, and around the water's edge was a mass of green. Nations that had little or no water now had plenty and were able to feed themselves and export the surpluses for the first time in decades. The earths underground aquifers were full, resulting in truly little seepage into the ground, so effectively microclimates had formed around what were the hottest places in the world and were now enormous oases and ten degrees cooler. The nomadic way of life for these people had changed; they did not have to follow the traditional routes of following the pasture and water they required for their animals and themselves. Water was in abundance; boats were of more use than camels.

The United Nations had only ratified seventy per cent of the countries of the world into full membership. Despite all countries being members, only full members could vote and become part of its infrastructure. Russia, China, and the Indian sub-continent were still coming to terms with the implications of its charter on human rights; over 3 billion people were being denied these rights, half the world's population. Strange allegiances formed inside the United Nations with full members and those not formally recognised because of the charter. The General Secretary was adamant: "Unless you adopt the charter in full, you will remain non-voting members." He did not need their funds, so he could not be bullied by them, as big as they were. The USA had only become a full member 3 months ago. The federal government agreed at the same time as the UK and Europe to adopt the charter, but it was painfully slow getting the individual states to adopt it.

The peace had held for all this time and was nearing completion. The Messapth scrolls had been, in fact, detailed accounts going back nearly seven thousand years. They were so detailed that they had maps of where the people came from, as Dark Seven had to let some through with their riches, otherwise there would be no trade from that area if deemed too risky an investment. At least 40% made it home and was deemed acceptable by the merchants that put the trade caravans together. So, exact knowledge was obtained—whence they came, on their way to the Far East. Dark Sevens hospitality was legendary and insured that they would stop on their way back. Their maps helped solve many of the problems over whose land it really was. Once the map was redrawn using all this information, deals and financial repatriation were done.

Since the rains, all the land in question would be fertile, and the eagerness to settle was enormous—even the religious problems were resolved, as each new country would democratically elect the government. If the majority wanted to choose a religious doctrine, the minority could choose to stay or go to a country of their choice. The largest financial cost was Israel's, mounting to nearly 17 billion dollars. The majority of it went to Palestine—a small price to pay for peace in the middle east.

At home, all the legislation in both manifestos had received Royal Ascent and now were law. The cost of this legislation to the government was enormous; bringing about the living wage was expensive and government borrowings had doubled. Over the course of this parliament, the new treasury model had shown a further increase in Year 2; Year 3 showed a small reduction in borrowings. Years 3, 4 and 5 showed a massive reduction, and by Year 5, revenue would exceed borrowings with a surplus of cash in excess of £50 billion.

I was incredibly happy, but Sue was not. She yearned to go back to a life she had before all this happened. "Life can never be the same again I remind her."

"Even when you're here, you're always in your office. I don't cook anymore; everything is done for me."

"I will try and spend more time at home. It shouldn't be that hard, apart from the business. I don't have any pressing problems, and I do have the right people. I could take a break. It's over 3 years since our last holiday, and that might make you feel better. Where would you like to go? The world is your oyster."

"Mundesly," she said. "The Royal Hotel. I love North Norfolk, and it's just us two and the dogs."

I agreed, knowing that it would not be that easy. I could tell she was happier.

I turned the news on—the national and international I knew; it was the local news I missed. We watched an article on a young Muslim girl, about 4 years old, who had a rare blood disease, and although there was a treatment to stabilise the condition, there was no known cure. The treatment cost £400,000 a year and NICE had now refused to pay for the treatment, as they could not warrant this type of expenditure. There were a further six children in the UK that had the same condition—life expectancy was a year without the treatment. The mother begged, on television, for NICE to change its mind; it was her only daughter, and she could not have anymore because of complications at the birth of her daughter. her tearful husband was holding her hand.

I turned to Sue, who was also crying—tears were in my eyes too.

Sue turned to me and said, "I thought the NHS had all the money it needed."

"So did I." I spoke with the Prime Minister, asking, "What's all this that NICE won't allow this treatment on the NHS?"

I knew he could hear the anger in my voice. He said, "All the people on the NICE council are doctors, parents and scientists. They knew their decision was to condemn seven children to death. We still have to be accountable for the money the NHS spends, and £2.8 million a month buys a lot more time on kidney dialysis. The prognosis is that these children will never leave hospital and cannot be subjected to an outside environment; the treatment is the only thing keeping them alive. NICE did not come to their decision lightly; they have to live with it, knowing they have sentenced the seven children to death."

Sue was still angry and was about to say something when Monk came into the lounge. He read our minds and was immediately up to speed, and then Sue continued, "We will pay for the treatment for all seven children. Phone the hospital now and tell them."

"You know I have no problem doing what you ask, but put yourself in the shoes of the children. If no cure is found, they live there whole long life in a tent in a hospital. It's probably fun for them with all this attention, but 6 years on, will it be so much fun? Twenty years on with no cure, it won't be fun at all. It's like life imprisonment."

Monk said, "Best we cure them."

"Are we able to?"

"I see no reason why not. It's just a blood disorder, very complex, but curable."

"We'll let us go."

"Can I come?" Sue asked.

"Of course."

"Give me a couple of minutes to change."

I said, "Meet us in the enclosed garden."

Ten minutes later, we were at the back of the of the Royal Manchester Children's Hospital. The verticular had dropped us off at the rear of the staff car park. We walked to the main entrance, and it was packed with TV cameras and crew; there was no way of us getting past them without being filmed, or worse identified.

Sue said, "There must be a staff or rear entrance," so back we went. It was not long before a door opened and a female staff member came out. We hurried towards the door, but we were not quick enough. Sue asked the staff member if she could let us in, but she declined on security grounds. Sue explained that we wanted to see the parents of the little girl who had the rare blood disease. "...we are going to pay for her medical treatment, including the other six children suffering from the same ailment. If we go through the front entrance, my husband is bound to be recognised with all the press there."

The nurse took a good look at me and recognised me. "You're the guy that gave us our second MRI scanner."

"So will you let us in?"

"Yes, and I will show you the way."

We followed her past the doctors' restroom, where there were several doctors' coats hanging up. We borrowed three and put them on—now we looked the part. We would give them back; this should only take a few minutes.

We got to the specialist ward; both parents were just outside the hermetically sealed isolation unit. Special sealed suits had to be worn to attend to their daughter's need. The medical team assigned to the little girl were conversing with the parents. Our presence was noticed, and I signalled them to come and meet us. We all went to the parents' room and introduced ourselves before the doctors did the same. One of the team was the head of research producing the drug keeping the children alive.

I asked him, "How far are you from finding a cure?"

"A very long way, I'm afraid."

"Is it funding?"

"No, I am a sub-contractor for GSK and have all the funds I need. I make the serum that keeps the children alive. It is so expensive to produce; at £400,000 a year, it is still being subsidised by GSK from their charitable budget."

"What do you need to make a break through?"

"The impossible! Someone that has recovered from the disease, and as yet, no one has."

I turned to the parents. "I will pay for this treatment for as long as it's needed and for every child in the world that has it." It took a few moments for it to sink in and then the tears of joy started. I asked the parents, "Do you have faith?"

They nodded. "My friend here has a rare gift and would like to see your daughter. He and I would be alone with your daughter to use his gift on your daughter; it will take no longer than ten minutes. If successful, your daughter will be cured."

The doctor in charge said, "No way. We can't risk any infections."

"We will wear your suits. All we need is to be close to be effective."

"No, I can't allow it. The responsibility is mine alone."

I looked at Monk, and he quickly changed the doctor's mind. We were now dressed in suits, and we entered the tent. The little girl smiled as we approached—no apprehension—it is as if she knew why we had come. Monk entered her mind and started making the repairs to her immune system. He fixed the mechanism that had been damaged in her brain possibly at birth and got the brain to produce a chemical that would destroy the virus quickly. I, on the other hand, was intrigued by the smile and found out that she had dreamt this moment of being cured. *How interesting,* I thought. As we said goodbye, we could see the smile had turned into a huge grin.

We told her parents that Monk may have cured her. "Would you take some blood in 15 minutes and have it analysed?" We waited until the results of the blood test, which proved beyond doubt that the little girl was cured, came back.

I turned to the sub-contractor. "You now have your first survivor; now find a cure. If you need anything—I mean anything—here's my number," and I gave him my card. "I am sure it would be easier if all suffering from this illness were bought here. If you arrange it, I will pay for it and their repatriation."

The doctor said, "None can leave their sterile environment."

"The suits we wore... can't they be adapted?"

"I suppose so."

"That is settled. One more thing: we have never been here, and what we have done must never be known outside this room." The parents agreed. There was some wavering from the medical staff—we couldn't allow that, and to be safe, we wiped their minds of the last 30 minutes, but I left the sub-contractor a memory to contact me tomorrow.

We left the way we came, leaving the coats where we found them, and returned to Assington. Sue felt good—it is the first mission she had been on, and it had been a huge success. It was seconds after our arrival back that we got Stephen's full wrath; leaving without any security or even checking with him was breaking the 11th commandment.

I said, "It was done on the spur of the moment, and I didn't consider there would be any risk."

"It's not for you to assess that's my job."

"Stephen, for over a year, there has been no threats or attempts to remove Sue and I and those I hold dear."

"Correct! I have you in a security bubble that no one is able to penetrate."

"Have there been any attempts?"

"No! That's not the point. You're all safe."

"Sue is unhappy—so much so, she would like to revert to what now seems a simple life, to go back to our home in Stanningfield, where she can meet her friends, go shopping with them, go on trips and other ordinary stuff. She wants to make my dinner and meet me in our local pub. She wants to be a housewife and be ordinary. I have agreed to have a holiday on our own—no security, just the two of us and our dogs. We won't be going abroad, and I will keep in touch"—I saw Sue grimace, and I continued—"if necessary." The smile came back on Sue's face. I put my hands up to block Stephen's interjection and told him this would happen, and soon.

I got a call from the sub-contractor, who was unsure why he was phoning me. "Because I asked you to call me when you were near a breakthrough with this terrible disease affecting children," I told him. "I know you have a survivor of the disease, and you should be able to find the antidote for it quickly."

"The parents have agreed for me to take a pint of blood from their daughter. From that, I should be able compare with her last blood test, identify the change and fabricate an antidote."

I asked, "How long will this take?"

"It could be days, weeks or months. It may even be years." This, I didn't want to hear.

"If you had unlimited resources at your disposal, would that make a difference?"

"It's not resources. I have told you GSK will let me use all their facilities, the problem will be identifying the change in the blood to make a vaccine."

"What about people to help you?"

"The people I would need are busy on their own projects, trying to do the same as I on incurable diseases."

"Give me their names, and I will get them to help you."

"How can you know they will help?"

"No one has ever refused my invitation to assist. Have you heard of a Russian professor called Daplynov?"

"Not recently, but he was one of the best clinicians in the world."

"He will be with you tomorrow to land a hand. Now, I want you to organise all the children suffering from this illness to come to your clinic and be cured."

"We don't have that type of facility."

"Well, get one or hire something suitable and have it ready ASAP. Charter as many aircraft as you need and employ as many people as you need to make it a safe place for the children. It does not have to be permanent; temporary sterile will do fine. Do not worry about the cost; I will pick up all the bills. If any of the children cannot travel, let me know straight away."

I turned to Stephen. "Do you have Daplynov's whereabouts?" He nodded. "We're going to need his expertise. Get him to Manchester by tomorrow to link up with the sub-contractor."

I gave Sue the list of names the sub-contractor wanted and told her make appointments today. "Tell them it would be very advantageous to see me today." The appointments were duly made, our first being in America at Berkeley

Campus. The second was in Cambridge at 11:00. The third at Oxford at noon.

I said to Sue, "Do want to see this project through?" A big grin appeared. I added, "If you're coming, you have just over an hour to get ready. We are leaving at 8 am."

We left for America. The professor there was hooked—he had been studying the disease, as a friend of his had a child suffering from it. A child that had been cured had to be a giant leap forward, and the professor was pleased to assist. He would catch the first plane to Manchester, but I told him we would pick him up with my transport at just after 9 this morning, our time, which was midnight in California. His house was in the Berkeley campus. The verticular arrived in his back garden, and I said to Sue, "Do you fancy something to eat while where here? There's bound to be something on campus."

We all walked round to his front door and rang the bell. He came to the door almost immediately—we had been expected. Sue introduced us to him. I said, "Is there anywhere close we can get a snack?"

"There's a Frankie & Benny's down the road, five minutes' walk. I will take you there." Five minutes later, we sat down and ordered. Sue and I wanted breakfast, but it was only served until 11:30, so we settled for a pasta bake. Stephen and Monk ordered enormous meals, and the professor had coffee.

The professor asked all sorts of questions while we ate—some we could answer, some we could not. "You will have the answer to all your questions soon," I said.

He paid the bill after breakfast, and we walked back to his house. I told him the next thing was highly classified. "Are you able to keep a secret? It is of the magnitude of the miraculous cure of the little girl." He said he could. There were so many scientists working for Earth Corp who knew of Utopia's existence, and it was still the best kept secret. "Our next appointment is in Cambridge at 11 am. Have you any luggage?"

"Just a suitcase," he said.

"Are there any weapons or electronic items in it?"

"Just my laptop."

"Can you access your laptop remotely?"

"Of course."

"Please leave it behind as our transport is highly sophisticated and will not travel with electronic devices. Flight mode will not do." He took his laptop out and left in his house. We approached the verticular, the portal opened, and we all stepped in and took our seats. "King's College Cambridge Science facility," I said. It would take about 25 to 30 minutes.

Sue had asked the other two professors to meet at the science facility at King's; all three were waiting for us in Professor Jackson's meeting room. After introductions, we got down to business.

"I want to co-opt you to help in finding a vaccine. The young child that was on national television has made a miraculous recovery; I need your expertise in finding this vaccine, so that all the children suffering from this disease in the world can be cured. I want you to drop everything you are doing and travel to Manchester today to help in the search for the antidote."

Unanimously they said impossible. Monk and I had read their minds; money would not influence, as they were well off. Money for research, a totally different matter. All their research was on forms of incurable cancers and had mega resources from the drug industry and charities. None needed any expensive equipment; they had it all. We had to dig a little further and found something on each of them—just might get them to agree. I told them I had a case of 1869 Chateau Laffite, and it would be theirs if they went to Manchester. "Just talk with the sub-contractor and help him. You may be able to bring the work back to Cambridge, but I need an all-out effort as 167 children will be in Manchester, dependent on your expertise to make them better." I told them who else would be collaborating on the project, and they were impressed. "I will pick up your expenses. You will all be my guests at the Lowery and will have cars, at your disposal, to take you to the research facilities. If the Lowery is not up to your standard and you want to stay somewhere else let me know. If you want to charter a plane from Cambridge, that is ok too."

We left for Oxford, met with professors with a similar outcome all would meet up in Manchester this afternoon, but now, I had to find two cases of 1869 Chateau Laffite. I remembered that a great deal of fine wine was removed from Messapth. I contacted Herr Hoffman, and after two rings, he answered—as always. "Robin, how can I help you?"

"I recall that from the Messapth horde we took, there

were some fine wines."

"Correct. A substantial amount. Their wine cellar was amazing."

"By chance, was there any 1869 Chateau Laffite?"

"Let me look... Yes. Nine cases."

"Could you bring three of them to the Lowery in Manchester? I'll book a suite for you and your wife if she's free, as Sue will be a little outnumbered at dinner tonight."

"We should be there just after 3. I will check with the chateau in question to ensure that the wine we have is authentic and get them to document it."

"Fine. See you this afternoon."

We took our American professor to the Lowery. He checked in—he had been up now nearly 20 hours and was going to take a nap. I said, "Dinner is booked for eight this evening, and at 5, we are going to the research facilities here in Manchester."

"A couple of hours should be enough."

"Don't worry. If you don't make it, you can catch up at dinner."

He went up to his room, and I asked to see the hotel manager, who came promptly. I said to the manager, "At tonight's dinner, we would like to have a very fine wine, in particular an 1869 Chateaux Laffite. Do you have any?"

"I am not sure but will ask the maître d." The maître d duly arrived and said, "We do have Chateau Laffite but not of that age. It's over £120,000 a bottle. It's more of an investment than a drinking wine."

"Would you mind if I supplied it? If we paid corkage on

each bottle drank of say... £100, would that be acceptable?"

"Don't worry about any corkage," said the manager. "It will be an honour to serve it to you and your guests."

The maître d face drained of blood the responsibility of opening a bottle this expensive without corking it. A cork that's been in the bottle for a 150 years... anything could happen, and he would be responsible. I had read his mind and told him not to worry, as the wine itself might not be drinkable.

The manager asked, "Have you ordered a special meal to go with this wine?"

"No, we were going to order off the restaurant menu."

"Why don't I ask chef to do something really special to complement this wine?" the manager said.

"No problem, but as long as we are at liberty of eating off the menu, if any of us wants to, without the chef feeling disappointed."

We had to go back to Assington to pick up some clothes for this evening and were back at the hotel just before three. We checked into our room—it was massive. While Sue explored, the phone went; Her Hoffman had arrived with three people from Chateau Lafitte to prove the provenance and to serve the wine.

Sue had finished exploring, and I told her that Herr Hoffman had arrived, so we both went down to meet him and his wife. Herr Hoffman pointed to the three people from the Chateau: "Two were Sommeliers and the other I think is a guard. They weren't very talkative on the way. The wine was in the cargo hold when I dropped into

Bordeaux airport to pick them up. They still haven't seen the wine as it has to go through customs and will be delivered by Securicor within the next hour."

I said, "Dinner is at eight. The chef is going to do something special to complement the wine."

"I had better tell the Sommeliers to get down to the kitchen for them to check the chef's menu."

"I'm thirsty. We will be in the bar."

We started walking across the foyer to the bar, when our other guests, the seven professors, came through the main entrance. I told them we would be in the bar after they had checked in. "Cars are laid on at five to take you to the research facilities, and dinner is at 8."

We ordered our drinks; Herr Hoffman arrived and ordered his, our wives started talking, so we started to talk shop. I had been spending and promising so much I asked, "Is there any money left?"

He just smiled. "It's been nearly 3 years since we first spoke and told you had £4.7 trillion. You have indeed spent billions and given away millions. Our half year end results show that Earth Corp is now worth £5.8 trillion."

"Before or after tax?"

"After."

"How come? I've been spending billions on land acquisitions all over the world—my people have started to build the infrastructure—billions more on over site and final completion."

"Because of the rains. The salination plants are now on hold. The geographical survey of Earth Corps land to find deep underground water is also on hold. Simply, there now is enough fresh water to support the land you have acquired."

"How much land do we own?"

"To date, Earth Corp owns 5.1 billion hectares or 10% of Earth. At the time, we paid around $10 an acre for dessert, a massive £126 billion. Each country couldn't believe that we would pay such a high figure for land they thought was completely worthless. Every year, our assets must be re-valued. Because of the rain, we have and had agreed with the tax authorities a £100 acre."

"That seems quite excessive."

"The best is yet to come. Ivan is negotiating with major property conglomerates, and on the table, as we speak, is $15,000 a hectare. Ivan's sure that it will reach $20,000 a hectare. If we release a third of our land to property developers, 1.7 billon hectares would amass $8.4 trillion."

"That's just extrapolating figures," I said.

"True, but look at its potential."

"I cannot make a profit on luck. Should we realise this amount of money, we will take what is reasonable—ten to fifteen per cent. The rest goes into separate bank accounts, controlled by Earth Corp for each country we have land in, to be used additionally to what we are already doing. Governments can go to them and put a case for this money, and our local representative will decide"

The hotel manager came into the bar and said the wine had arrived. We followed him. The Sommeliers were already there, inspecting. Everything looked authentic—

numbers matched—it was wine from the Chateau, and indeed, the year was correct. What they couldn't reconcile was wine of this value just appearing. Herr Hoffman put them out of their misery. He reached inside suit jacket and handed them an envelope carrying a letter and invoice signed by Baron Rothschild for the nine cases of wine. The letter said, "Thank you. A case of our very best wine, one for each enchanting day we spent together." The invoice showed nine cases of wine. There was no value, but the signature was that of the Baron. The authenticity was confirmed.

We went back to the bar, and all eight professors were there. I told them that the wine had arrived, and the authenticity had been confirmed. Plus, two Sommeliers from the Chateau had come to serve the wine at tonight's dinner. The sub-contractor had turned up with the cars. He mentioned that the other children had arrived and were at Manchester Children's hospital. We arrived at his research facility. They were a bit blasé about it; one research facility is much like another, and I was impressed. They soon got down to business. Consensus was they needed more blood from the little girl. She had already given a pint, and any more now could harm her. It would take a month to naturally replenish and be safe. I looked at Monk and he nodded. Six miraculous cures were needed. We took our leave and said we would meet back at the hotel in time for dinner. Not knowing how far the hospital was, we summoned our transport. We arrived the moment we entered it. We waited at the rear entrance as someone came out. We used the same back entrance as last time and picked up our doctors' coats on the way to the isolation unit. The medical team was the same as yesterday. I asked them to come to the parents' room, where I again asked them all if they had faith and asked if they would allow my friend to talk to their child. They all agreed. We put the isolation suits on, and one by one, met the children, and Monk did the same as yesterday. It took just over 20 minutes. We asked the medical team to take blood in 15 minutes, knowing the results would be good, and asked the parents for a pint of blood from each child in the morning. We wiped their minds of everything else that happened in the last half hour.

It was just after 18:00 when we arrived back at the hotel. Herr Hoffman came over and told me what all the commotion was about. Apparently, someone from the hotel had told the press that we were about to consume nearly £2 million worth of wine over dinner. "Every anarchist, anti-capitalist, save the world... you name it, is outside condemning us big time. This whole situation must be defused."

"I will go outside and talk to them."

"No," said Stephen. "We cannot protect you outside. Not enough manpower, and inside the hotel would be better."

I told the hotel manager, "I am prepared to give an interview to the press and ten protesters picked at random here in the foyer."

Ten minutes later, I met with the press and demonstrators. I told them that they had been misinformed.

"The wine that will be drunk tonight was a gift from the owner of the Chateau to a certain lady friend of his over 140 years ago. Her descendants, however, have been guilty of funding illegal activities across the globe, have been caught and all their assets have been confiscated. Stolen items were reunited with their rightful owners. The wine we drink tonight has no intrinsic value as such. Wine of this year and vintage is extremely expensive, but nine cases of it on the open market would make the price plummet. All those people and pension funds would lose a considerable amount of money. On the other hand, if it is drunk, then the scarcity of it would remain the same and would not affect the price."

One of the protesters shouted, "Why should you drink it."

I said "Quite simply, I have it and you don't." I felt an angry exchange brewing. "At my disposal, I have close to 10,000 bottles of rare wine. If I were to give you a bottle of this wine, would you drink it or sell it? You could easily get over £100,000."

"I would sell it. It's a life-changing amount."

"Exactly. You would sell it and undermine the price, so by drinking it, the price will remain the same. The wine was brought here as a gift for people who will help find a cure for the disease that affected the little girl here in Manchester. She is cured, and her blood holds the secret for a vaccine that will cure all that suffers from this ailment. They were all busy on their own worthy projects and the wine was a clincher in getting them here to assess and appraise the little girl's blood. They are at the research facilities now, and over dinner, we will be discussing our next steps. To answer your question fully, all 10,000 bottles will be drank. I shall be proposing a raffle to win a place to drink a glass of rare wine, and all proceeds will go to charity chosen by the people who have bought a ticket. It will all be done online. I cannot give you any more details other than a ticket will cost a pound for a place at a table, and there should be 35,000 to 40,000 winners."

Another question came from the press—Rachel James, Manchester Echo. "Why are you in Manchester?"

"My wife and I saw the plight of the little girl on the news yesterday. The mother's plea to NICE moved us to come to Manchester and tell her that she need not worry; all the funds she needs we would pay."

"Did you go to the hospital?"

"Yes."

"Did you see the parents?"

"Yes, of course."

"Did you see the little girl?"

"Briefly."

"Have you been back to the hospital today?" I did not like the way this was going, but before I could answer, the fire alarm went. The hotel manager took us to the fire exit, and my impromptu press conference came to an abrupt stop. Stephen had seen my discomfort and had hit the fire alarm. It got me off the hook for the time being, but more people would be putting two and two together. It was best for us to not be around to answer any more questions. The foyer was now clear—some protesters had taken cover and others had dispersed because of the torrential rain. We were all allowed back into the hotel. We went to our rooms to get changed for dinner. An idea occurred to me. I spoke with **Conrad head of Media Corp**, "I know I said I would never interfere, but I would like you to consider giving Rachel James of the Manchester Echo a job on our and the country's flagship daily newspaper, **The Globe**. She is getting too close to the miraculous cure of the children in Manchester. Double her salary and get her on the first train south. She will still want to pursue this story; you can tell her the truth if necessary, but it must be kept a secret. We are working on a plan similar to what we have done in Manchester. It will take time, but it is a priority. I will talk to her when she is in London if necessary."

On our way to dinner, Conrad got in touch and said she had accepted the new job. She said that she was on the verge of an amazing story, and I asked her "have you confided with anyone else?"

"No," she said. "It's my scoop; nobody is aware of it."

I said I was intrigued and told her to come to my office as soon as she arrived in London.

"That's great, see you sometime tomorrow."

We met my guests in the bar and then walked to the restaurant. Sue and Herr Hoffman's wife sat down at the huge round table in the middle of the restaurant first. We sat beside them, and our guests filtered in and around the table. The seven-course menu was in French and English and was very elegant. The first six courses were all types of different red meats to accompany the red wine. The first course was served—a massive plate in the middle was about a tablespoon full of food. The two Sommeliers started to pour the hopefully amazing wine. When everyone's glass was filled, I stood and toasted the team and wished them success in finding a cure. I took a large sip. Our professors rolled the wine around their mouths and slowly swallowed. They took mouthfuls of food and another savouring slurp. "Well, what do you think" I asked.

"I think it's a bit early to tell. The first course is a bit over-flavoursome." The Sommelier agreed. I told chef that the seasoning was too much, and they assured that the next course would be better. Not really being a wine drinker, I thought it was ok. Would I pay over £100,000 for a bottle? Certainly not.

I asked Sue what she thought, and she replied, "It's very nice. At this price, it should be the best wine I have ever tasted, but it's not." Hoffman's agreed.

The second course arrived—it was wild goat, so thinly sliced you could nearly see through it, with the asparagus spears and sauce. It was an utterly amazing taste—I could have eaten a lot more of this course—and the wine started to improve. This course with the wine were perfect complements. We all agreed that the wine had improved from the first course. Throughout the meal, the wine improved, the third glass possibly had something to do with it. We had consumed a bottle each, and the conversation was very amicable. I asked the professors if they were willing to help, and they all agreed. The professors from

Cambridge and Oxford would use their own facilities. The sub-contractor, Professor Daplynov, and the American would work in Manchester.

The sub-contractor said, "That with only one pint of blood, which I will share, is not enough and it will be at least a month before we can get another."

I said, "Have you spoken to the hospital this afternoon?"

"No, I have had my phone switched off. I didn't want to be interrupted with outside interference; I respect these people."

"Is it still off?"

"Yes."

"I would turn it on if I were you." he did so. The phone pinged with urgent calls from hospital, so he rang the isolation ward and was told that the remaining children were all showing signs of being cured. "We're taking bloods every two hours, but they have significantly improved. By the morning, they should be completely cured in the same way as the little girl yesterday."

"That is incredible," he replied and told us all round the table.

"That is excellent news. You will all have enough blood to work with."

"That's very convenient," said Professor Jackson. "You left us at the research centre, as soon as we said we would need more blood, and miraculously, six more children were cured."

I did not want to lie to these people as I wanted their help. "What I am about to say is for your ears only. I am telepathic; I can read your minds as well as wipe them clean. I am still learning how to use this resource, but Monk has been a telepath for an exceptionally long time. He can cure every ailment that plagues mankind. He can enter the mind and find what has failed, correct the problem, and get the brain to produce a signal to the immune system and eradicate whatever is causing the problem. Monk's abilities are secret and must remain so, but you are all researching cures for debilitating diseases, some which can be fatal. I know you have clinical trials, and after the help you give us in coming up with an antidote for this crippling children's disease, we will help you in a similar manner. Monk's abilities will enable you all to find cures for all known ailments, on one especially important proviso: it's shared freely around the world."

Professor Jackson said, "Most of us are tied to a pharmaceutical company for research funding and our cures are for them to decide who gets the information and at what price."

"But Monk will have given the cure to you free. You will only need to research the cure and not find it."

"Over the years, they have spent millions, and they will need a return on investment. Their shareholders would insist upon it."

"Well, we will cross that bridge as and when." I turned to Herr Hoffman. "Can you find out how much it will cost to buy all the pharmaceutical companies, just in case they become a problem with releasing information on the cures?"

"Whatever the cost," he said, "you can afford it."

"Well, that's solved that problem!"

The meal had been a success. We all went to the bar for a night cap, the professors had said they did not really want the wine I promised, now they had tasted it. "We have given it a thorough tasting, so return it all to the raffle. I will certainly be buying tickets. We stayed talking at the bar until it was time to go to our rooms. It had been a long but successful day. As I lay in bed, Sue said, "Why do you need to buy all these pharmaceutical companies? Why don't you buy a small one, or start one, then all the cures will be ours, and we will be able to give them free to all that needs them?"

"Nothing is that simple. If we find cures for all these ailments that plague us, that in itself is a huge problem. I know you have not been to Utopia for a visit—they have no hospitals, no doctors, and no illness; they heal themselves if a bug makes them ill. Now imagine 10 years on, we have medicines and treatments that make people well so no one's ill anymore."

"That would be marvellous," said Sue.

"But would it? A complete reversal to our NHS and medical care around the world; hospitals, doctors and nurses with no patients; there would be no need for drugs other than recreational."

"It would be gradual; it wouldn't happen overnight."

"I know, but the markets would. The children we just cured would not be noticed in the scheme of things. Just supposing this cure also helps those that are suffering from Leukaemia, let's say, there are one million suffering the disease, and the average cost of treatment is £1000, £52,000 a year, £5.2 billion per annum. The markets would do the same sums and start dumping shares in anything connected in some way to the medical industry. Their share value would go down in the short-term. It would only plummet when more cures are found and dividends are not sustainable. Most pension funds would have a considerable amount of investment in the medical industry, as the return on investment over the years has been excellent. I would suggest, but do not know for certain, that their portfolios would between 30 to 40 per cent of their total investment package. Possibly £200 billion would be wiped out when nobody gets sick anymore. That would affect every company's pension scheme, and ultimately, the employee that has and or will retire in the future."

"Everything becomes so complicated, so if we buy all these companies, long term we will take the hit?"

"Correct, and we can afford it."

"I have enjoyed today, being part of your business. Can I do something on a permanent basis? It will take my mind off missing all my friends."

"Well, I normally ask Herr Hoffman's trading team to do all my buying, but I see no reason why you can't be my Director of Acquisitions. I will tell Herr Hoffman. You can fly back with him tomorrow and introduce yourself to his trading team."

"Are you sure I can do this?"

"Of course. Any difficulty, just ask. That's why you have the bracelet. Always remember the bigger picture."

During breakfast the next morning, I told Herr

Hoffman that Sue had joined the team as Acquisitions Director and would work alongside the trading team to buy all the pharmaceutical companies. He held his hand out and said, "Welcome to the team. What time's your flight back to Switzerland?"

"14:30."

"Do you need anything from Assington, Sue?"

"Yes."

"After breakfast, I will take you back and bring you back here to catch the flight."

I asked the waiter about my other guests, and he said they had an early breakfast and had checked out. The sub-contractor's team was still there, waiting on the new blood from the hospital, and were keen to start. We finished breakfast and left for Assington. Four suitcases later, we were back in Manchester, where I left Sue and told her to contact me via the bracelet in case of anything. We met up with the Hoffmans at the private terminal at Manchester Airport. Herr Hoffman had made an appointment for Sue at one of Switzerland pharmaceutical; this was totally Swiss owned, unlike the rest, which were part of the global pharmaceutical industry. On the flight, he handed her a dossier on the company, and she got up to speed. They arrived in Zurich and sailed through customs, and Sue was dropped off at the company. She would be collected after the business meeting.

The head office and factory were located at a business park close to the University of Zurich. She walked to reception and signed in. The CEO was notified, and within a couple of minutes, his secretary came and escorted her to his office. Sue looked elegant, but she felt somewhat overdressed. The sharply dressed secretary was intelligent, and upon reaching the office, Sue noticed another woman dressed similarly.

Note to oneself: shopping tomorrow, she thought.

The CEO introduced himself and his two colleagues—one was the director of finance, and the woman was director of research. The secretary asked if they wanted anything, all declined, and the meeting started. Sue began by asking them if they had heard of the miraculous cure of the seven children in the UK. All three nodded—it had been international news. "Our company was involved in that cure, suffice it to say we cured those children. I cannot tell you how, as it's immaterial to our meeting today, but Earth Corp have the capability of curing all known diseases, including Alzheimer's and dementia, with no requirement for further treatment; once cured they stay cured.

"Impossible," said the research director.

"We figure it might take up to ten years, as there will be need of companies like yours to produce the antidotes. The main reason I am here today is commercial. As we see it, the long-term prospect for the industry is bleak, and the need for drugs other than recreational will be minute compared with today. About £46 billion is invested by pension companies to pay pensions to their hard-working retired employees. We believe that, as the cures are found, for example kidney dialysis, it'll bring a global cost of about £5 billion, and that is probably on the low side. It will not take long before the global stock markets adjust accordingly the price of pharmaceutical stock. We believe the share price will halve in the short-term and could have a disastrous effect on global pension funds. I would like to make you an offer for your business. Simply put, our offer is the highest price your stock has traded in the last 12 months plus a 5% bonus: 2.3 billion Swiss francs."

The CEO said he need to first consult the other directors; those not on site for a board meeting would be on a conference call. "Why don't you have a look round our factory?" He buzzed his secretary and told her to show their guest around. She led Sue to the door and the factory tour began. The secretary took her floor to floor—marketing, sales, and the research laboratory on the ground. She was impressed, having never seen a working laboratory. It was state-of-the-art. The secretary pointed out that the lab worked on different projects, but they did not use animals in any of their research. This bought a smile to her face; it took a few minutes to walk the length of the laboratory, which joined the factory. They were met by the production manager at the other end, and he took over the tour.

He explained, "We have ten assembly lines—five for our products and five for products we make under licence." The first stop was the raw chemical store., which could only be viewed from the outside. It had every drug, in concentrate form, you could imagine, a drug addict's heaven. From there, they went to look at where the raw materials were made into compounds. The chemists closely watched the machine make up a batch of compound and then test it thoroughly to ensure it was correct. Once checked, it made its way to the production line. "The assembly line is sterile. All operatives change from day clothes to sterile clothes and do so every time they have to leave their station for a call of nature, but most leave it to official break times as it can take 30 minutes. We have floater people that step in when some have to leave or official breaks. We work a flexi shift system, and all operatives are trained to do each other's jobs, but must work a central block of four hours continuously. But either side can choose when they start and when they finish, providing they complete 35 hours a week. It's 24 hours, seven days a week on a rota, which means they have to work weekends six times a year."

Sue said, "It seems to be highly automated. Do you really need people?"

"Yes—to reset machines, blockages and basic maintenance."

"It looks pretty boring just watching and waiting."

"They are paid very well to be bored, and our health and safety people insist they have a break away from their workplace every two hours. It may look boring but they are concentrating on their part of the assembly line."

"How many tablets do you make a day?"

"It can vary"—he pointed to the far assembly line—"it's currently making Aspirin, and the line is working flat out, at 400 by 100 milligram tablets a minute, 576,000 a day. It will take just over 9 days to fulfil the order from your NHS for 5 million tablets."

"That's incredible."

"The Dutch manufacturer who makes the machines has informed us that the latest replacements are five times faster."

"Will you be replacing them with the new machine?"

"It's a 250-million-Swiss-francs investment and will reduce staff numbers by 80%. The machines are so quick they have their own robots, free from human interface."

"That's extremely interesting." They neared the end of the production line. "Those pretty-looking blue pills... what are they?"

"Viagra." She wished she hadn't asked that question as her face turned bright red. She thanked the production and returned to the boardroom with the secretary.

Sue thanked the CEO for the factory visit. The CEO said, "That Earth Corp offer was in principle acceptable, barring a few questions. Will you replace the board and how many redundancies would you make?"

Sue smiled, "We want to buy your shares, not to run your business. We expect you all continue as you are. Our people may occasionally look over your shoulders, but they will not interfere in the day-to-day running of your business. Your production manager says you are looking at new equipment that will be five times as fast, and it is a considerable investment; we would have no problem with that, and if needed, fund it."

The employees' representative spoke, "This new machinery will result in 80% of the work force being made redundant. That is not acceptable."

"I understand that 27% of the stock is held by people around this table and the work force. That is 850 million Swiss francs which will make all the work force millionaires and the board multimillionaires. I have no idea about Swiss redundancies or the companies but a reasonable rate of redundancy would be 5 weeks for every year worked."

"What about the people that have not reached the qualifying level for shares and redundancy? They will be left high and dry."

"To me, I would take 10% off the total, giving you an 85 million hardship chest to do what you want with and help these people."

The CEO asked if there were any more questions, but none came. Sue thought they were all trying to work out how much they were worth. "One other thing we will control is the price of every drug you market. It will never be more than cost plus 10%."

The marketing director, who was on a conference call, asked, "How will we make enough money to continue research?"

"You will always have sufficient funds for research. The cost will not be reflected in the price; it will be a business expense and written off against the companies tax liability. It will never reflect in the price of the drug. My husband is emphatic about essential drugs being free. No one will suffer from their inability to pay."

The CEO said, "If we are giving our drugs freely, we will be inundated with orders from all over the world."

"Hopefully not. You're the first of all the

pharmaceutical manufactures I shall be visiting over the next few days to offer similar deals."

The CEO finished the meeting and asked if Sue needed a lift anywhere. She said "No. Herr Hoffman's chauffer is waiting to take me to their residence where I am staying the night. His people will be coming tomorrow to do all the legal bit."

Back at the Hoffman's residence, Heidi, Herr Hoffman's wife, asked how everything went. "Fine," Sue said, "but I felt a little bit overdressed. My clothes are just not business clothes."

"I have the perfect answer for you. There is a marvellous dress shop I use. They are closed now but would reopen if I ask them."

"No, we will go in the morning. I should have plenty of time, judging by the appointments your husband has set up."

She showed Sue to my room and asked, "Would you like to go out for dinner or eat here? I have bought so many evening dresses that it would be a waste of money if I didn't wear them." They both chuckled. "I will book a table Haus zum Ruden. It's a lovely Swiss cuisine restaurant. Heinricht and I just love it. I will book it for nine o'clock."

They really had a great time. The food was superb, and the company excellent. I just love this couple. It was past midnight when Sue finally got into bed. Sleep came straight away.

CHAPTER 20

SECURITY WAS TIGHT AT MEDIA CORP headquarters, but we sailed through. We met Conrad in his office; Rachel James had agreed to be our leading investigative journalist on the condition that she could continue her investigation into the miraculous cure of the seven children and me. "Best I have a chat with her, as that cannot happen. Where is she?"

"She's on the news floor—the end alcove on the right."

"Does she know that I own Media Corp?"

"Not sure. Certainly didn't come up at her very brief interview."

"Is there anywhere we can talk without interruption?"

"There are three interview rooms on the left as you go out of the newsroom". I walked through the news floor. Despite it being busy as usual, I got some acknowledgement, but most people were too concerned with their tasks and deadlines. I approached the alcove and looked over the top. She was staring at the computer screen. She nearly fell off her chair when I said hi. I added, "Have we not got an interview to finish? The last one was saved by the bell." I chuckled. She knew the fire alarm had been set off deliberately, so that I didn't have to answer her questions.

"How did you get in?" she said.

"That bit's easy—I own Media Corps. I told Conrad to employ you so we could finish our chat. Let us go to one of the interview rooms and finish our chat. Conrad says you only took the job if you could pursue the story you were working on, so let us finish it."

We went into the interview room. I introduced Monk—he was always by my side; he was like my shadow come minder. "He goes everywhere with me, and he has a unique gift: he is telepathic, and so am I, to a lesser extent. He makes sure that I use my abilities correctly as I am still learning. And sometimes, anger can cloud my mind, as I found out some years ago when a gang of crooks tried to rob my wife in Cheltenham. Monk had a hard job putting their minds back together."

Rachel said, "You can't expect me to believe that. I have seen so many magicians that say they can do that; it's a trick." I entered her mind, and deeply embedded in her subconscious was something that really shocked me.

"Why did you murder your uncle," I asked. A look of shock came over her face. I rattled off several of her passwords and sheer disbelief and horror took over. "I can tell you how and why you killed him. He was your mother's youngest brother, only 5 years difference in age. You grew up together and were really close. Inevitably, you became lovers, and you were infatuated with him—this was a closely guarded secret that you both held; none of your family had any hint of the love affair. When you got your first car, he had met someone else, he broke off the relationship, and you were devastated, bitter, and jealously took hold. You had an opportunity and took it when you saw him crossing the road. You ran him over, and he died a few days later. The police and family treated it as a terrible accident, knowing that you had grown up with him. He was like a brother to you, and they did not realise it was a crime of passion. Your remorse has eaten you. You put yourself in harm's way at every opportunity, and you are punishing yourself as you were not punished properly for your crime."

"Are you going to tell the police?"

"Certainly not. You have suffered for more than any custodial sentence would have placed on you."

"Do I still have this job?"

"Of course! You're a fine journalist, and you can ask me those questions that you tried to ask in Manchester."

"Did you cure the young girl in Manchester?"

"Yes—Monk did. My wife had seen the plea on the television, and it seemed to be a money thing, of which I have plenty, and we would have paid for the treatment.

Simple but nothing is simple in this life; everything has a knock-on effect. We were told that there is no cure in sight, and it might take decades to find. At four years old, she is getting constant attention—it is not a problem now—but when she is older, she will be a prisoner in an isolation ward and will have no life at all, so we had to cure her instead. She could not supply enough blood for the team, so we cured the other six to provide the blood necessary. The team feels that a cure for this rare disease will be quick and the disease eradicated."

"So you have the ability to cure all disease."

"Yes, we think so."

"Are you going to pick and choose those that you want too, acting like a god?"

"You are not seeing the bigger picture. We want to help the World Health Organisation. We told the team that's working on the cure for the girl's disease we would help them find a cure for all the projects they are working on and has the backing of the WHO."

"But you will let people die now when you have the ability to save them?"

"It's pure logistics. Let's say there are hundred incurable diseases and two billion of Earth's population are suffering from them: it takes about two minutes for Monk to enact a cure on an individual, 4 billion minutes to cure everybody. It would take 700 years. Our way is to cure the 100 diseases and make the cure available freely to all suffering."

"But you will still control the timetable?"

"Not so. It is in the hands of the team and the WHO.

They are prioritising the order; all I am asking is the cure for the girl's disease be first as it's a promise I made to all those suffering and have bought them all under one roof."

"it's still a great story and should be told."

"What will happen if your story is published: desperate people will be dragging their loved ones in search for Monk to make them better. They will never get close as security will see to that. Thousands of people will congregate around the Earth Corp properties in the hope of a cure for loved ones that will not happen. Could you live with that misery your article will cause? I have no editorial power over any of my media; it's down to individual editors. If they think your story is newsworthy, they will print it, or you can take it to any media I don't own, all I ask is you think about it for 24 hours, and I will see you tomorrow."

"OK, I will see you tomorrow."

I returned to Assington and checked through my inbox. Ivan had put some offers of land that he had received, and the amounts of money was truly staggering. I gave him the green light on all the projects. He also reminded me that acquiring all the pharmaceutical companies would bring me into conflict with the monopoly's commissions. "If you owned them all, you could monopolise the drug price to your advantage. That is how they would see it and prevent you from taking them all over. I needed to talk to the Prime Minister and the American President to smooth the path of the acquisitions that Sue is brokering."

I got to see the PM after his cabinet meeting and explained our plans. He said he would see to it that the monopoly commission would not intervene in the UK. I spoke to the President, and he likewise supported our proposals. I left Herr Hoffman to talk to the heads of governments in the EU as he was fluent in French, German, and Italian. He did not think there would be a problem.

CHAPTER 21

OVER A HUNDRED cataloguing professionals were employed specifically to catalogue the treasure of Messapth when it arrived in Switzerland. Due care was taken in background checks for the recruitment process. One group of five succumbed to the temptation—since the treasure was being catalogued for the first time, it would be easy to steal an item, but getting it out would be the problem. The metal detectors at the entrance to the warehouse would set of alarms as all personal metal objects were to be left in their lockers. The toilets were inside the warehouse and there were several WCs with small windows against the outside wall. An alley divided one warehouse from another, and at each end of the alley were two CCTV cameras pointing towards the parking lots of the different warehouses. It would be easy for someone to slip into the alley without being seen and wait to catch the item thrown from the toilet window—this is how their plan worked and had been successful three times.

One of the team knew an Alsace-based jeweller who handled most of the expensive stolen jewellery in Europe. They made the two-hour journey to deliver the first piece of jewellery to him and arrived just after six. The shop was closed, but they made a phone call to the jeweller, and the lights came on in the shop before the door opened. He greeted them all and took them to his office. The member of the team that knew the jeweller handed the piece to him; he could not believe his luck. He took them into another office for further scrutiny, checked his computer to see whether it had been stolen and got nothing. He got his eye glass out—there were no hallmarks on the gold setting, the diamonds and sapphires were genuine. There were over 200 gems in the piece, each of which he estimated to be worth over ten thousand euros, but the piece was unique— he had many clients that would pay four million euros for this item.

His clients found that they could take their fortune wherever they went, far less bulky than cash and an investment. He told them he was interested and asked how much they wanted for it. He could see they did not have a clue about its true worth.

"I pay 20% of trade value. The gems I value at two

million euros, and as I might have to break this piece up—and the gold has no hallmarks—so will four hundred thousand euros buy it?"

It was ten times what they had thought, so they eagerly agreed. He got up and went to his vault ten minutes later he came back with a bag with the money and handed it to them. He told them he would take all the pieces they brought, provided they were of the same quality. They left for Zurich, and the jeweller took the piece back to his office. He knew the piece was old, but how old? He scoured his computer, looking for something similar. After an hour of searching his files, he came across a photo of a wall in Cleopatra burial chamber; a Roman was kneeling, handing her what look like the bracelet. His heart pounded—if he were correct, the piece would be priceless. He knew an ancient Egypt scholar, who he sent a picture of the piece and a copy of the burial chamber, asking for his opinion.

The team arrived back in Zurich and went to their local bar, overwhelmed, and then greed took over—they would keep stealing until they all had amassed a million euros. Two more pieces got them one-and-a-half-million euros, but what they did not appreciate that the Swiss logistic team that put the pieces in the boxes had made a detailed manifest of the quantity and a brief description of all that was inside each box. After cataloguing each box, it went to another person whose job was to check the manifest against catalogue. It was time-consuming and boring until he found a discrepancy two weeks in—a bracelet had not been catalogued. He took his findings to security, and they told him not to mention a word but check all there cataloguing first. Two hours later he returned and said a further two pieces of jewellery were unaccounted for. Herr Hoffman was advised; he asked Stephen Shefford for advice and acted on it accordingly. When all the employees had left, security placed TV cameras around the warehouse, canteen, toilet areas, and offices. There was not a metre of the building inside and out that was not filmed. When the suspect team arrived in their cars, all of them were bugged. Stephen had advised to let them steal a fourth piece and film every movement. He had said. "Once you know the end game, let them steal a fifth. Call me and we will both go to the fence and wait for their arrival."

The fifth piece was stolen, and Stephen was informed. He assembled his team, and I went along with Monk. After the 80-minute flight, we arrived at the jewellers just before closing, and Stephen deployed his men around the streets and alleys to seal all escape routes. Herr Hoffman had asked for it to be kept in-house, and he would deal with the thieves. The French police were not to be involved. The dossier on the jeweller showed that he had a licence to carry a firearm and that there was a panic button direct to police headquarters.

We entered the shop while his three female assistants prepared to leave. He advised us that he was about to close, but I changed his mind easily and he told his staff they could leave—he would deal with us.

I told him it was my wedding anniversary and needed something special.

"How much do you want to spend?"

"Depends on the item; the money is irrelevant." He came from behind the counter, towards me, then Stephen and Monk went to either end of the counter, stopping him from reaching the panic button. I knew he was not armed but finding the guns or weapons was important as no one needed to be hurt. His mind told me that they were in his desk and two more in the vault. While in his mind I got the vault combination and told him to lock up. He did it without thinking. Alarm now appeared on his face. I told him that he had fenced four pieces of jewellery that indirectly belong to me. "You are waiting for the fifth piece this evening and we're here to film its arrival and arrest the culprits." Colour drained from his face. "We need to talk. Stephen, he has one gun in his desk and a further two in the vault." I gave him the combination. The look of horror on the jeweller's face was better than a prison sentence. "We are not here to rob you; just to get our property back."

With the brief description on the manifest, it was easy to locate our items—he had kept them together. We went into his office. Stephen had the weapons and jewellery and sat down. The jeweller was trembling, and I told him to relax.

"How much did you pay for all this jewellery," I asked.

"Two million euros in cash."

"What do you think they're worth?" I noticed that he was beginning to relax a little.

"If I am right about the first piece they bought me that it's a gift from Caesar or Mark Anthony to Cleopatra, it would be priceless."

"How much is it worth as a jewellery item?"

"I could get at least 4 million for it with just one phone call."

"What would it make if it went to auction with a proven providence?"

"It could go through the roof. We have so many billionaires; they would fight in the streets to own it."

"What about the other three pieces?"

"They are old, and if a similar providence could be found, the sky's the limit."

"If I told you that there were over ten thousand pieces, I am assuming of the same quality, would they realise the same kind money?"

"It would flood the market, and prices would drop possibly. There's a lot of people out there with bundles of cash, and it's hard to transport. Look in my vault, I carry ten million cash. It fills up most of the vault. I have one shelf of jewellery worth over 300 million and could get all of it in a suitcase and take it with me wherever I go. There's a lot of people out there that do just that."

"I have a dilemma. This treasure trove came from an ancient sect that has been around for at least five thousand years. It is all ill-gotten gains, so it has been confiscated as it is the proceeds from evil and crime. We need to realise this asset in the best way, as all of it will go to a new independent United Nations. So, what do we with you? I know all your wealth is in your vault and stock in the shop, which makes you a wealthy individual. If we confiscate it, as proceeds from crime, which I am quite sure I can do, you will be penniless when you come out of prison. Trust me, I know you have no secret stash anywhere, and Monk agreed with me. Now this is my offer: you can keep all your money and work for us on getting the best price. You will no longer fence stolen items; your role ends when the last piece of jewellery is sold. The time span is under your control. You can employ as many people as necessary at your expense. Any commission you seek will be paid by the buyer. Do you agree?" After a few minutes of thought, he agreed.

The jeweller's phone rang—the thieves had arrived and were outside the shop. He let them in as normal and did not lock the door behind them as per instructions. He took them to his office, where the three of us were. They weren't overly concerned about our presence as they didn't know us. It soon changed when Herr Hoffman arrived. They tried to make a run for it but just bumped into Stephens men. They were all searched, and the fifth piece was found. The jeweller picked up the fifth item and commented, "remarkable," and put it down. Herr Hoffman nodded, and the thieves were taken outside and put in a Swiss unmarked police van and would be dealt with in Switzerland. They would have fared a lot better had they been arrested by the French police.

I suggested to the jeweller that he might go back with Herr Hoffman to look at the treasure. There was still a great deal to catalogue.

CHAPTER 22

ON THE WAY BACK to the UK, we discussed why such a jeweller would fence stolen property; he and twenty-four other jewellers around the world did it similarly. Monk delved into his mind far more than I had and said, "It appears to be an arrangement they have with the criminal underworld and prevents them from being robbed, as the jewel thieves need to turn gems into cash. They know that should they hit any of them, the other jewellers will not entertain fencing jewels of a fellow jeweller in the group. It appears that if the thieves hurt, maim or kill anyone in the course of the robbery, they will not touch the jewels, and the thieves know it and without anywhere to take the jewels, they are normally caught."

Stephen chipped in. "It gets better than that: my firm was asked to act on behalf of a consortium of insurance companies to buy back jewels stolen from safety deposit boxes from a London bank a few years ago. The publicised value was £100 million, and the thieves got £20 million in cash from, no doubt, some of this group of jewellers."

He rattled four names off and Monk nodded. "The actual amount the insurers were liable for was £800 million. The policy holders wanted to downplay the amount for tax reasons; otherwise, it would have gone down in history as the largest robbery ever. We were asked to deliver the cash and get the jewels back which we did. Thinking about it now, they had £800 million at risk and got it back for £25 million plus our hefty fee—they were quid's in. I bet you they do this for every robbery; it would make commercial sense. The jewellers give the thieves 20%, and they receive 25% and no doubt push up the owner's premium by 10%. It's a win for all concerned."

CHAPTER 23

HERR HOFFMAN PHONED the Swiss police commissioner and organised a night stay in a Zurich jail for the five disgraced employees. When the commissioner asked why, he said, "It is an internal problem—quite serious—and I do not want them to leave the country until I have dealt with them tomorrow."

"Ok, I will organise it."

They reached Zurich just after 22:00. The police van stopped. Herr Hoffman opened the van and asked, "Where's the money?" Silence. "If you don't tell where the money is, I will turn this into a police matter. I have told them that it is a serious internal matter and will be dealt with internally." Silence. "Fair enough. When you signed your employment contract; in the event of proven dishonesty, you can be searched at your work place your car and your home. We don't need a search warrant to do this, and our own security people can use any means necessary to gain access to any property belonging to you." Silence. Some of the condemned thought the money would never be found and were confident, so they were not going to say anything; it was what they all agreed in the van on their way back to Zurich. If they pleaded guilty, they would get 3 years and be let out after one year served. Two million euros would be worth the inconvenience of a prison term.

Herr Hoffman could see that they would not be helping him in finding the money. He called me I had just got back home. "They won't tell me where the two million is."

"Oh!" I turned to Monk; he was already shaking his head. Neither of us had entered their minds, so we had to go back to Zurich. It took us just over ten minutes to get there using the verticular. Monk and I confronted the thieves and discovered that all had split the money up and hidden it in some clever and peculiar places. In their presence I told Herr Hoffman's security team where to find the money. Colour drained from their faces; their criminal nest egg was no more. Herr Hoffman said that it was now a truly an internal matter. He thanked us, and we were back home. It had all taken just 40 minutes.

Herr Hoffman told his security team to get the money. He went with the thieves to police headquarters, where they were expected. The custody sergeant showed them to their cells and locked them in. Herr Hoffman said he would collect them at 9 am the following day. "On no account should you allow them access to a phone or a lawyer. They are your guests for tonight only. Feed them only if they ask. Do not enter any dialogue with them, and that goes for all that may encounter them."

The five were put in separate cells. They tried to shout to each other, but the cells were well insulated for noise. They were asked if they would like something to eat, and they all declined and spent most of the night wondering how on Earth Corp knew where they hid the money. Since none of the others knew, it left them with only one thought: those two guys can read minds.

None got much sleep. They accepted a coffee each before they left with Herr Hoffman's security team. All their work colleagues gathered in the cataloguing room. Herr Hoffman started his well-rehearsed diatribe on how low a Swiss national can be to steal from his employer. It went on for 15 minutes, and by the time he had finished, they just wished they could have melted into the floor.

"Finally, as all items and monies have been retrieved, it will not be a police matter. You will clear your lockers, and any monies owed to you will be paid, but you will never work for a Swiss company ever again. You have bought shame on Switzerland. Now, get out."

As they left the cataloguing room, all their colleagues turned their backs on them and booed them until they had left the room. The humiliation of the five rankled them so much they swore to get their revenge. All their Swiss friends had disappeared; they were on their own—outcasts in their own city. It was as if they had Leprosy; no Swiss would talk to them. With their severance pay and savings, they would last 3 months if they all moved into one flat. Getting work was impossible with the skill sets they had. They were forced to look into the minimum wage jobs, most of which were held by imported labour since the Swiss did not want them. The rent on their apartment was over three thousand Swiss francs. Eventually, the three men found work in a laundry in the old part of Zurich, and the two women, office and shop cleaning jobs, respectively. Combining all their wages, they were able to just survive in Zurich, and they had to be in Zurich to get the revenge on Herr Hoffman.

Over dinner one night, the women had said they were cleaning a fashion shop in the old town when a woman came in, and everybody stopped what they were doing to attend to her. I asked one of the seamstresses who the woman was, and I was told it was Frau Hoffman. "I asked, 'Does she come to the shop often?' and they told me maybe once a month, but she apparently has been known to come weekly." They got the street map of Zurich, and the women showed them where the shop was. It was not too far from the laundry where they worked.

After dinner, the men said they would go and see how close it was. Two were dropped off outside the shop, and they walked in either direction to navigate around the building. When they got to the end of the building, they turned left and right, respectively. In about two hundred metres, they came across an alley separating both buildings.

It would have looked suspicious to go down the alley so they continued. Both had recognised where they were, and sure enough at the next junction, they turned and there, waiting for them, was the driver who had parked in the goods outwards of the laundry where they all worked. The news that the fashion shop and the laundry were back-to-back divided by an alley lifted their spirits. On arriving home, they told the women of the coincidence that possibly the shop and the laundry may be back-to-back or certainly close. The kidnapping of Frau Hoffman was a distinct possibility. Tomorrow would be the first day of getting their money and revenge. It did not have to be right away; meticulous planning was the key and time, and well they had that in abundance.

Eight weeks later, the women got a text on where to go, and they got to the fashion shop. It was a lot easier for the men, and they were there every day. The emergency exit was alarmed. It was amazingly simple magnetic device at the top of the door. The magnet was screwed to the door, which had a lever attached to the door frame. If the door opened, the magnet would separate from the lever, and the alarmed would sound. It was the simplest of things to overcome; at break they removed the two screws, cut the threads off and super-glued the screw caps back in place. It looked like they were attached, but if you pushed the door opening bar, it would open without the alarm going off.

At lunch time, they walked the alley and paced it. It was easy to see where the laundry was with the steam bellowing out of the extraction fan, but locating their emergency exit, not so easy from the other side. There were doors that could be a possibility. They had so many other problems within the laundry. The emergency door was in the ironing room, and they worked in the wash house and needed to get transferred to the ironing room. Also, if the kidnap were to be successful, one of them would have to become a driver to collect and deliver the laundry.

The women cleaning the fashion shop, at their first opportunity, had replaced the screws and taken photos of the fitting rooms and sewing rooms. All were at the rear of the shop and awfully close to the emergency exit. To ensure they had the right emergency door, they placed a piece of silver foil under the door, in such a way that it could not be seen from inside, only from the alley. They phoned the men, and one of them went down the alley at break and collected the silver foil and noted it was the middle door of the three. Perfect. All were confident that the disabling of the alarms in both buildings would hold unless there was a fire in either building or would be secure until they needed it for the kidnapping.

It was not hard for one of the men to get the driving job. He had the knowledge of a Zurich taxi driver, so when the driver called in sick and the Turkish replacement came back with 80% of the load undelivered, the man stepped up and volunteered to finish the delivery. It took him just over two hours to finish the delivery. The Turkish owner was well pleased and retained him as the spare driver. Since the usual driver was still sick, he did the whole delivery and was back at lunchtime. This went on for a week, and his knowledge of Zurich insured that he completed the delivery round by lunchtime.

One of the other men suggested to the owner, "Why don't you have a second delivery in the afternoon?"

"We don't have enough business customers at the moment."

"I am sure if you offered next day delivery, restaurants and hotels around the airport would jump at the chance for next day delivery."

"I will make some phone calls and see what I can drum up."

He was amazed at how many new customers he gained by the next day delivery service. The following day, the boss called him into his office and told him he had been right—they had an additional thirty customers on the other side of Zurich, but there was no way the existing driver could do it and the profit margin did not allow for a second van and driver.

"Could you not get him to work in the laundry and my friend be the main driver?"

"The driver is my brother, and he hates the laundry work."

"Well, why don't you make him sales rep—uses his own car, same salary, and commission on any new business he brings in. It will be a promotion for him."

The laundry really prospered, and all three were given pay rises, and one was made foreman to oversee the entire workforce, which gave the owner time to expand his business, as he had left the day-to-day running of the laundry to the Swiss.

The two women had enrolled in night school to study tailoring for women, which gave them the necessary skills to get work in the dress shop. The owner of the dress shop was wonderful with her customers but somewhat of a tyrant when it came to her staff. She required perfection and speed, which do not necessarily go hand in hand. The staff turnover was quite large, so when two cleaners said they were able to make alterations quickly and could clean the shop as well, it was win-win for her, and they were employed full time.

The two women did the same thing to the fire escape door as the men had done in the laundry. All this had taken time, but none had worried about it, making sure everything was exactly right. Their perfection was even down to the making of the homemade chloroform, which they tested on each other, firstly to see that it worked and to see how long the hostage would be unconscious. The laundry emergency exit was camouflage to look like a wall and a wheelie bin chained to the handle, all to give them more minutes to get away with the hostage. They had several sites that could take them to, which would depend on the kidnapping day. All had agreed it would be best for the hostage to be unconscious for an hour. The van would take 20 minutes to reach any of the hideouts, to tie and gag them would take no more than 5 minutes for the van driver, and at lunch, the other two could check on the hostage. Everything was in place, and now they only needed an opportunity.

CHAPTER 24

FRAU HOFFMAN AND SUE LEFT for the dress shop soon after breakfast. The chauffeur was Hilde's personal bodyguard. Sue had insisted her security was minimum, which consisted of two vehicles front and back, with two armed bodyguards in each. The security team had agreed that the chauffeur would be the inside man. From his knowledge, they would deploy both cars at either end of the alley and two men would be outside the shop. Hilde Hoffman had phoned the dress shop and informed them that she was bringing a friend that needed several stylish business suits and dresses and would like them to be ready today at about 10:00.

At just after 09:00, the owner of the dress shop told all

the staff to be ready for their most important clients. The convoy arrived just before 10, and the women called the men at the laundry and told them of a second person with their target, and they all agreed she would also be taken as hostage as well. Sue and Hilde took their seats and watched the business suits and dresses as they were modelled. Sue, with Hilde's, help choose about fourteen suits and dresses, which she elected to try on. The fitting room was at the rear of the shop, and Hilde's chauffeur and bodyguard were used to their principal disappearing into the fitting room, so thought nothing of it.

The three of them went into the fitting room and would in there for some time. The two female accomplices were already in the fitting room, and they sent a text to the laundry as the customers entered. The timing could not be more perfect—the laundry delivery van leaves around midday for the afternoon run. The fitting was going well. No one heard the fire exit open. The door to the fitting room silently opened, and three men entered and chloroformed the three women. It only took seconds, and the women did not have a chance. As silently as they entered, they left with the hostages over their shoulders, across the alley into the laundry. The hostages were put into two laundry baskets and were wheeled to despatch. They placed laundry over the lifeless bodies and wheeled them round to the despatch area and straight onto the van, which was on its way for the afternoon delivery. The female accomplices had chloroformed themselves so they would wake up with the shop owner and appear to be victims as well.

They had chosen a hotel that had recently been bought by a large hotel chain for refurbishment in the old part of the city. It had slowly gone downhill, from a 5-star rating to three stars. A contract company that was in line to refurb it could wait no longer for a decision, so they had started another refurb while waiting for a decision. This meant that the hotel would be completely empty. What made this such a good place to keep the hostages was that the laundry room was accessible from the street and one of their customers had keys to the laundry room. The van arrived, and the laundry baskets were wheeled into the room. Using plastic ties, he bound hands and legs together and put gaffer tape over their mouths. Confident he had done well, he left to carry on with the deliveries. From kidnap to the laundry room, it had taken less than 20 minutes. At twelve it was the normal lunch break for the kidnappers, and they made their way to the hotel laundry room. They had made duplicates keys of all possible kidnap hidey holes. Inside the laundry room, they lifted the unconscious hostages out of the baskets and sat them on the floor against the wall and used the laundry for them to sit on. The hostages would be out for another 30 minutes. They still had no identification on the second hostage, but they both felt she must be important and would find out soon enough. It was a successful day for them.

At the dress shop, it was not until someone took some coffee into the fitting room, some 20 minutes since the kidnap, that the alarm raised. The chauffeur rushed into the fitting room, saw the unconscious females and rushed out of the emergency exit. He noted that the alarm had been doctored and ran to one end of the alley to tell the other car to contact Stephen. They had seen nothing, and no one had come out of the alley this end. He rushed to the other end, and similarly, no one had exited the alley. He radioed the men outside the shop and bought them up to speed—they would check all the shops their street side.

The chauffeur walked back down the alley, trying the door handles of the emergency exits of all the other shops and businesses while the other security guys checked the shops and businesses the other side of the alley. He walked round the wheelie bin, not thinking it was concealing a handle, and all the other emergency exits were locked. He radioed the other bodyguards to check the emergency exits of all the shops and to see if they alarmed; one by one the emergency doors opened and alarmed except for the laundry. It was hard to open. The chauffeur heard the struggle and saw the wheelie bin and the camouflaged door that he had missed initially. They were pleased they had found the laundry and people there must have known something, only to find that all the staff were Turkish and did not speak the languages of Switzerland. The foreman was at lunch and due back at 14:00 was about as much as anyone could understand.

I was in my office when Stephen rushed in. "Sue's been kidnapped with Hilde Hoffman 30 minutes ago." We were in Zurich in 15 minutes. The chauffeur said she, along with the women in the shop, had been chloroformed, and that was why I could not make mental contact with Sue. I asked Monk if it would be safe to wake them; he could not answer as he had no knowledge of chloroform.

The chauffeur asked one of the assistants, "Have you a medical cabinet?" She led us to it, and the chauffeur rummaged through it and found what he was looking for—the smelling salts. He took it back to the fitting room and woke the women, they had seen nothing, and we did not want to press them just yet. We left them recovering and went across the alley to the laundry.

Stephen had called the police, and we met them in the laundry. Interviewing the employees, none had any knowledge of any wrongdoing, and Monk and I confirmed this by interrogating them mentally. All had said the only other workers were the three Swiss employees: two were at lunch, and one was doing the afternoon deliveries. It had to be them. No one had seen anything, and they worked so close to the fire exit.

Stephen said, "It has to be them. Look at the size of these laundry baskets. You could get two people in their easily and wheel them straight onto the van in front of all these workers, and they wouldn't suspect a thing." He turned to the chief of police. "We need to find that van." The police incident vehicle was parked outside and told the officer to get the CCTV up. He logged into the Zurich CCTV road system; an all systems alert was sent to all the mobile units. It would not be long before the van was found.

I still could not contact Sue through our bracelets, and it had been nearly an hour. The Turkish man who owned the laundry turned up and was quickly appraised of the situation. He gave the addresses of the employees. Two police cars were sent to these addresses, which later turned out to be false. Stephen asked the laundry owner if he knew the route the van would take.

"The driver normally chooses when he's delivering as the Zurich traffic can change day-to-day."

"Have you a list of his drops this afternoon?"

He went into his office and came back with the day's deliveries. It was only the afternoon deliveries we were interested in; the police chief gave the list and told them to contact all on the list and to narrow the search area.

We went back to the dress shop. The women may be feeling better to answer some more questions. The owner had said that she had ordered a taxi to take them home. I asked for their address, and she gave it to me. It was the same address of the Swiss from the laundry. I showed it to Stephen. "Damn", he commented, and I passed to the chief of police.

As soon as Stephen and I entered the fitting room, the two female accomplices immediately recognised us. They knew Monk and I could read minds and were so relieved that we had not interrogated them before going to the laundry. They could not believe their luck when the owner of the dress shop said they could go. Their taxi arrived, and they told the driver to take them to the nearest supermarket as they needed some items. As soon as they were dropped off, they phoned their men and told them, "The guys that read our minds are here, and it seems the other woman is the wife of one of them."

The men were not duly concerned; it would only be a problem if we were face-to-face, and that is not likely at all. "Just in case, do not go home as they will soon realise the address held will be false just like ours. Go to the pictures until you here from us."

The men had put masks on when the women were coming too. They knew who Hilde was but had no idea who the other woman was. They went over to the women and removed the gaffer tape, so Sue soon made sure that they knew who the other woman was in no uncertain terms. She said, "You haven't hurt us; just a bit of inconvenience, so let us go now before my husband gets involved, and we will say no more about it."

Both men laughed. "He will never find you."

"He will have found us before 4 o'clock. Last chance, or we will wait to be rescued as it won't be long."

The kidnappers conferred then one phoned the third accomplice and told him to dump the van. "It's too hot, and police are looking for it. Hide if you can, but ditch it as soon as possible and meet us here."

He got another phone, put a new sim in it and phoned Herr Hoffman to tell him the safe return of his wife would cost him 5 million Swiss francs. He then handed the phone to Hilde, who told him they were both ok. He took the phone back and said, "We will be in touch about where to leave the money," and hung up.

I had seen all that had transpired as I was mentally in touch with Sue. I told her to scan where they were, and her eyes had scanned the whole room—it was a laundry room. On the first scan, there was no visible name of where they were and no clues at all.

Stephen asked, "Can you see any fire extinguishers?" which I relayed to Sue. She started scanning and soon saw a fire extinguisher. It was Permafix and had a number on. It was PM 006.

Stephen phoned the CEO of Permafix, explained the position and said he would wait while he did the checking. After 6 minutes, he came back and told him, "It is an old extinguisher but PM006 was placed in Hotel Atlas in the old town, and according to our records, it can be found in their laundry room." Bingo! We knew they were being held in the laundry room of Hotel Atlas, and he told the police.

I phoned Herr Hoffman and told him we now knew where they were being held. "Would you tell the chief of police that we will handle the recapture of our ladies and will hand the kidnappers to them afterwards?" He rang the police chief and told him we would be handling it. He eventually agreed; the police would take the kidnappers after the rescue. We had plenty of men for the rescue. We needed plans of the Atlas Hotel.

I asked Herr Hoffman to have a word with the city architect as a matter of urgency, and the plans were emailed back to us. The ground floor showed the laundry room had a door to the street and another to the hotel. The city architect had also told us the hotel was closed for refurbishment, so it was empty. The kidnappers must have known, so that is why they choose it.

"Where is the hotel?" I asked.

"It's about 15 minutes from here. Still in the old part of Zurich, about a 15-minute drive in traffic, quicker if no traffic," replied the chief of police.

"There is a multi-storey car park a 2 minutes' walk to the hotel," Herr Hoffman said.

Stephen said, "I reckon there will be three guys max. We go in through the main hotel entrance and make our way to the laundry room from the inside. Sue's security team will watch the street entrance, Hilde's chauffeur, Robin, Monk and I will do the rescue."

Herr Hoffman said, "I am coming too."

We reached the hotel, and the security team took their positions and went to the front entrance. It was heavily chained with padlocks. It never ceased to amaze me how simple Stephen made of locks of any kind, and it was seconds before we were through to the actual hotel entrance door. In our haste, we forgot our torches, and all the windows and doors had been boarded up for extra security measures. It was pitch black inside. Stephen got his phone out and put the torch on. Herr Hoffman and the chauffeur did the same.

The laundry was opposite the kitchens, and our best route would be through the restaurant and through the kitchens. All the internal doors were unlocked, so we made easy progress and were in the kitchen in no time. We had to be a bit more careful from now on. I connected with Sue and told her we were outside and asked her to look at the kidnappers so we could see where they were, in relationship to the internal laundry door.

Have they any weapons?

She thought *no* or at least she and Hilde had not been threatened with any weapons. Both had only been conscious for no more than 30 minutes. "We must assume that they have and will use them," said the chauffeur, who was itching to put a bullet into the kidnappers.

"Well, this is what is going to happen: Stephen will unlock the door, Monk and I will disable the kidnappers"— I pointed to the chauffeur—"You will cover us. Stephen and Herr Hoffman will go and untie the hostages."

The chauffeur said, "Surely I should go in and take them out. You're not even armed."

Stephen said, "Believe me, they are heavily armed." I told Sue to get the kidnappers' attention when we were about to open the door. I will let you know. The five us made our way down the corridor; the laundry door was the last one on the right. We approached it silently, and Stephen used his universal key to unlock the door. He slowly turned the key, and a faint clonk was heard. I told Sue now, and she asked the kidnappers if they could do anything about the cable tie they were cutting into her wrists and ankles. As the kidnappers went to have a look, Monk and I quickly went through the door. They were still bending over the hostages as they felt our presence. We disabled them mentally—they could not use their arm and legs, and they nearly fell on top of Sue and Hilde.

Sue looked at the kidnappers and said, "I told you so." Stephen and Herr Hoffman went over and cut the ties.

There was a sudden dawning on the kidnapper's face who Monk and I were, and the colour drained out of their face. I probed a bit more into their minds and all became clear.

I asked Herr Hoffman, "Do you recognise them?"

It had been sometime, and he said, "Yes, these are the people who stole the Messapth treasure, but there were five of them."

Stephen said, "I think the driver will be the third guy, and the two women from the dress shop will be the female part of the gang."

"Hilde, Sue, what would you like done to these kidnappers? We can hand them over to the police, or I could really hurt them like the gang in Cheltenham. I am a lot better with this mind control now. It wouldn't be so messy."

Sue said, "I don't have the stomach for that again."

Hilde said, "We should decide when they are all caught." Looking into their minds again, the driver should be here shortly, and the women are at the pictures. However, the guys do not know which one.

Stephen rang the dress shop and asked the owner which taxi service she used for her two staff. She told him and asked if there was any news about her clients. He told her that they were safe and reunited with their husbands.

Sue said, "I need to get back to the dress shop. I have not finished shopping and need the clothes for my other appointments." She was not fazed at all; it had merely been an inconvenience.

I told the chauffeur to take them back to the dress shop

so they could finish shopping. I told her I would see her back at the dress shop as soon as we had rounded up the rest of the gang.

Stephen phoned the taxi company and soon found out where they were dropped off. The supermarket was in a shopping mall with a cinema. It had to be that one. He took the mobiles from both the guys and looked at the call history and two recently dialled numbers; he asked them which was which. No answer. If we sent the text to the wrong one, the other three would know something was amiss.

"Stephen, Robin, there a bit reluctant. Can you assist? Controlled tweak of their central nervous system should do it," and it did. They had never known such pain.

A text was sent to them to meet them at the south entrance of the shopping mall at 15:00. The driver turned up at the laundry room and joined his friends, similarly the two females were picked up brought to the room. All five of the gang had been caught in just over three hours. I turned to Herr Hoffman. "What are we going to do with them? Dealing with them the last time a non-custodial sentence didn't work, and their hatred towards you is eating them away. Our wives have not been really harmed they are back shopping. What sort of prison sentence would they get?"

"Ten to twelve years."

"Probably out in six with good behaviour, maybe earlier with a tag and more time to fester the hatred and seek revenge on you or Hilde."

"What do you have in mind instead?" he asked.

"Well, what if Monk and I removed that hatred, the jewel heist, and working for you and only leaving in their minds they work in a laundry and the two women in a dress shop? We'd leave them really happy working in their jobs."

"I want them punished."

"Don't you think working in a laundry and dress shop for five educated Swiss is a punishment?"

"I suppose so."

"Do you agreed?"

"Yes." It took 15 minutes to change them into happy laundry and dress shop workers.

I contacted Sue and told her what had been decided and said, "The seamstresses will be coming back to the dress shop, and tell the owner that you are happy for them to do the alterations. I will have a word with the laundry owner; I am sure he will be happy having them back." I went from talking to the Turkish owner to the dress shop, and it was if nothing had happened. They started on the alteration of Sue's clothes, which would be available about 19:00 the same evening. Herr Hoffman said he would get them collected and sent to England. Three of the outfits had been altered, and she took them with her. We said our farewells to the Hoffmans and got back to Assington just before 5.

Sue would show me her new outfits. Monk and I went to the kitchen. There was always something available as the security team were always changing shifts—two large hostess trolleys of hot food. Monk was there like a shot, grabbing a plate and lifting each lid and putting a bit of food on his plate, quickly running out of room.

I said, "We will be eating properly at eight tonight so don't eat too much." He just smiled. For a small guy, he could really eat. I just grabbed a sausage put it in a buttered roll, with loads of fried onions topped with my favourite brown sauce. I took my roll back to my office, and Stephen joined me.

"Now you can understand why the security is so large to protect you," he said.

"The problem in the shop was that Sue didn't have Pat and Sheflin, as they were on their honeymoon. Had Sheflin been there, she would have gone with Sue into the fitting room and prevented the kidnap in the first place and hospitalised the lot of them."

"It was Sue's idea to let them have two months off, not mine," Stephen said. "You can't do Australia in a week; it's just to big."

I replied, "It's over now, and no harm's been done."

CHAPTER 25

THE TEMPLE OF KRURS CHENDO-DA had in its 4000-year history had never known the amount of snow that fell in a month. A month when there was hardly any snowfall. It had taken them over a year to make a snow tunnel to get below the snow line. They thought that Messapth organise a similar dig towards them from the snow line. It was obvious, for some reason, they were not going to pick up the daughters of Messapth. The daughters were now ready to leave as they could not be taught anymore. The high priest was concerned since they brought new recruits and enough supplies for their children and the monks. The monastery was self-sufficient in all, but there were certain items they would start to miss.

He summoned all to the great hall and spoke, looking directly at his students. "I do not know what has happened to your mothers or at least the mother that should have collected you last year. At first, I thought it must be the snow, but now we have reached the snow line, nothing has been up the pass as far as we can tell. I am afraid we must assume something has happened and there not coming."

He could see their disappointment in their faces. He continued, "However, we are extremely low on some essential supplies. It is my intention to send ten monks down the mountain to purchase supplies, and you can go with them and make your way back to Messapth. The journey is over 2500 miles and will take you weeks." He opened a large trunk beside his chair asked the students to come forward one by one. The trunk was full to the brim with ancient gold taels. He told them to put their arms out straight and carefully placed the taels on their outstretched hands. Most of them could manage around twenty-five pounds before dropping them. You will need these taels which are pure gold to get you the things you need for your journey. The students picked up the gold and shared equally amongst themselves. The ten chosen monks also received five taels each for the purchase of supplies, and all would leave in the morning. The problem with the pure gold taels was that the tael itself could have been worth more than the gold, because of its rarity. No one knew the actual value since Messapth paid for everything as payment for teaching their children this incredibly special martial art.

The temple could only be reached in high summer,

there was about a three-week window, but now with the snow tunnel to the end of the snowline, they would be immune to the worst weather the mountain can through at them. The daughter's state-of-the-art, cold weather gear they had arrived in was of no use, so they had to wear the traditional garb of the monks.

The daughters were given belts to hold the gold taels which they wore around their waists and set off down the mountain with enough supplies to last the three weeks the journey would take. However, the snow tunnel protections enabled them to travel longer and further and were at the snow line in four days. The daughters set the pace for the monks, they wanted to get to civilisation as quickly as possible and set a formidable pace. All of them were super fit and made civilisation or at least a small village the one the daughters stopped at on their way to the temple. The monks and daughters were treated with the highest respect, all the village knew that they were deadly and lethal weapons, but they also paid them well, as this village provided the manpower to get all the supplies up the mountain. They would rest here and make their way to Kathmandu in the morning. The monks asked the elder of the village for guides and horses so they could get there quicker.

The elder asked if they would be able to pay for this, and a monk bought out a single gold tael and showed it to him. The elder took it and said it was far too much—the gold was worth two million Nepalese rupees. "I only want a hundred thousand for your horses and guides, and do not have the ability to give you change."

The monk said, "Keep it as security, and on our return, we will pay you in rupees."

"American dollars would be better."

"Ok," the monk said. "Be very careful as there will be many people that want cheat you out of the taels' correct value. I have told you what the gold's worth, but these are so ancient, the rarity may be greater than the gold value, so you need to find that out as well."

"Do you know anyone in Kathmandu that you trust who would do it for us?"

"I am afraid not, but if someone tries to cheat you, he will have that knowledge you seek and no doubt with your skills, you will able to get it from easily."

They had a fine meal, and all rested well. It would take another week to reach Kathmandu.

The journey was a lot more pleasant. It was warm, and they made good progress the guides found and paid for their food and accommodation. It was late afternoon when they reached Kathmandu. The guides were now out of their comfort zone—they had never been there—so their usefulness had expired, and they said their farewells and would meet them when ready to return to the temple. It was a long trek back to the village.

Ten monks and seven beautiful girls left on the outskirts of the city stuck out, and it was not long before a taxi stopped and asked if he could take them somewhere. The guides had given the monks five thousand Nepalese rupees to see them through until they were able to change up the taels.

The monks asked the taxi driver to order up three more cabs, so they could all travel in convoy. When their taxis arrived, the whole group boarded. "Take us to someone that deals in gold and will convert it into cash, please."

"I will confer with the other drivers to see who would be best."

They all agreed a shop in the middle of Kathmandu was the best choice, and there were a not many legitimate bullion dealers, so they went to the biggest one. Deflin of all the daughters was that much better than the others and had taken the role of the senior daughter and her and two monks entered the shop. The others went with the drivers for a coffee.

It was not busy inside the shop. The monks approached the counter and rang a bell for service. A middle-age guy came out from the back office and asked, "How could I be of help?"

"We would like to convert some gold into dollars."

"That's what we do. Can I see what you have?"

The monk gave him a single tael. Immediately he recognised it as the purest gold, and the coin was ancient. He would have to check but thought it was at least 2000 years old and could be worth more than the gold itself. Unfortunately, the expression on his face showed this and was easily seen by his customers. He took the gold to some scales and weighed the tael—one pound. He picked up a calculator, punched in the numbers and told then the gold was worth $1,150 dollars. Before he finished the sentence, the monk flew over the counter and pinned the guy to the wall with his index finger. The owner had never known such pain and was screaming in agony. The monk released the pressure, and the screaming stopped.

Deflin went over to the door and put the bolt on the door as the monks pushed the owner into the back office. There was a huge relatively modern safe and a couple of filling cabinets, his desk with a computer and a printer. A photo of his large family took pride of place on the desk.

"Sit down. You have just tried to rob us with that valuation. We have been told that the gold alone should be worth $15,000 dollars, and the coin itself may be worth even more, so we know you're a crook, and we are happy with that."

"What are you going to do with me?"

"Proper business."

The monk told him the order he belonged too was not religious. The martial art was ancient and dealt in death.

"We are very good at it," Deflin said. "We want you to act for us, as our broker and get the best deal for these taels."

"How many do you have?"

"About 200."

"That's close to three million dollars, but as a coin, it could be worth three times the gold price."

"Your brokerage fee will be a generous 20%, and will make you even richer. Should you cheat us, we will wipe you and all your family out; don't even think that we can't."

"Have you bank accounts?"

"No."

"Have you passports?"

"No."

"Any means of official identification?"

"No."

"That makes things extremely difficult. You need a passport to book into a hotel and definitely a bank as you will need a truck to carry all that currency."

The monk said, "We don't need any official documentation, as we are only here to bring our charges back to civilisation. We will complete our shopping and go back to our monastery. These girls will need everything for them to move freely and without fear so they can get back home."

"I think I know someone that can do all of that, but he's in Delhi." He went to his safe and took out $10,000 and gave it to the monk. "I will book you into a hotel. I shall tell them you have just come off the mountain, and all your papers and clothes were lost in an avalanche. I will arrange dinner tonight and would suggest you retain your taxi drivers while you're here, 50 dollars a day is more than enough."

Deflin removed another tael from her waist band and said, "We need to do a lot of shopping as well."

He went back to the safe and handed her another $10,000 dollars.

"We will need to change all our taels up for our journey home," said Deflin.

"We will change all ours up as well. What cash we don't use you can have the remainder," said the monk.

"Thank you, brother," the broker said. "Would you like

to keep them in my safe? You really don't want to carrying that amount of gold. Violent crime here has escalated over 40% in the last year."

"We will keep it on us at the moment. If you want to see all 200, that won't be a problem, but until we are close to finding the value of the taels, they will be safe with us."

"As you wish," the broker said.

They left the shop and met up with the rest. "We are booked into the Hyatt Regency until our documentation arrives."

They sat in a café for tea. Deflin got out the money and shared it equally amongst the girls. Everyone in the café saw the distribution of the cash to the girls. It did not take long before it got to the attention of the criminal underworld.

Deflin and the sisters had some cake with more tea, and while they ate, the broker came over and said he had spoken with his man in Delhi. "It seems he knows you. He has all your documentation ready, and he wants to see you, so he is coming here on the next plane."

He handed Deflin a piece of paper, on which were the new identity names. Now they did not have to invent names. The taxis took the girls to a shopping mall where they spent a glorious couple of hours shopping; they had bought so much the taxis had to make two trips to the hotel. The daughters all booked in under their new names and went up to their separate rooms. The taxis were picking them up at eight to take them to dinner; it did not leave them much time, all showered quickly and could not wait to put on their new clothes. They had no time for makeup, but with their beauty, they really did not need it. They all met in the hotel's foyer, and the taxis took them to the restaurant. The broker had asked for a private room so they could speak freely and on the advice of the man from Delhi. The taxis arrived and dropped them off; all were ushered into the private dining room.

The man from Delhi had checked the room for bugs, and it was clean. The broker said, "May I introduce you to Jojhinda Ravagit?" He went round to each daughter asked for their house name and each was given a large manila envelope. All sat around this enormous round table. Waiters came round and asked what they would like to drink. All the daughters wanted Coca Col—it had been a long 8 years—and the monks ordered fruit juice. The broker informed them he had ordered everything that was on the menu for them to try, "and if more is required, just ask."

The first course was a variety of pickles and coulis with poppadum's, the banquet was next and was huge, as each was placed on the table, the waiter explained what it was, none of the daughters or monks had anything like it before and it was readily devoured, only the chicken dishes were left. The broker asked why they did not like the chicken dishes.

A monk replied, "Chicken is our staple diet. It's chicken this and chicken that. Everything is chicken. Now, given the chance of something else to eat, we all took it." They all laughed. Jojhinda got all the daughter's attention and handed them envelopes. "Inside you will find your new identities. Bank accounts have been set up. There are debit, credit and charge cards, birth certificates. You will notice you have aged three years for your full driving licences to be valid. There is a history of your false life, schooling, exams friends you do not have, but you must learn it all before you travel. You have £10,000 in your bank accounts or the equivalent in your own currency; I assumed that you will be taking up your family's business in their sphere of influence. The credit card has a limit of £50,000 and the charge card has no limit but needs to pay in full at the end of each month. I shall be here for a couple of days to help you adapt."

A great deal of noise came from the restaurant, and the door to the private dining room burst open. Six armed men entered and demanded all the money. The monk looked at Deflin: "It is your turn to prove the training, and you have not killed yet." He spoke in the temple dialect so only they would know what was said.

In unison the girls leapt from the table and killed the gunmen inside three seconds. They never knew what hit them. Their noses had been pushed so far into their brain, and they died instantly. The monks nodded with approval. The broker had never seen anything like it, Jojhinda had heard about their skills but had never seen it in action, and both were suitably impressed. The broker went into the restaurant and summoned the taxi drivers and a waiter to the private dining room. They all noticed the dead gunmen. A monk went to one of the drivers and asked, "Do you know anything about this hold-up."

"No, we tried to stop them until they pulled a gun on us," the driver said, and the waiter added, "We all tried until they pulled the guns. There are two more in the Land Cruisers on the other side of the road. Must be the getaway drivers."

The broker went to the one of the dead men, rolled up the sleeve and saw the tattoo; all six had the same tattoo. "They are members of the Mongoose gang," he said. "They are going to be really pissed off losing six of their gang."

The monk said, "eight," and turned to Deflin. "Go take the other two out." Sheflin, who had not killed, went with her. The waiter showed them into the kitchen and out the back door. Quietly, they made their way along the alley, where it reached the road, and crossed the road. Using the shadows to their advantage, Deflin would take the driver in the first car and Sheflin the second car. Both drivers windows were open. Deflin and Sheflin took four lightening steps toward the car and smashed the larynx and windpipe, which stopped air reaching the lungs and it took the drivers a couple of minutes to die. They put the heads of the drivers back into an upright position, so they looked alive apart from the blue-white facial colour.

They walked back across the road to the restaurant and into the private dining room. "What would happen if we took the whole gang out tonight? Our charges need the practice, and they seem to deserve it, spoiling our meal," said a monk.

The broker said, "The gang feels invincible, and the police will not touch them—the officers are afraid for their families."

"So we would be doing them a service?"

"I suppose so," the broker said.

The monk turned to the daughters, "Are you up for ridding Kathmandu of some mongooses? Will you need our help?"

Deflin said, "I don't think so, we will whittle the numbers down slowly to a more manageable number."

"We will be nearby should you need us."

A taxi driver knew where the gang hung out—it was a no-go area apart from gang members. "We will need to change into something more fitting for annihilating mongoose."

The broker asked, "What are we to do with these bodies?"

"We will drag them into the alley and park the Land Cruisers in front of them. When we have despatched the rest of the gang, we will put the bodies in the vehicles and take them to the gangs hung out."

The monks started dragging the bodies out through the kitchen into the alley, and a couple of taxi drivers reversed the Land Cruisers into the alley. The taxis took them back to the hotel, and they changed into black all-in-one suits. They would get proper stealth suits in time, but these would do for now.

The gang's headquarters were a three-storey building at the end of a cul-de-sac. Either side of the building were boarded up industrial units. There was no light from these buildings, but the gangs place was lit up like a Christmas tree, leaving so much shadow it would be so easy to penetrate. The taxi driver had told them that they usually put two lookouts at the beginning of the cul-de-sac.

Deflin spoke with the daughters: "I think we should take them out, but not kill them. They may have to make regular contact to their leader. Once we have found that out, we either kill them now or kill them later."

"If they have to make regular contact, it can't be every five minutes, guessing we would have at least 30 minutes—maybe more. We need to find that out first," Sheflin said. "That's easily done."

The taxis dropped them off about 400 yards from cul-de-sac. Three daughters kept to the shadows and incapacitated the lookouts. They dragged them back a couple of hundred yards so their screaming would not be heard. They interrogated them on when the next call was to be made. To hurry it up, they painfully killed one in front of the other, and the other told them everything they needed to know.

Deflin was just about to send him to his maker, when Sheflin said, "We might need him. Put him in a taxi and ask the monks to look after him until we get back."

The seven walked back to the cul-de-sac and entered bandit territory. No one was to be left alive. From what the lookout said, there should not be many on any of the floors, but they needed to be checked. Four daughters easily climbed to the third floor. They entered through an open window and checked all the rooms—there were five in total on that floor, already unconscious either through drugs or alcohol, and they would never wake up again.

The stairs were dark, which worked a treat for the daughters. Nothing was found on the second floor, so they proceeded to the first. They knew this could be busy as it was where the toilets were. There were only two couples in separate rooms, and it would be the last time they would be making love. The toilet blocks on each floor were in the same place, as the ones before. The mirrors were over the sinks and the urinals were against the furthest wall. The two men urinating had their backs to door and did not notice the door open, and they died. One of the doors was locked, and someone was inside. One of the daughters kicked down the door, then a four-finger jab to the throat followed by a palm push of his nose into his brain robbed him of life.

All floors were now cleared and were now on the ground floor waiting for Deflin and the other two daughters to do their part. Deflin and the other daughters walked straight through the main entrance in a triangular formation and into a large open area covered with sofas and chairs; a quick estimate was 45 to 50 guys and girls. The daughters had certainly got the attention of the men—their black body suits left nothing to the imagination, and it only enhanced their beauty.

Deflin said, "Who's the leader of this gang called rodents, with a symbol of a rat on their arms?"

"We are the mongoose gang, not rats," said a guy sitting on a sofa with two prostitutes either side.

"Are you the leader of these rats?"

He nodded.

"Why did you send eight men to rob us at the

restaurant?" Meanwhile, the other four spread themselves around the perimeter of the room and picked off the gang members. Deflin noticed.

The gang leader denied sending the robbers, saying, "What are you going to do about it?"

"I am undecided at the moment," she lied, it just came so naturally. "How did you know we had a considerable amount of cash with us?"

"One of my guys saw you distributing it at the café and followed you all to the shopping centre. You filled four taxis twice, so you have plenty of money, and we want it."

"As you can see, we don't have any with us so how to you propose to get it."

"Well after my men strip search you and find nothing, we will hold the other two hostages until you return with the money." The leader nodded to some of his men, who started to move towards Deflin and the others, still unaware of what was going on behind them.

Deflin said, "Do not kill the leader. I want more information from him."

While they stood there, they summoned up their chi. It took a couple of seconds for the aura to surround them. All the men thought it would be easy to overcome these beautiful women, and it was not until half of them were dead that weapons appeared—which were easily disarmed. It was too late when they realised they were being attacked from the rear too. The leader was roughed up but alive.

Deflin went over to him, "As you can see, we don't take too kindly to being robbed. You chose the wrong people this evening—we are Messapth, evil personified. Are these girls whores or family?"

"All are whores," he said. That answer saved their lives. Deflin went over to trembling prostitutes. "My gut reaction is to kill you all. However, if we can be assured that you have seen nothing"—all were nodding—"we will let you live."

One of the whores plucked up courage to speak: "Who would believe us? Seven girls did this."

"You have a point. Does this low life owe you money?"

"He's never paid us anything."

Deflin walked back to the leader. "Where's your safe?" Silence. "Come on now, aren't you in enough pain?" Silence. "That's a pity." She went over and found the nerve that would give him so much pain that he wish he were dead. He pointed to an office at the back of the room. Sheflin went over to it. Against the wall was an exceptionally large safe, surrounded by what one must be stolen goods. She went over to the safe checked the handle. Of course it was locked. She went back outside and asked the leader for the combination. Silence. Deflin drew close, and he blurted out the combination. Sheflin went back inside the office and opened the safe; it was full of cash and documents. She returned and told Deflin what was in the safe, and Deflin asked the prostitutes, "How much money would you need to stop whoring and live a normal life in Kathmandu?" They did not have a clue.

"How much does a shop assistant earn?"

"About 10,000 Nepalese rupees a year," one said, as she had been one before the prostitution. The leader had no more use and went to see his maker. Deflin said to one of the daughters, "Go and fetch the monks; they will need to assess us. Tell the taxi drivers to put the bodies in the Land Cruisers and bring them here and dump them in here." Deflin and Sheflin went back into the office and to the safe—there was extraordinarily little local currency; it was mostly all dollars and euros. The dollars were in packets of a thousand. They took $50,000 out and gave each of the prostitutes $5000 each. "You will leave Kathmandu tonight by any means. If you can drive, take the cars outside, but if your here in the morning, you will face the same fate as the gang. Now go." Most could drive and went for the cars.

The broker and Jojhinda came in with the monks, who assessed how well the daughters had done. Deflin took them to the safe, and the broker let out a whistle when he saw the contents. The safe was a similar size to his and contained about $2 million. The broker checked the documents and found that they were related to the cars. They found black dustbin sacks and put all the cash in them.

"The Land Cruisers are nearly new according to the paperwork," said the broker.

"That's handy you will not have to buy vehicles for your journey to Messapth," Jojhinda said.

The monks returned with smiles over their faces. "You have passed with flying colours. We could not have done better. We all concur; you seven are the best we have ever trained, and most of us have trained at least five sets of daughters." It was praise of the highest order.

The taxi drivers had returned in the Land Cruisers, and

the monks helped disperse the bodies amongst the other corpses. The taxi drivers were given $5000 dollars each and told to do the same as the prostitutes; they would not need them anymore as they had their own transport, albeit they could not drive. The money was loaded in the back of one of the Land Cruisers, and they made their way back to the hotel. They parked up in the underground car park and took the lift, with the money, into Deflin room; it would be counted in the morning.

It was nearly midnight but the adrenalin in the daughters was still high and no sleep would ensue until the level reduced. The monks had all gone to their rooms, and the broker had said his farewells, so it just left Jojhinda. He went to the mini bar and got himself a scotch and American dry. The daughters would have coke, but there were only four cans, so they rushed to their rooms and gathered up more coke and came back to Deflin's room.

"Tomorrow I must take your photographs for your passports and driving licences. Your new identities will cost $25000 dollars each. Remember I have put £10,000 or its equivalent in your bank account. I normally charge £50,000 as I thought something must have happened, having not heard anything from your mothers in over 7 years. And when the broker phoned about you, I was truly elated and thought you would not have any money until you got home. Your family and mine have for a few hundred years been in business together, and I was prepared to wait."

"Do you know what's happened to Messapth?" Sheflin

asked.

"Not very much, I'm afraid. Normally, I hear from your high council to prepare your documentation a year before you leave the temple so there is no rush in preparing your papers. In between your sisters across the world, order two or three additional identities for reasons I never ask, but nothing it is as if Messapth has disappeared. What I do know is your mother Deflin was shot in London, trying to assassinate the CEO of Earth Corp. This is only rumour, but your mother with your sisters robbed a Columbian drug baron and took all his cash about $700 million dollars. It went to the Cayman Islands bank which your mother used, and the bank owner was a very intimate friend of hers. The money was taken electronically from the bank, they do not know how, and went to Earth Corp. it is why you are your mother Deflin tried to kill him and failed. What happened to your sisters no one knows? The answer must be in Messapth."

The daughters nodded along. They had to get back home as quickly as possible—it was there they would find all the answers. He said his goodnights and left before they went to their own rooms and eventually slept.

They all met at six o'clock in the hotel fitness spa, after a relentless hour of training they returned to their rooms, showered, and changed and went down to breakfast. The monks told them that they were going to get the stores for the temple and would meet them this evening.

Jojhinda joined them at breakfast and told them, "The cash they had would be difficult to handle here. The broker may know of a way, but I can help you legitimised the money. I have contacts in India. When I return home, I will be in a chartered aircraft."

The daughters agreed carrying that amount of cash was asking for trouble, so unless the broker has a better idea. They would take the money to India, before setting off to Messapth. It took an hour for the photographs and a further hour to complete the passports, driving licences and identity cards where necessary.

Deflin asked, "We all need to be bought up to date with phones and computers. I assume there have been many advances."

"I assume you don't have any, so we better go shopping before the driving lessons." Jojhinda asked reception for the best place for phones and laptops. On the way there, he phoned his nephew in India and asked him what sort of kit they needed. He said he would text the types of electronics he thought. They needed to be usable anywhere in the world without contract. They went to both shops, but none did the standalone, so the daughters were bitterly disappointed that they would have to wait a few more days.

On their way back to the hotel, they passed the gangs headquarters. Every police car in Kathmandu must have been there. The taxi had to queue to get past. Several body bags could be seen—there were so many bodies that they had overwhelmed the local mortuary and were having to find alternative places. The taxi driver told them a whole gang was killed last night.

"I would think someone has done Kathmandu a favour,"

Jojhinda said.

"Too bloody true; it saved me 500 Nepalese rupees a week to keep my cab safe from those bastards. Sometimes it was more than I took but they didn't care."

The traffic started moving, and they were back at the hotel. The broker was waiting in reception for them. They all went into the hotel lounge and ordered drinks. The broker said, "it's probably not a good idea to use the Land Cruisers for driving lessons, the police know the vehicles and if we are found in them, we really do not need to attract their attention" "we will hire a couple then" Deflin said. Jojhinda went to reception and asked for two four-by-four hire cars, the broker would hire one and he the other.

The broker updated them on the shenanigans of the previous night. More prostitutes had turned up after midnight and found all the corpses.

"It is a major crime scene. I spoke to the police inspector in charge of the investigation, and he reckons that whoever did this used their vehicles to escape. So, I do not think using the Land Cruisers would be wise in the short-term and even long term. They have asked Nepal to help and have put an all-points bulletin on the vehicles. I am sure no one saw us in the vehicles, so leave them where they are, I will pop down and wipe all the surfaces in both vehicles."

Jojhinda said, "There is a possibly all our prints are all over them. I think that we really ought to torch them to be safe."

"We can't torch them here at the hotel; they have to be driven somewhere," the broker said.

"What we need to do is change the registration plates," said Jojhinda.

Deflin said, "There were several rental four-by-fours in the underground car park...why do we not we just swap them over tonight?"

"Good idea, but I will get some people I know to do it tonight."

"Well that's sorted," Jojhinda said.

The broker added, "A Chinese billionaire has offered $39,000 for each coin, a £25000 premium on each for the coin. I have done some research and believe them to be from the Zhou dynasty at least 3000 years old. I can find the Ying and Yang symbols on them, but these coin and taels have never been in circulation—the ones I have seen on the net are of extremely poor quality due to their age, but yours seem to be in mint condition, as if they have never been in circulation. We need to get the coins carbon dated to prove their age. I have no doubt in my mind they are what you say they are, but anyone interested will need the providence and age authenticated. I will be able to do the providence and get the university here to carbon date them officially." He then turned to Deflin. "Have the monks given you their taels?"

"Yes." she said. "Also, the cash is in our bedrooms still in the black sack. It's not been counted yet. We put 'do not disturb' signs up, so the chambermaids will not have come in."

Jojhinda said to the broker, "Now that all their travel documents are correct, there is really no reason why the daughters should remain here. They can stay at my country house outside Delhi—it's empty and has plenty of room. We can bring you up to date, electronically. I shall launder the cash and the daughters should hold on to the taels simply because no one could steal them away from them. It would be suicide."

"I have never been robbed at my shop and my safe is new and burglar proof."

"It didn't take long for us to get the combination off the gang leader now did it?" Jojhinda said. "My charter to Kathmandu costs $7000, and it's an hour and a half away."

"But no one knows I will have them," the broker replied, "apart from the Chinese billionaire and all the people at the university involved in carbon dating."

"They are sure to tell their families until everyone's knows you have some awfully expensive coins in your safe."

"Put like that, it would be best," the broker said.

"We need some large suitcases. We can't book out of the hotel with several black sacks."

Jojhinda went to reception told them they would be checking out as something urgent needed his attention in India. He then asked where he could buy new suitcases and was directed to the shopping mall. He added, "We do not have time for the rental cars. When they arrive, apologise and give them this for their trouble." He handed her two twenty-dollar notes. He went back into the lounge and told the broker to buy thirty-five large suitcases and seven small ones. "I shall go down to the carpark and change over the number plates and then go up to your rooms and help you count the cash."

Everyone departed to their assigned tasks, and the daughters returned to their rooms. The counting was relatively easy as the cash was in 1,000-dollar bundles and the higher denomination notes were in 10,000s, which they put in 100,000-dollar piles. It had not taken Jojhinda long to change the plates and was back to check to see whether the cash was genuine. It was. The final count was 1,995,550 dollars and 675330 euros.

"Just under two-point-seven million. Not a bad day's work," Jojhinda said. "With the money from the taels, less the brokers generous commission, you should be worth ten million cash, one-point-four million each."

The broker arrived with the cases.

"We will tell when we are packed." Deflin said.

By the time everything was packed, the monks had arrived and were told that they were leaving for Delhi. The monks had finished all their shopping, which would be delivered to the village they first stayed at on their way down from the mountain. The monks would wait there until the supplies arrived.

Jojhinda phoned reception and told them he required four taxis for the journey to the airport. By the time all suitcases were in the lobby, the taxis had arrived. They loaded up and said their goodbyes to the monks, and left for the airport. A daughter rode in each taxi as security. At the airport, Jojhinda asked for their passports and took them to the VIP passport control. The taxis took them directly to the aircraft, and fifteen minutes later, they were

35000 feet and landed just after seven in the evening.

The heat and humidity was overwhelming. *What is it going to be like during the day,* Deflin thought.

Jojhinda's grandsons met them at the aircraft. A minibus for the passengers and a van for the luggage were just nodded through customs.

"My nephews work in customs, and they are always on shift when I travel. It saves a lot of time that way." As they proceeded, he added, "My family extends to every major country in the world. All can help me when asked. I pay for all their tuition fees and give them a stipend to live reasonably well—they are extremely grateful and will do what I ask when I ask. It is so much easier than having to find a corrupt official or blackmailing to get what I want, family just do it. Even if they have reached the pinnacle of their career, they will always do what I ask. While you at my house, you will have plenty of time to read and learn your new roles. It is especially important that this information becomes second nature to you. My two grandsons will look after your IT training and anything else you may need. I have several servants to look after you, so enjoy your stay."

The house was large and modern construction, set in about four acres of well-kept gardens. The electric gates opened, and they went through and up to the house, where the servants greeted their guests. Inside was heaven—the air conditioning cooled the place exceptionally well, the interior was modern and tastefully so.

The daughters were shown to their rooms, where they unpacked their clothes. The money fitted nicely into three suitcases and was collected by the servants and loaded into the van that took it to Jojhinda's nephew, the money laundering bank manager.

The daughters were shown around the rest of the house—it was impressive, and the pool was huge and could be accessed anywhere from the ground floor. Inside the pool changing room were swimming costumes of all shapes and sizes; something was bound to suit them. However, none of the daughters could swim, and they told Jojhinda so.

"No problem. My cousin's son is a lifeguard, and he will be here tomorrow for your first lessons."

From there, they went to the garage and found eight expensive cars. He pointed to a Range Rover and said, "This is what you will learn to drive in. It's a manual transmission, which takes a bit more practice. Dinner is at 8:00, so go and freshen up, and see you at dinner."

The dinner was traditional Indian, not elaborate but very enjoyable. It had been a long day, and after dinner, they watched a film and were asleep thirty minutes in. Deflin was the first to wake up, and she woke the others to go to their rooms.

The next two weeks followed the same routine, starting with their martial art training, which lasted two hours. IT lessons followed breakfast. Before lunch, they had swimming lessons, after lunch: driving lessons, then relaxation around the pool. The daughters were fast learners, so the relaxation period got longer and longer— the exposure to the sun tanned their skins.

Deflin told Jojhinda that they would start their journey to Messapth on Monday morning. He had found two nearly new Range Rovers like the ones they learned to drive in. When they arrived at the house, they looked as if ready for the Dakar rally. The guys that delivered them showed the daughters how each bit of equipment worked. With the extra fuel they carried, it would give them 1500 miles before refuelling.

A delivery guy said, "When you are travelling, never pass a fuel stop. Keep the tank topped up and use the extra fuel only in emergency. When the fuel gauge is on half, start looking for a fuel stop."

Monday soon came round. The previous night, they planned a route with Jojhinda. He advised not to travel through Iran. "No matter how good you are, you cannot beat an army filled with religious despots." So, they'd travel through Turkestan, Azerbaijanian, a ferry to Baku, from there to Igdir, Turkey, then onto Messapth.

They left just after daybreak and made good progress through India and were allowed through to Pakistan. They soon arrived at the Afghanistan border and made good time to Kabul where they'd find a hotel. They found one, which was more like a motel near the airport so their vehicles could be seem from their rooms. About three in the morning, the alarms on their cars sounded. Some would-be thieves thought it was their birthday and were trying to steal both vehicles. On hearing the alarm, the daughters were at their vehicles in less than 30 seconds, to the surprise of the thieves who thought they would have several minutes easily enough time to disable the car alarm and make off with the vehicles. Being confronted by seven scantily clad young women was a bonus.

Deflin said, "Please stop what you are doing and leave, and no harm will come to you."

A guy who Deflin assumed was the leader spoke, "And if we don't?"

"At worst, you will be dead or hospitalised. Probably the latter, as we don't want trouble with the police. After all, we are only protecting our property?"

"Hand us the keys to these vehicles or..."

"Or what?" Deflin asked, walking closer to the leader.

He pulled a knife, which was a signal for his men to do so, "Before I cut you into pieces. I am going to rape you," he added as he took his last step forward in this life—Deflin turned the knife against him, using his own hand to stick it through his throat. In the second he took to hit the floor, the five other men were neutralised.

"We must have been seen, so best we call the police and ambulances for the wounded."

The daughters returned to the rooms and rang reception to tell them what had happened.

The police arrived at the scene and recognised the victims. They were taken to hospital and would be interviewed after their recovery. Reception had told the daughters the police wanted to question them and asked them to bring their papers. The daughters dressed and went downstairs to their vehicles where the police were.

Several guests had witnessed what had happened, and

they came down too. Each daughter was interviewed and told the same story. "We heard the alarm go off on our vehicles, came down to see and were confronted by this gang. We told them to leave and warned them they would be hurt if they did not leave, they came at us with knives, and we had to defend ourselves." The only story that differed slightly was Geflin's, as her assailant was that much closer, and she had to push his knife away—unfortunately into his neck. The hotel guests that witness the event supported the story.

"How long are you staying in Kabul?"

"We are leaving in the morning. We are making our way to the Caspian Sea."

"The man that died is the brother of a warlord, who will not be happy about the death. It seems unless you find another way, you most certainly will bump into him."

"Does he have many men?"

"Close to a hundred of well-armed men that even the Russians and Taliban couldn't defeat and took the American side in our last war?"

"Can you show us on a map where his citadel is?" The officer went and got out his map and directed Deflin. The officer was right; they would be driving directly towards them.

"We will bring the statements to you, and if you agree and sign, you can be on your way."

The daughters went back to Deflin room. "Do we change course or continue, and if we have to confront this warlord, his soldiers are good. What are our chances of winning, for all of us to be safe?"

Geflin said, "He won't rest until the people responsible for his brother's death are caught and punished, which is almost certain death."

"What are you proposing?"

"Take them all out in a stealth attack at night. We have all the gear. It would be easy." All were in agreement, so meticulous planning had to be done.

The statements arrived while the daughters had breakfast, and they signed. As the police left, a car sped by the hotel entrance and two machine guns sprayed the hotel. The face of the hotel was a glassy mess. The daughters heard the gunfire and came rushing out. "What happened?"

"The warlord has just found out about his brother's death, and this is his first warning shot. He means to find and kill those that caused his death," an officer crouching behind a pillar said.

The warlord's enclave was just over 250 miles towards the Turkmenistan border—they would reach well before nightfall. It would give them time to assess the defence of the enclave. The drones that they had were the latest American technology, almost silent. They were specifically designed for the special forces. Daughters Tewlin and Feflin had really mastered the controls when practising at the house. Looking at the map, five miles before the enclave, there is a road off to the right. Looking at it seemed to go up the same mountain and finished at another small village. The enclave would be directly the other side of the mountain.

"All we need to do is climb up to the top and come down the other side and attack them from the rear. It would be the last thing they expect, and if its late enough, most will be asleep."

The main road to the border had a few small villages and small towns. Deflin studied the map. "We are about 30 miles from the enclave, so we need to start looking out for the turning that will take us behind the mountain."

As they drove closer to their turning, they were amazed to find that the valley and mountains were a brilliant red. Just before their turning, a couple of cars had stopped at some sort of roadblock. Deflin came to a stop some 100 yards away. Through binoculars, she could see it was not official, and it seemed that the driver of the vehicle at the roadblock was ranting and raving at the people stopping him. She could see much pushing and shoving by both men until the guy stopping him pulled out a gun and shot him.

The drivers behind leapt out of their cars and fired at the guys at the roadblock. The guys at the roadblock were exceptionally good, and nine more joined their mate on the floor. Deflin went to their other car and told them what she had seen.

"I have only seen five guys, but they are good. They just clinically shot all ten and were not afraid of the other parties firing at them. We need to keep one alive for questioning."

The daughters approached the roadblock and got out of their vehicles to walk the rest of the way towards the roadblock. The guys had not seen such beauty in a long time and were taken off guard.

Deflin asked, "Why are you stopping us? This is a public road."

"This road runs through our territory, and a toll has to be paid for each person travelling along it."

"How much is the toll?"

"A thousand Afghanis."

"Do you take dollars?"

"Ten American dollars each."

"That's rather expensive. We are on a strict budget, and this toll hasn't been envisaged."

"You are not passing until you have paid."

Deflin got close to him. The daughters saw the signal and took out the other four. The guy went for his gun, but a jab as sharp as a knife hit his solar plexus, and he crumpled to the ground. As he fell, she broke his jaw.

"Get rid of the bodies, where they disposed of the others. I need to talk to this man." He was slowly recovering, but his jaw hurt like hell. "Now I need some information, is this roadblock manned at night?" No answer. She broke his right arm...still nothing. He was tough, so she broke his left arm...still nothing. "You're being very foolish. No one will be left alive for you to worry about; we are here to kill them all. You will tell me what I want to know. I promise you, there is a point with pain, that your body just can't take anymore, and you will tell me. Why put yourself through this?" Still nothing. She took the right broken arm—it was a clean break at the top of his arm—and twisted it so the broken bone jammed the nerves in the arm against the bone. The pain was horrendous, and his bladder emptied.

He could no longer contain the pain, so he cried for her to stop. He told her everything, and she killed him after she had gathered enough information. They moved the cars blocking the road. Their original plan was no longer any good since someone would come to look for the deceased guys if they weren't back by sunset. Deflin said, "We have two options: we can put as much distance between us and not stop till we reach the Turkmenistan border or bring forward our plan and attack while they are awake, which for us will be far more dangerous."

Geflin said, "I don't like the idea of running away. We just have to be more careful and plan accordingly"

"Our best plan is to attack in the early hours. If these guys don't return, they will send some more to see what's happened to them."

"If they don't return, they will send the whole army."

"What if one of us take the Range Rover to the enclave and tell them what we saw? A gunfight and all are dead."

Lanlin said, "They will be angry, but not necessarily anxious, as there is not a lot they can do for their dead comrades."

"We do have a problem though if he knows who killed his brother. There can't be too many unaccompanied females making their way to the border," Deflin said. "And if they put two and two together, it could be dangerous."

"Well, I volunteer to go to the enclave," Geflin said.

"I will be the other," Deflin said. "If they have heard about the seven women who killed the gang, we will say Geflin and I are travelling together and know nothing about seven females."

Lanlin added, "If they don't believe you, and it starts getting nasty, you could always say that your parents are extremely wealthy and would pay any amount for your safe return. Even if the warlords want you dead, his closest friends will advise him to get the money and then kill you."

"Good point. So we will either be guests or prisoners. If we are guests, we will make ourselves seen by the drone just before sunset so that you know all is well, otherwise you will have to use the transponder to locate us."

Tewlin said, "There is no blood on the bodies of the men we took out, and if the bodies are collected, no bullet holes."

"Best we put some in them, but not sure how much they will bleed as they are dead, and best use the weapons of the unfortunate ten victims."

Lanlin scampered to retrieve three pistols and emptied them into the corpses of the warlord's men, then put them back on the bodies.

"It's about three and half hours to sunset so the rest of you make your way to the other side of the mountain and get into position as soon as you can."

Deflin and Geflin got into the other Range Rover and cruised to the enclave. Neither was nervous nor drove straight into the beginning of the enclave. They were stopped just inside; they told the guy what they had seen on the main road and come here for help for the poor victims. The guy pointed to where some other cars were parked, and they drove there and parked. Two other guys escorted them to the warlord's house. Walking across, they counted fourteen armed men in and around the house. After a quick look around, they confirmed that there were no lookout towers but plenty of CCTV. Apart from the guy that stopped them, security was rather laxed.

Inside the house, there was a large lounge, with nine men either playing on their phone or reading. They looked up at the sight of two beautiful women and their eyes followed them into the warlord's study.

The warlord was nothing like his men or his late brother—he was clean shaven, had a primped full head of hair and was quite good looking. He was about fifty. He looked up from his desk. "What on Earth are two beautiful women doing out here?"

"We are making our way to Turkey overland. It's more adventurous."

"It certainly is that," he replied. "Are you going via Iran?"

"No, we were advised against that."

"And you find travelling through Afghanistan not a problem?"

"It is relatively peaceful, and we have only been treated with kindness...until what we came across a few miles from here. Our sat-nav told us there was a village ahead closer than going back to the other village we just fuelled up in."

"Very hi-tech."

"We had to have it, or we were not allowed to go."

"So what did you see?"

"Not a lot. We heard more than we could see, but as we approached, there were lots of bodies. We checked them for a pulse, but all were dead."

"Were there any other vehicles involved?"

"No, but when we left to go for help, some other vehicles had stopped."

He told the guy that had bought them to take some men and fetch the cars and bodies.

"So, what are you going to do now?" he asked.

"Push on to the border. There is another large village about seventy-five miles from here, and we should make it before dark."

"I have a better idea. Why don't you stay here tonight and join me for dinner? It's not often I can entertain and certainly with such beautiful guests."

"That would be lovely," Deflin said.

"I will get a couple of rooms made up for you. There's plenty of hot water so you can bathe or shower."

"We will need some things from our car, and it's been a tiring day. Could we have a look round before dinner?"

"Of course I will give you a guided tour of my little domain."

A guy went with them to the car and carried the suitcases to their rooms. The rooms were genuinely nice, both ensuite with large queen-size beds. Without being obvious, she laid on the bed and scanned the room for hidden cameras. She found three so there could be more and there were—two in the bathroom. She thought, is this to keep tabs on us, or is the guy a pervert? The latter would be better, as he appears quite nice and much harder to kill.

They both showered and dressed, ignoring the

cameras—if he was watching, he got a show. Deflin went to Geflin's room, and they both went down together. Deflin asked if they could be shown around. Out of sight of the cameras, they wore their communication earpieces, which they covered with their hair. Whatever was said now could be heard by the other daughters, and a running commentary of the enclave begun. He told them that he grew opium poppies. When harvesting, all these outbuildings would be full of seasonal workers.

"In three weeks', time this place will be heaving with people. It's labour intensive, and the workers come from all over the region for the poppy harvest. There are several poppy fields in the region, and all my poppy seeds go to America. Since the decriminalisation of all drugs, our business has boomed, but the price is low, but I have negotiated a deal with the American pharmaceutical companies that guarantees me a premium over the market price. It has another five years to run so I am sitting pretty."

Both the daughters heard the faint buzz overhead, but he had not or had pretended he had not. The large buildings to the right posed no threat to the other daughters, and they concentrated on the other part of the enclave. He took them to see his stables, and there were at least a dozen beautiful horses which were well cared for.

"Why do you need so many men since all the problems are now sorted?"

"Insurance. The Taliban are always a threat. I sided with the Americans in the war and fought alongside them against the Taliban and the other warlords. They all have exceptionally long memories; I need to protect my workers and my poppy fields." They continued walking, and several of his soldiers came out of their billets to see the women. Deflin counted thirty-eight billets, all seemed to be fully equipped so there was no large Mess hall for the soldiers, so they would be in their billets tonight, apart from those on guard duty. The daughters would take them out first, to give them more freedom to move around the enclave.

The tour had nearly ended and neither Deflin nor Geflin had come across a communications centre, so it had to be in the house. The house was large but only two storeys. They assumed the central staircase led to bedrooms, so the communication centre had to be on the ground floor.

It was just getting dark when they got back to the house. The warlord offered them drinks, and they followed him to the bar. The warlord went behind the bar and asked them what they would like and opened a couple of cokes, and he had an orange juice. Four soldiers were relaxing by the large lounge windows, and the warlord walked over to them with Geflin and Deflin. The soldiers jumped to attention before he introduced his officers to the women. "Are our men back from the roadblock with the bodies?"

"We haven't heard from them, but the police are there and made it into a crime scene."

"Do we know why the police are so far out of town? It's very unlike them."

"No."

"And what about our men?"

"There being taken back to the village with the other

bodies for a post-mortem."

"We will be able to collect the bodies tomorrow afternoon." That was music to their ears. The warlord was unaware of his brother's death. They scrutinised the ground floor layout while they relaxed. There were five doors off the lounge—they knew one was the office, one had to be the kitchen, one had to be a toilet. His office was opposite the kitchen, next to his office that door would be the toilet. The two doors facing them must be the comms centre, and the other another office. They would have a better look at the mystery doors as the large dining table was close to the kitchen.

Dinner was served, and they were shown to the table, which could seat twelve. The warlord sat at the head with his two guests either side of him, and the other officers sat at the other end of the table. The warlord explained that he did not drink alcohol, as it was against his religion.

"We don't either. It's not a religious conviction; we have just chosen not to. There is so much for us to see and do, pretty sure we would miss something if we drank alcohol, so we will stick with coke, thank you."

The meal was delicious, the conversation pleasant, and they all have acted like perfect gentlemen. It was a shame they had to die.

Geflin asked if there was a bathroom downstairs and was pointed to the door next to the office. Both excused themselves and walked to the bathroom, Geflin went in first and Deflin got close to the two mysterious doors. There was noise coming from the right-hand door and nothing from the other, so the right-hand door had to be the communication centre. The kitchen door opened, and she got a good view—there were eight, possibly nine, servants working in there. Geflin came out and Deflin went in, used the toilet and went to the sink and turned the taps on. She spoke with the other daughters and told them to find the servants quarters. "They do not propose a threat so they need not be killed," she said.

It was acknowledged, and she returned to the lounge. It was nearly eleven o'clock when they finished coffee. They thanked their host for the fine food and the company and decided to retire, as they have a long journey ahead of them in the morning. It was the first time that they sensed something other than friendship. As they were about to leave the table the four officers closed in on the daughters, both looked at the warlord and he shrugged his shoulders, which inferred that his men were going to have some fun with the daughters and watch the antics of his officers.

The officers got to the sides of each of the daughters and each placed a hand on the daughter's shoulders. The daughters spun so quickly, and with two lethal jabs, the four officers were dead, so quickly the warlord did not have time to react and was also completely incapacitated. They tied him to the chair gagged and searched him. He would be unconscious for some time. It had all happened so quick. Deflin rushed to the comm centre door and Geflin to the kitchen door. Deflin opened the door and walked in, the surprise looks on the faces of the two guys was still on their faces when they died. She pulled all the plugs out of the equipment and then joined Geflin. They both entered the kitchen, Geflin quickly went to the only other door to block any escape. All in the kitchen were staring at them, none were armed but plenty of knives.

The surprise turned to terror as Deflin explained what they had done to the warlord and his officers. "We mean you no harm, as long as you tell us what we need to know." They received reluctant nods from all concerned in response. "How many other servants are there?"

What appeared to be the woman in charge of the kitchen replied, "a further eight people."

"Are they all in the servants quarters?"

"Yes."

"Let's be totally clear, the servants quarters are the three buildings directly behind this building and to the right?"

"Yes."

"So all the houses to the left of this building are his soldiers'?"

"Yes."

"Are there any other people here?"

"Eighteen women, whores for the men."

"Have they got their own accommodation?"

"No, they stay with whoever they go with. It's mostly the single men."

"Is there any way we could tell where they are within the enclave?"

"No, not really," the woman said.

"I don't want you take any risks. If the women present a risk, take them out as well. It's always far easier to kill all quickly than having to sort out which ones to kill," the daughters outside advised.

"There were two men in the comms room...when do they change shift?"

"Six in the morning."

"Will anybody else come to this building tonight?"

"Not normally. It's dinner and bed; the boss and the officers may stay up working, but no one comes till the morning."

"So, unless something changes drastically, we can revert back to the timetable." All the daughters outside agreed.

It was now 23:30. They searched all the kitchen staff, took their phones, and told them they would be locked up in the bedrooms upstairs. Any attempt to contact anyone would result in lethal force.

"I have an idea that just maybe the chance of your lifetime, if you do as your told."

Out of the kitchen and up the staircase, they saw the handiwork of these women, the four dead officers and the warlord still out for the count and viciously tied to his chair. Once locked into bedrooms, they had time to explore his office and the other mysterious room. They searched the office but found no safe, and his desk only contained books. After searching the filing cabinet, they found the deeds to the enclave and the land surrounding it. It was just short but thorough search, but they knew nothing of value was in his office. The deeds proved there was no safe, since they would be in it if there were one.

The mysterious room was locked, and they found no

keys in his office. They searched the warlord and found the keys. He started to come round and was put back to sleep. Deflin opened the door and found the light switch. The light illuminated upon a storeroom—it had no windows, and it was full of cubic metre parcels wrapped in black plastic. Geflin tore a hole in one of the parcels and managed to remove what was inside: hundred-dollar bills. They checked a couple more boxes and found the same thing. Deflin spoke with Jojhinda and told him what they were doing and what they had come across.

"It seems," he said, "that they are parcelled up in million dollars. A rough estimate, you have found $300 million. That's going to take a lot of laundering, so it will take some time."

"We still have to neutralise his army, which we will do in a couple of hours' time."

"I have your location, and the only way to get that amount money out is by a Chinook helicopter. I will have to talk to my nephew—he's a colonel in the Indian air force—and get back to you."

Just before three, the daughters swept through the billets. It was almost a biblical Passover, slaying all the males and leaving the females—some of which they incapacitated. Upon reaching the other servants' quarters, the daughters woke them up and told them to go to the house at once. When they all got to the house, Geflin went upstairs and got the kitchen staff and told them to prepare something for the other daughters. Deflin did not need to ask how it went—the mere fact of being there told her the job had been done, but she needed to ask about the women.

"Some had to be knocked out, the others are still in the billets," said Lanlin.

"Round them all up and bring them here," Deflin said.

Fifteen minutes later, all were assembled in the house. In that time, Geflin had dragged in one of the money parcels and stacked the money on the large table. The kitchen signalled that the food was ready, and the daughters went to eat.

Deflin addressed them all, "It was not our intention to do this, but the warlords brother tried to rob us. We told him not do, but he would not listen, so we killed him and his gangsters. We were told by the police that the warlord would seek revenge, which forced our hand, and we had to do what we have done tonight. No soldiers are left alive. We could have killed you, but choose not to, as we do not believe you are a threat to us. We have a proposition for you all. Firstly, there are a lot of bodies that need to be buried before the stench becomes overpowering. Secondly, the poppy harvest is three weeks away and needs to be harvested, and finally, there is a large amount of cash. What we propose is that you take over the business. You all have been around to know enough to run it. You will all have equal shares in the business, starting from this year's harvest. The income to be divided fifty-fifty. We will...or our agent will come and collect our fifty percent when you receive it from America. We are sure that you will all be dollar millionaires after this harvest. Are you in agreement?"

There was truly little reaction from all of them—they

must still have been in shock.

"We need to know whether you are interested," and she turned and asked them individually. Slowly they came round to the proposition and agreed. One of the prostitutes asked whether this applied to them too.

"What do you know about the opium business? The servants have been around it for a long time...what can you do for them?" Deflin turned to the servants, she could see greed surfacing in all their eyes.

The chef insisted that all the servants would be able to run the business but unless the prostitutes could do something apart from opening their legs, it would not be fair on the rest of the team. They all nodded.

"Well, I am afraid that rules you women out. How much money did the soldiers pay you?"

"We are yet to be paid."

Deflin asked the prostitutes to come forward and handed them $20,000 dollars each. "This money is to buy your silence. Never utter a word of what has happened here. We will send you all a further $10000 each year for your silence. Any one of you to breaks this agreement lose their pay, and death is all they must look forward too."

Deflin then handed $20000 to the rest of the servants. "This is to tide you over until the cash comes in. How much cash do you need for the harvest?"

"The pickers get $5 a day, others $7."

"Is that reasonable pay for what they do?"

"It's the same as we get, less board and lodgings."

"Well, let's budget $10 a day and free board and lodging

for the seasonal workers. The warlord told us about a thousand people are required to harvest the crop. Forty-five days at $10,000 a day, that's $450,000. What are the freight charges?"

"Freight charges are paid by the pharmaceutical companies, so half a million dollars should cover all contingency."

"A word of warning: we can monitor this area from satellites 24/7, with such accuracy we can read the number plates of cars. So, our eyes will be on you all the time."

Deflin's phone rang—it was Jojhinda saying he had organised a Chinook helicopter and would be with them in the morning.

"Can you bring a lawyer? We need to get legal on the transition of ownership from the warlord to his servants, who have agreed to take over the running his business with us as silent fifty-fifty partners."

"Ok, I will see you in the morning."

Deflin said to the workers, "You have heard that I am making this legal for you all. It may take time. All you have to say to the authorities is that the warlord simply took his money, paid off his soldiers and us. He just cracked, when he heard of his brother's death. He could no longer stay here, probably fearful for his life. I don't think many people are going to ask questions. You will have enough money to hire the best lawyers to make this business yours"

"Has anyone any suggestions as where to put the corpses?"

"There is a JCB we use as a fork lift. It has a bucket and

dig attachment and could dig a giant grave and put them all in there."

"Have you any quicklime to help the bodies decompose quickly?"

"No, but I know where to get some."

"Good, how quickly can you get it?"

"As soon as they open in the morning, I can take the tractor and trailer we use for the poppy harvest."

"How far is the place?"

"It's the next town along the main road. It's about 25 miles away."

"So it will take you about three hours there and back plus loading. You will leave to be there at opening and you should be back by nine-thirty."

One of the gardeners said, "I think the best place to bury the corpses would be at the back of the warlords house. He has a beautiful garden. It could take up about 10 metres of lawn and flowerbeds. No one other than the select few were ever allowed near it, so there would be no prying eyes to see the newly covered hole."

"Any better ideas?"

"Right who can drive and use the JCB?" Another guy put his hand up. "You go with the gardener and start digging the hole, as deep as you can." Deflin pointed to the guy who was going to get the quicklime. "Bring the tractor and trailer to the soldiers billets. We can use the trailer to carry the bodies to the hole, so let's get to it."

Two hours later, all the bodies had been moved to the soon-to-be mass grave. Another hour and the grave would be finished. The hole was complete and the JCB unceremoniously pushed the bodies into the grave. The tractor driver went off to get the quicklime, and they all made their way back to the house. Deflin asked Tewlin and Feflin to take their car and pick up the other car. It was approaching four in the morning, and all the daughters could do with some sleep. The remaining daughters went upstairs to get some sleep.

CHAPTER 26

DEFLIN HAD BEEN UP ALL NIGHT. The servants had gone back to their rooms, terrified of their new partners. Moreover, none would do anything to compromise a possible fortune. They had already received more money than they had ever had, so none would upset the apple cart. The kitchen staff came back at eight in the morning and prepared breakfast for all.

Jojhinda had hired a Chinook helicopter from Gujarat airport, and it had to refuel at Kabul before proceeding to the poppy farm. He rang the daughters and told them he would be with them about eleven in the morning and asked if there was any aviation fuel at the farm since stopping at Kabul to refuel was not an option when loaded, considering the cargo. Deflin replayed the question to the workers, and the answer was "yes."

"Can you find out how much?"

"They are always full, as the pharmaceutical companies use American Air Force transport to fly the crop to an American base in Pakistan and fly it directly to the United States. Deflin told Jojhinda there was enough to refuel the helicopter.

"Great! See you at eleven."

The tractor driver had returned, and three tonnes of quicklime were emptied over the corpses. It was levelled, and the gardeners planted over the mass grave—it looked just like a mature flower bed.

The helicopter arrived just after eleven and landed on the helipad, which was some distance from the house. The pallets were larger than the only exit out of the room into the lounge, so Deflin told the JCB driver to knock a hole where the French windows had been. They loaded the pallets onto the tractor, which took them to the helipad for loading. It would take a couple of hours to load the Chinook.

Jojhinda and the lawyer were in the warlord's study. It was so easy to access his accounts—he had elaborate passwords but kept a written record of them all on index cards. The total of his cash in the three bank accounts amounted to $37 million dollars; the pharmaceutical companies paid into his bank, and he used the earnings just for wages for his army servants and seasonal workers. It did not take long for Jojhinda to work out that the cash being loaded onto the helicopter were the proceeds of his illegal drug dealing. He made net about $5.5 million a year legally, and there were even tax payments made. Armed with this information, he could formalise the transfer of ownership to his ex-employees. It was quite apparent that the ex-employees were out of their depth and really had no idea of running the company.

Jojhinda turned to Deflin and said, "To make this work, we need a businessman."

The lawyer said that if there were no objections, he would run the business on their behalf for a negotiable fee of around 10% of net profit. Jojhinda had to make it much simpler for them. Each year since the legalisation of the drug trade, the profit was around $5.5 million. The lawyer's fee would £550,000 for running the company and ensuring all legal and taxation is complied with, leaving $4.950,000 to be shared. "$2,475,000 will go to your partners and the remainder shared amongst you, $137,500 each."

A large part of the costs was paying for the army and weapons and the workers didn't need an army. "If you need extra security while waiting for shipment of the crop when harvested, the lawyer can organise that." Heads had started nodding, and there was eventually an understanding.

One brave servant asked the question all wanted to ask, "It seems that you get far more than we do, and we do all the work."

Jojhinda explained, "It's quite simple. If you would like more, kill some of your colleagues, which ones don't you like, point to them and our ladies will oblige you, and you will have a bigger share. If there is only one, you will get close to $2.5 million. So where shall we start?" Silence. He continued, "In five years, when the guaranteed price for your product runs out, you can decide to continue or sell the business. Whatever you decide, you will be rich enough to do anything you want."

Deflin joined the conversation: "You have seen what we have done here, so you should be dead. We have given you an opportunity of this business. Once you sign the necessary papers, you will all be accomplices in what's happened here, and there will be no going back. Those that don't sign will join the warlord. It's that simple."

The lawyer said that it would take a few days to finalise everything and would stay on until it was all complete. Jojhinda and the lawyer explained to the daughters about opening shell companies and saw the expression on their faces.

Geflin stopped them and said, "We trust you. Do whatever you have to make the money safe so we can use it."

"When it's all settled, you should individually be worth about $35 million." The amount of money really did not register with them, but they all knew it would be enough to whatever they wanted.

Deflin asked the lawyer, "Do we need to be here till everything is signed?"

"No, when the paperwork is complete, I can email it for you to sign and return to me."

"That will be great." she turned and told the other daughters, "We are leaving as we are now behind schedule.

we will leave at the same time as Jojhinda"

The helicopter was refuelled and loaded just after two in the afternoon. All the servants came out to see off their silent but deadly partners. The daughters got into their vehicles and set off for the Turkistan border. Deflin got into the back of the Range Rover and was asleep within five minutes.

CHAPTER 27

STEPHEN SHEFFORD WENT THROUGH his daily brief his staff routinely prepared for him. The brief looked for business opportunities and business risks worldwide. Whether it was instinct or luck, but he was drawn to an unsolved crime in Kathmandu—according to Kathmandu Post, over seventy people had been killed. Curiosity got the better of him He got the reporter's name and phoned him. The reporter was only too happy to fill in the bits he could not print; there was no hard proof, and the police were not trying that hard since the mass murder was a service to Kathmandu.

"So, what's missing?" he asked.

"It is all circumstantial—no facts, no proof." He outlined what had taken place at the restaurant. The restaurant owner told them that the gang would seek revenge for the murder of its members.

"How many people were involved?"

The owner replied, "The private table was booked for twenty, but only nineteen dined: twelve men and seven beautiful young women."

"Definitely seven young women!"

"Yes."

"How were the rest of the gang killed?"

"In a similar fashion—hardly any blood, and they are still waiting for the post-mortem results."

"Where are these people now?"

"The seven women flew to Delhi, and the ten monks went back to the monastery."

"Do you know the names of the other two men?"

"Not quite, but one was Indian, the other a local bullion dealer."

"Have you got the address of the bullion dealer?"

"Yes."

Stephen made a note of the address. "Do you by chance have the names of the females?"

"No. They said that all their documents were lost in an avalanche, and the names they gave when booking in didn't check out."

"Did this gang have a lot of cash?"

"There were a lot of stolen property there, and a large safe."

"Was there anything in the safe?"

"No one knows. They can't open it and are still waiting for the manufacturer to send someone to open it."

"Have you any idea of the size or model?"

"It was relatively new. It's why they are having a problem opening it. I have seen it; it had the name Hamilton on it. It was two metres high, a metre deep and a metre width."

"Well, thanks for all that. If you can let me know when you have heard the autopsy results..."

"Ok."

Stephen contacted me and told me the remaining Dark Seven women had surfaced and had wiped out a criminal gang.

"Should we be concerned?" I asked.

"When they find out what we have done to Messapth, pretty sure they're going to be somewhat pissed off and come after you. You know how close Geflin got to turning your lights out, and there's now seven more."

"Let's try and find them. Once we know where they are, we can keep tabs on them."

"If the gang had any cash, it would have been kept in the safe, which no one can open, but I have checked with the manufacturers and given the size of it, they tell me that it would hold in excess of $3 million dollars. I'm bloody sure they would have secured the combination before they killed however had it."

"So our young adversaries have a potential $3 million war chest to fight us with," I said.

"It gets worse. A bullion dealer has several gold taels, which are over 4000 years old and in pristine condition. These could have only come from one place: The Krurs Chendo-Da temple."

"So they have plenty of money, but we have that plus the technology to find them, so let's get to it."

CHAPTER 28

THE KIDNAP HAD NOT PHASED SUE at all. Stephen assembled a security team for her since Monk and I would not be with her, and I approved, much to the annoyance of her. The meetings continued with the pharmaceutical companies in America. She faced tremendous scepticism at each appointment until she explained that Earth Corp did not want to take over their businesses but absorb the financial fallout. She told them, "When the need for medicinal drugs declines, whether it's next year or five, your stock will bottom and will hurt the major pension companies and hurt the people that rely on their pension. You will use your cash reserves to bolster your stock so that you're unable to pay dividends, which will send your stock further down. We will buy the stock at ten percent above the highest price it reached last year or this year. When the pharmaceutical markets regularise, we will sell all that stock back to you at the current market price."

"You will lose billions," they told her, and Sue always enjoyed telling them we have billions to lose.

The American leg of her meetings was over, and she was on to South America, then Australia and East Asia. For China, she met up with Chou En Li. His corporation had merged with Earth Corp eight years ago, and he had been a regular visitor to Assington. It would be difficult—they just did not believe it would happen. Sue left, saying the offer was open should they need it.

It was over dinner that Chou told her of the Chinese taels. He had purchased one and wanted more. He carried his with him and showed it to her. Sue was surprised how heavy it was for its size. He told her that it is from the Xia Dynasty, and his ancestry dated to that time. He had been advised by a guy in Kathmandu that another 199 were available. He had bought this one for $45,000 but intended to buy them all, no matter how much it would cost him.

The house of Li had always been close to every emperor, and he had influence within the politics of China.

"It's a pity the leaders of the pharmaceutical companies didn't listen," Sue said.

"When I have my weekly meeting with the Premier of State, I shall tell him of your offer and their point-blank refusal. If they cause the Han San to dive, I am quite sure he will have their heads, literally."

They finished the meal, and his chauffeur took her back to the hotel. When I spoke with Sue spoke, I could tell she was disappointed with the outcome in China. "We just have to wait and see," I said.

"I should be home by the weekend. Only India and Africa to go.

"You know if you had used my transport, it with have been a lot quicker."

"The Learjet is fine, and they look after me very well. See you at the weekend"

CHAPTER 29

IT WAS MID-AFTERNOON when Stephen updated me on the young women. "They stayed at Jojhinda's country house and left in two Range Rovers. I am almost certain that they are heading for Messapth. The vehicle entered Pakistan and left the same day at the border with Afghanistan. I am sure they would not go through Iran and would make their way to Turkistan, Azerbaijan, and then Turkey as the foot entrance to Messapth is on the Turkish side."

I chuckled. "If there not pissed off about the money, they will certainly be about the concrete we used to seal the foot entrance—we pumped over a thousand tonnes of concrete into the entrance, so it will only leave them either a big climb up and into Messapth or a helicopter."

"You know what?" Stephen said, "it has to be a helicopter. The nearest town to Messapth is Igdir, about 400 miles, and they will hire a helicopter to get there. Even if they travel first and find the entrance blocked, they will return and use the helicopter as it really is there only option."

"I think you're right. I don't think they will want to stay there even for one night as it's really primitive now."

"What else have you got?"

"My sources in Kabul tell me that seven young women were staying at a hotel some two hundred mile west of Kabul, and a group of men attempted to steal their vehicles and ended up dead in the process. One of the dead men was the brother of a warlord. Apparently, the police have put it down to self-defence, but that morning, there was an attack on the hotel—it was sprayed with automatic gunfire. No one was hurt, and the girls continued their journey west, or so it is assumed. My people now say this is complete conjecture on their part, putting snip bits of information together to make a story. Three days ago, a Chinook helicopter landed at Kabul for refuelling and went west, nothing unusual about that as the Americans airlift all the poppy crop, but the crops not ready for another three weeks. So why the big helicopter? This is all conjecture from now. My people say it must be cash, tons of it. The remnants of the illegal poppy trade, they think. It has been a legitimate business now for eight years—bank accounts, taxes, wages...it's now all squeaky clean, but he kept an army to protect something, and my people reckon it was cash."

"Do they keep satellite footage of that area for any length of time? If they did, we could watch what happened."

"Well, the only people that would keep it would be either the military or the CIA. Through the whole Afghan conflict, the warlord sided with the Americans, ever since the Russian invasion of Afghanistan, and were deemed an asset by America, so it is possible."

"Who do we need to talk to find out?" I asked.

"Well, I think the quickest would be for you to have a word with Rodbridge and for him to talk to his son, the President, which I did, and we had a week's footage of the warlord's domain, which confirmed conjecture into fact. So, we know what has happened to the warlord and his army—they're all buried in a mass grave. We counted nearly three hundred pallets onto the helicopter, which amounted to a serious amount of cash."

"We must locate them and quickly and find out where all that cash went. Can you get a team together to bug their vehicles as we did with Russians?"

"I am not sure how many border crossings there are. I would think they would travel through Georgia, but there are also crossings from Armenia and Azerbaijan."

"We will cover all border crossing points in the Black and Caspian sea areas, and a team in Igdir, just in case we miss them at the border."

Stephen called his office in Istanbul. It would take about four hours to get the teams in place. "This Indian guy Jojhinda is proving to be a problem," Stephen said.

"Did we get any evidence against him from the last business with Geflin? After all, he supplied forged documents for her and the rest of the daughters eight years ago," I enquired.

"No nothing, even the smashed hard drive, we were unable to find anything incriminating. The damage was far too great. He is a very wealthy businessman, he pays his taxes and has the ear of all those important people in government, not only in India."

"How much do you estimate was on the helicopter?"

"Close to $300 million."

"Well, he must have a big problem laundering that amount of cash."

"if we can find out what's happened to the cash, we might be able to get him on money laundering."

"My company has a lot of assets in India. We really didn't use them, other than recovering of the hard drive, as the guy was not a main player at that time."

"Well let's put all our resources and get this guy."

CHAPTER 30

JOJHINDA WAS WELL PLEASED with the transfer of the cash; everything worked like clockwork. The helicopter got to Gujarat without refuelling, and Jojhinda went to see his brother, the bank manager, at the Bank of Gujarat. It was a paper chase that would need a forensic accountant, with acute knowledge of the Indian banking system to trace the origin the money. Its destination was the foreign currency reserve of the Bank of India. The money had passed through at least six banks, on paper, each taking the correct amount of commission leaving a final sum of $287 million dollars deposited in the foreign exchange. It had only taken $12 million to clean the money, which left him a hefty, but extremely healthy commission of around $46 million. He transferred $37.2 million to each of the daughters and phoned Deflin. He asked where they were and was told they were waiting for the ferry to take them to Baku. Deflin reckoned that another two days and they would be at Messapth.

"Will you let me know what you find?"

"Of course," she said.

When he returned from the Caymans after delivering the new identities to Geflin over eight years ago, he discovered his hard drive had been removed from the waste bin. He became concerned about what Geflin had told him about how her money was transferred from a bank with state-of-the-art security, and they could do nothing to stop it. The security system he had was extremely good. He ran the CCTV tape while he was away but could not see anything—no one had been in his office, but the hard drive was gone.

His grandson and great nephew had finished their first-class degrees in IT at Oxford and had been head hunted by two of the largest IT companies. Jojhinda had summoned them to Delhi. He told them the story of Geflin, how money had been transferred, and the break-in to his office. It did not take them long to find a missing 40 minutes on the tape. His grandson highlighted that the wall clock showed a time of 01:30 and the next frame showed 02:10. "That's when your hard drive disappeared, and no doubt a thorough search of your office. It must have been a professional job."

"Who would have been able to do this?"

The grandson said, "It could not be Indian secret service

or the government. You would have been tipped off, so it has to be an outside source."

Jojhinda said, "I think I know who it might have been. The transfer of my client's money went to Earth Corp, and Shefford Securities are their security company."

"I know of them. It would be easy for Shefford to do this—they are the best in the business."

"Would they have been able to hack and transfer the money without alarms and anyone noticing?"

"Yes," said the great nephew. "This is a whole different ball game. To hack into that bank in particular would be impossible; their security is impregnable. But it was, as we know, and someone must have a back door key that overrode all the security of the bank. It is the only explanation."

"So what your saying is someone in Earth Corp or Shefford securities have a way into that bank unseen?"

"It is a key and would possibly open or bypass security of any computer. It is the holy grail of hackers around the world, and it seems they have one."

"Could they get into my computer?"

"If they needed to, yes."

"Could I prevent it?"

"No, and they could do it from the other side of the world without you even knowing."

"How are they able to do that?"

"I am only guessing, but I would think they have something in every computer they can access which bypasses the security algorithm and moves straight to the programme."

"How can I prevent this happening?"

"Simply if you use any manufactured computer, it's likely it will have the key, and you're subject to attack. The only way to avoid it is to build your own computer. No sourcing of parts; they all must be made, so you know their integrity, or you could be importing the key into your device."

"Can this be done?"

"Yes and no. Yes, I can build you your own computer, but no, we would have to use imported parts. Currently the Indian computer industry is self-assembly or made under licence. We have no manufacturing infrastructure of our own to make a purely designed and manufactured Indian computer."

"How much would it cost?"

"It would be a massive investment. I really do not have a clue, but we could be talking in the billions."

"How creditable is this back door key problem? Would we be able to frighten the government and military into funding a solely Indian-based computer industry?"

"We know of three such attacks: CIA, GCHQ and the bank of Cayman Brac."

"Do we have any hard proof other than hearsay?"

"We have family in both the organisations. I will ask them to find out. I need you both here to start the Indian computer industry. While we are waiting for collaboration on the attacks, you will visit the existing infrastructure to see whether we can assimilate it into the new fledgling industry."

In the eight years following that inaugural meeting, the Indian computer industry leapt to fifth in the world. The government and military took the back door key seriously and funded the initiative in partnership with a private enterprise business initiative. The existing IT infrastructure joined when their licences expired, and Jojhinda was one of the first to have an Indian made computer with no back door key.

CHAPTER 31

THE DAUGHTERS ARRIVED at the Turkistan border the following day. The journey to the border proved to be uneventful. However, the previous night's accommodation was a bit on the rustic side. The vehicles were thoroughly searched. Also held up at the border crossing were four Australians guys in a VW campervan. While waiting, they struck up a conversation with the daughters. The Australians were on a round-the-world trip and wanted to take in as many countries as they could. They had been on the road for over a year and had another year of travelling. They were medical students and had come top in their chosen specialisations. All had been offered positions in several hospitals in Australia. They all had decided they would need a break, after seven years of intense studying, and told the hospitals they would start in two years.

The Australians asked where the daughters were travelling to, and perhaps they could travel in convoy if going the same way. Deflin said they preferred to travel alone, and the look of disappointment on the other daughters' faces was plain to see. But how could they resist an opportunity to travel with four doctors? "From the border, we travelling to Mary then on to Ashgabat, and then to Turkmenistan to catch the ferry to Baku. We could travel with you as far as Ashgabat then we are heading North and going round the Caspian Sea."

The Australians introduced themselves—Mike, Tom, Darren and Damien and the daughters responded with their new identities. Leaving the border and heading for Mary, the camper van struggled to keep up with the powerful Range Rovers. At the first pit stop, they decided that the convoy would not work—they would meet up in Mary—and they swapped phone numbers. They would let them know when they found accommodation. The extra fuel they carried and the amount of gear was taking a toll on fuel consumption. They would fill up at every opportunity, which meant the camper van was just an hour behind. The daughters booked into the Hotel Mary, phoned the Australians and told them which hotel they were booked in. the hotel had a fitness centre and pool, which they made good use of. The fitness centre was a good size but had so much exercise paraphernalia they would not be able to work out as they wish. They asked if they could move the equipment out as they had no need for it. The hotel obliged and moved the equipment.

Two hours of a rigorous workout attracted quite a few spectators. They were wearing Krurs Chendo-Gi, like a karate-Gi, so the spectators were looking at their technique and not their bodies. After the workout, they changed into their swimming costumes and went swimming. The Australians had checked in and were watching the training and hurriedly changed into their trunks and joined them in the pool. Most Australians are good swimmers, and these four were not exception—they all had swum for their university, two for their state and one was just point one of a second from qualifying for the 2016 Olympics. The daughters did length after length; the guys started showing their swimming abilities, and overtook the daughters, so a race began. The daughters quickened their pace, which was slightly slower than the men's, and the men were soon a length in front and started to slow. The daughters kept to the same pace, and the lead got smaller. The guys quickened again but soon ran out of puff, while the daughters kept to their pace, overtook them, and continued swimming at that pace for another 30 lengths. The guys were exhausted, but by the time the daughters had finished, their breath had come back.

Mike said, "Well done. Outfoxed by the tortoise and hare syndrome. You are tremendously fit young ladies." The other guys nodded in agreement. "I didn't recognise the martial art that you were practising in the gym."

"It is a unique martial art. Only a few people know of it," Geflin said.

"It looks quite deadly if you were up against it."

"It is meant to be," she said. "We are going to have a look round Mary why it's still light."

Mike said, "We will spend another hour swimming if it's still light, we will come and look for you when we are finished."

After the pool, they showered and changed. With another two hours of daylight, they went in search of the Australians. It did not take them long to find them at a bar not far from the hotel. They pushed a couple of tables together, gathered up and placed chairs round them and asked what they would like to drink. All asked for coke.

Damien said, "Don't you want anything alcoholic? We are drinking the local Raki. It's very good."

"No, thank you. We don't drink alcohol. Cokes will be fine."

"Are you hungry?" Tom pointed to the large kebab machine. The daughters nodded. He asked, "How do want them? We like them hot and spicy."

"That sounds good," Geflin said.

Tom went over and ordered the kebabs. The waiter was about to take the already sliced meat when Tom told him no. "Slice it fresh from the hottest part of the rotating kebab."

He watched intently to ensure everything was freshly sliced. The waiter added pickles, peppers and the hot sauce and bought the food over to them. The buns were hard and were delivered with cheap but sharp knives so that you could easily cut them into edible sizes. They were extremely nice and hot, but no one would say—they all suffered in silence.

Deflin turned the conversation towards the next stop. The guys probed why the daughters were travelling by road to Turkey, and the daughters kept changing the conversation. A woman walked in and went up to a guy at the bar. He must have been a local. He pushed her away, but she came back and grabbed his arm, trying to pull him away from the bar. After a few repeats, the guy got angry and hit the woman hard, and she fell to the floor. Blood spilt from her mouth, but she got up again and tried to pull the guy from the bar. He was going to hit her again when Darren stood in front of her.

"I don't know what this is all about but you not going to hit her again," he said.

The guy shocked at being confronted and took some time to assess the problem. Darren was a big guy who showed no fear. The guy drew a knife and was about to stick it into Darren when Tewlin threw the kebab knife with such force it went through the guys hand. His knife fell to the floor, and his hand was impaled into the side of the bar. The knife was smothered in hot sauce, and it must have been agonising for the guy. Tom told Mike to fetch the med kit from the camper. Tom, an acute trauma doctor, went over to see the damage. There was not much blood as the knife was well embedded into the palm as well as the bar. He could not believe that Tewlin could throw that hard and accurately. He could not do much until the med kit came but asked the barman for a bottle of water to get the hot sauce off the knife.

Mike arrived with the kit and handed it over. Tom opened up and got a can of spray and numbed the area of the palm. He eased the knife out and sprayed the other side of the hand. Tom cleaned up the wound put two steri-strips on both sides and neatly bandaged up the palm. He then told the guy it would be painful once the spray wears off and gave him six strong painkillers.

The barman had told them that the woman was his wife, and it was okay to hit your wife if she was annoying you. She just wanted him to come home and stop drinking their money away. On hearing this, Deflin peeled off $500 and gave it to the woman for medical expenses. The shock on the woman's face—she had never seen so much money. She hurriedly put in her pocket and left; he was not going to get his hands on it. The guy was in so much pain that he took no notice.

Tom told the guy, "You should go to your doctor to have the dressing changed in two days and go there now for a tetanus shot just to be safe."

He shook his head and said he had no money for medical care, so Tom gave him 200 Manets, and he left the bar.

The barman said, "He will spend it all on booze and take his chance that you did a good job."

They continued talking, but the conversation kept turning to Tewlin's knife-throwing abilities. Eventually, Sheflin said, "Our parents are wealthy and would not allow us to go unless we could look after ourselves, so we were taught how. Throwing knives and defending ourselves now comes naturally to us all, to protect each other and those close to us. You were being threatened so it was logical for Tewlin to assist. She was closest and had the best chance of disabling the guy."

The conversations in the three days they had been travelling together had had a profound effect on the daughters. The guys had become doctors because their mission was to save life, and this bought some gravity and perspective into what they had done in Kathmandu and Afghanistan. None of the daughters had spoken about it, but they all knew what they had done would be reprehensible to the doctors and their philosophy that all life is sacred. The daughters had a real problem, growing up in Messapth was all fun; the only learning was languages. So, when they were taken to the temple, their minds had not formed love or hatred and there was no evil in them—the temple taught them how to kill, which they learned well. Had all been well, their next seven years at finishing school and trips back home would have programmed the evil into them. So, their minds could be programmed a different way, the influence of the Australian doctors on them made them all question their actions. It would not be long before they would speak openly about these new thoughts. The daughters were quite emotional when the goodbyes were said.

It was 700-kilometre slog to Turkmenbashi, but they had booked cabins on the ferry, which could take up to thirty hours. Custom formalities took an hour and were on the road, having decided to go via Tbilisi, Georgia, and cross into Turkey from Georgia. The distance was longer, but the roads were much better, and in theory take less time than the sat-nav said. They arrived at the Stamba Hotel after another long drive. Just one more stop, then the Turkish border, then on to Igdir, which they would make their base until they had spoken with their families in Messapth.

It was a further four hundred miles to the bottom of the valley and a good day walk to get inside the valley, if they could remember where that foot entrance was. Certainly, for their first seven years, helicopters were used all the time. Most of the women could fly helicopters. The consensus was that hiring them would be a risk, and the pilots would have to be eliminated to keep the place secret. Deflin spoke with Jojhinda and told her he would organise it and meet them in Igdir sometime the next day. The daughters arrived at the hotel late the following day. Deflin told Jojhinda where they were staying and asked to book them in. Now all they had to do was wait.

CHAPTER 32

THE TWO RANGE ROVERS ARRIVED at the Turkish border. The daughters were asked to take their documents into passport control. Meanwhile, Stephen's men easily tagged and bugged their cars; now we could keep proper tabs on the daughters. Stephen had tried to get into Jojhinda's computer, but even Court Leiston's back door key would not work. We had involved the world's best CIA officer Mossad and GCHQ, none could get into his system. We had the daughter's new identities from the first border crossing and found out their banks and realised they were seriously wealthy. As hard as we tried, we could not trace it back to Jojhinda. We kept tabs on him from a distance as he had friends in extremely high places, and we needed to be sure if we were ever to bring him to justice.

We knew he had chartered a plane to Esenboga Airport in Turkey and that he was meeting up with the daughters, but we didn't know why. He could easily land close to Messapth, but then a hard journey up and over into Messapth.

Stephen said, "They must be hiring a helicopter."

"Does the flight plan have the pilot's name?" I asked. We soon got it and checked it out. It was going to take nine hours to get to Esenboga and a twenty-minute hop by helicopter to Igdir, then a two-hour flight direct into Messapth. "Is Messapth still bugged"

"Of course."

"Well, I think we need to start listening to find out what's on their minds?"

"When they're all there, we should smart bomb it and turn it into a crater. Shall I organise it?"

"No."

He then told his team in Turkey to trace and bug the helicopter. "You have under nine hours to do so. It must be a nine-seater or above, that should reduce the workload."

It was now a matter of waiting. I searched for Sheflin—she and Pat had returned from their honeymoon. I asked, "What should we do with these cousins of yours? Were they taught evil at the temple?"

"Not only taught to kill without remorse."

"So for the first seven years, what do they do?"

"Play and learn languages."

"So when is the evil taught?"

"We do not see it the same way you do. It's business for us, and if someone needs removing, it's just business. We don't hate and seek revenge unless our backs are to the wall, and we can be really vicious, but evil no."

"So why have they killed so many on their way home?"

"Probably through necessity. Our doctrine says 'if all are killed, there will be no one seeking revenge'."

"But surely that has to be evil."

"No; good business practice. We have been doing it for thousands of years, and it's worked. Look how their wealth is now supporting a totally independent United Nations."

"If we hadn't stopped them over eight years ago, they would have wiped out ten of the richest men in the world, including the President of the United States."

"It was a business opportunity. Bruce Kennett had lost his business to you, and he wanted it back. He would have been in our pocket had we let him live."

"That's evil."

"Business."

"Well, I do have a major problem. Stephen wants that to turn Messapth into a crater with a powerful smart bomb as soon as their helicopter touches down."

It was plain to see the look of horror and shock on her face. "I must warn them," she said and tried to run.

I caught her arm. "I haven't agreed to anything, and Stephen takes orders from me. Your cousins have amassed a fortune on their way to Messapth, I can easily make them poor as you know, but I am inclined to let them keep it."

"Why would you do that?"

"The people they took out in Kathmandu...my intelligent reports say that it is no bad loss, and the police are not looking too hard for the perpetrators. Similarly the warlords cash was from illegal drug business before it became legal. It was a huge amount of cash, and they have set up his employees to run the now legal business and are partners with them, which will give them a reasonable income. Do you think these daughters pose any threat to us and the world if I let them keep the money?"

"I really don't know. All above the age of twenty-seven have pilots' licences for aircraft and helicopters, albeit out of date. But with a few hours flying, they will get their CPL quickly. That would give them mobility and ability to leave Messapth and disperse."

"Would that be a problem?"

"I don't think so. I still have my Krus skills and would use them to protect you and Susan and kill without thinking, to prevent an attack on you. But I don't have any anger for what you did to my mind."

"I think we might pay them a visit when the young ones arrive. I have an idea"

I had to speak with the Prime Minister and the President and run the idea by them. It was simple but could be so effective if it worked. So much crime still went on, and with the skills of Dark Seven, could help the police forces around the world as an impossible mission force when put to proper use—fighting fire with fire. In return, the daughters could keep the money they had acquired and any cash they'd come across in the line of duty. After a lot of persuading, they agreed to give it a trial. Now all I had to do was get Dark Seven to agree. I told Sheflin my preposition. "All we need is their cooperation. I will not mention it to Stephen just yet. I think they would prefer this to remaining as they are, but we will have to see. They may like their new lifestyle, as it's been over eight years."

CHAPTER 33

DEFLIN RECEIVED A MESSAGE from Jojhinda that they were forty minutes away. The daughters took a taxi to the outskirts of town and waited for the helicopter. It arrived on time and took off to Messapth. Jojhinda was talking to them, but the noise drowned his voice. He pointed to above their heads for earphones, and they put them on. He was asking for guidance. It had not occurred to the daughters that finding their home could prove exceedingly difficult, it being in a secret valley.

"What can you remember about its location?" he asked.

Tewlin said, "There is an oil pipeline and pumping station. Planes and helicopters can land."

Deflin said, "Igdir was the nearest town."

Jojhinda googled pipelines in Turkey. There were only two in this part of Turkey, one close to the Georgian border, the other a good two-hour flight time from Igdir. By process of elimination, it had to be that one. The pumping stations were 200 miles apart. Following the pipeline into Iran, the penultimate pumping station looked the most promising and had a fuel depot. He gave the pilot the co-ordinates, and they headed towards it.

Two hours later, they arrived and landed at the pumping station. The pilot refuelled while the daughters scanned the terrain. It all looked vastly different from Messapth—it was a clear blue sky over the mountains. Deflin said the there was always cloud cover over the valley, and it did not take long to reach from here if they were in the right place. They took off and climbed to eight thousand feet and flew over the mountains. After five minutes flight time, they saw a large cumulation of cloud below the ridge of a mountain range. It had to be Messapth. They flew through the cloud base, and below was indeed Messapth, but not how they remembered it—all the green spaces had been replaced with agriculture and the houses were neglected. Many people were working in the fields, and they all stopped as the helicopter landed and rushed towards it in excitement.

The daughters disembarked and could not believe what they saw. Their mothers were in rags and seemed to subsistence living. The beauty was still there, but their faces looked haggard from the hard work. The mothers immediately recognised their daughters and rushed to hug them; the daughters responded similarly. Jojhinda was also shocked as he knew most of them from past business dealings.

They walked towards the men's house, which was the largest of all the houses and could accommodate them all. The daughters were keen on learning what had happened, but their mothers said they did not really know—they awoke, and everything had gone, including all the men and servants; only three elderly male servants left. The work load these servants had took its toll, and there had been no men here for over six years.

"We have had to do everything ourselves," a mother explained. "A helicopter arrives monthly and drops off the supplies we ask for—no luxuries; simply basic living items, but we have coped. We are missing the mother that took you to the temple, and Sheflin who was on station in Prague. We have no idea what happened to them."

Jojhinda said, "Geflin was shot trying to assassinate those that stole all your wealth and are responsible for the way you are existing now, but I don't know what's happened to Sheflin." Jojhinda hoped for a reaction other than a shrug of the shoulders, but it appeared they were not that bothered on the surface.

The daughters then relayed their journey details and the fortune they had amassed which put a huge smile on the mother's faces. All the mothers had expired CPLs and helicopter licences. They were prisoners here as the only foot way out had been blocked. The fuel depot and pumping station had the phone removed, and walking did not seem to be an option. They needed to think about their next course of action carefully.

Daughter Deflin asked, "Are we going seek revenge for what's happened to you?"

Her mother replied, "We must think. The people that did this to us are more powerful than we are. Our skills did not help us. Had they chosen they could have wiped us out? We would if the situations had been reversed. What we do now must be well thought through."

CHAPTER 34

WE WERE IN MY OFFICE in Assington, watching and listening via satellite. I turned to Sheflin and said, "Shall we pay them a visit and see what they think of my offer?" Stephen had gone off to check something, which was a golden opportunity for us to visit Messapth, and so we arrived some twenty minutes later.

The verticular dropped us off, and as always, became invisible as we exited. We were about three hundred metres from the men's house. There was no one about; all were in the men's house. Sheflin, Monk, and I strolled into the men's house. Everyone inside was enthralled with the young daughters' return story and had not noticed our arrival.

Sheflin called her mother. At first, there seemed to be a hostile reaction, but it soon dissipated. Monk and I scanned minds for any danger but there was none. Sheflin waded through and embraced her mother. It had been over eight years. Tears streamed down both faces.

Jojhinda pointed. "That's the guy in charge of the company that stole all your money."

Monk and I could not feel any vibes from all assembled towards us. There certainly was no violence towards us. Sheflin spoke to her mother and asked that I could address them all with a proposition that may be of interest.

I explained, "Eight years ago, when we had the opportunity to eliminate you all, I used my resources to ensure your survival. For the mayhem you caused and the deaths of that stood in your way, world governments wanted you all to stand trial, but I used my influence for you to be isolated here. I'm here to make you an offer. Your newly returned daughters have amassed a small fortune in their journey here. I can take that money easily but have chosen not to. The last time we met, your beauty was overwhelming, but eight years of toil has taken its toll. Your organisation has caused so much suffering in your actions that all interested parties want you dead. I do not want that, and it is the reason I am here. The daughter's largess can rebuild Messapth to its former elegance, and you all will have freedom of movement around the world, but not to continue your previous trade.

The whole world has changed in the last eight years. Your wealth has made the United Nations a truly independent entity. No longer can they be bullied into the wishes of the major countries; the smallest country has the same clout as any other. My only problem now is the criminal activity that unfortunately still goes on. Your unique skills could put an end to organised criminality throughout the globe, like the daughter's whatever cash is found will be yours. You will finance all from your daughter's wealth and we will decide and give you all the intelligence we have for that task. I turned to Jojhinda we know what you do and currently we are unable to break into your system, rest assured that we are able to watch your every move. I have no intention of shutting you down as Messapth may still need your services. We are watching you. I will be back tomorrow for your answer."

I read Sheflin's mind, and she wanted to stay, so Monk and I made our way back to the verticular. We disappeared with the helicopter and returned to Assington. All was well until Stephen found out that we had been somewhere without him. I just shrugged and said we were back now and safe, and he did not press it further.

CHAPTER 35

THE ELDERS OF MESSAPTH DISCUSSED the details of my offer. Their concern increased tenfold when Jojhinda told them that his helicopter had vanished. They summoned Sheflin to answer questions, and she told them everything she knew about me and the organisation I represent. She was part of the security that saw Aunt Geflin try to assassinate the head of Earth Corp. Geflin managed to get two shots off before being killed.

"Stephen Shefford took them both in the heart, and I knew he was dead. He was scooped up, taken outside, and he returned five minutes later, alive and kicking, saying his bulletproof jacket had saved him. The press had no option but to swallow the story, but I knew he was dead. But he has no scars on his chest at all. Something special happened to him in those five minutes. If they are able to bring dead people back to life, make a helicopter disappear, reduced Messapth to Serfdom, taken everything of value we had and you are not seething and wanting revenge, they have changed you too, my opinion is to accept the offer. With **the daughters' fortune, you could leave here, or you could** rebuild Messapth to its former glory as you will no longer be prisoners and will be able to come and go as you please. The only problem is who they ask you to go after—it will be people you have dealt with in the past. On a personal note, I have found the changes they made to me acceptable and have married a man that I tortured cruelly, and we are deeply in love."

Sheflin was dismissed and caught up with the other daughters of her age. Their stories were all similar—they fell asleep, woke up here, and everything was gone. Two hours later, the elders returned. It was unanimous they would accept the offer.

CHAPTER 36

WHEN THE UNITED NATIONS BECAME INDEPENDENT, they set up an international justice department to tackle international crimes and had a mandate from every country to cross borders to track and tackle crime. As always, the criminal soldiers where easily caught, but no evidence could be found for those in charge. The guy in charge of the justice department was called Jon Bridges. I had contacted the Secretary-General and asked if we could meet up for a discussion on the deal I was trying to broker with Dark Seven.

The meeting I had asked for was confirmed for 14:00, their time. I arrived with Monk at the United Nations building, and we were shown up to the Secretary-General office. I had never met Jon Bridges before. I quickly entered his mind and found nothing but his mindset as a highly motivated man with a passion for justice of the highest integrity. After the formal greetings, I told them of my offer to what was the world's worst criminal gang.

"We visited them this morning and found no sign of hatred or evil in their minds. The reason for the visit was the seven missing girls had arrived back at Messapth with the forger, Jojhinda. On their journey there, they have amassed over $300 million. I told them I could take that money easily but would not if they turned their skills into bringing to justice the top people in crime."

"How do we know we can trust them?" asked Jon.

"I have told them they can keep the proceeds of anything found."

"That could be tens of millions."

"They will be funding all their actions, and that money is already lost to us as its illegal, so it makes no difference. We will get them the latest equipment and training at their expense. If the money gets to be a problem, I can easily take it."

"Will we be giving them free rein over everything."

"Correct. They will work better for us if their hands are not tied. All you need to do is keep them up to date with the latest intelligence and let them work the best use of it."

"We need these people brought to justice and tried."

"I agree, but sometime these criminals are too well protected, so that might never happen. So what do we do then? We just can't leave them to continue with their criminal activities. It will be your decision to remove the head of the snake, not theirs."

"How long will it take them to get up to speed?"

"At least three months."

"What sort of people should we get them to go after?"

"It occurs to me that now drugs are legalised and the cartels are now legal businesses. There has to be a load of illegal cash still in their system. Get them to get for us; it will be right up their street." The nodding of heads showed that we were all in agreement, so I could pursue my proposition the next day.

We arrived back home a little after nine. I told everyone what I was proposing to do with Dark Seven, and it did not go down well with Stephen and his security team; he would never fully trust them. I went out and found Pat Smith and told him that Sheflin would be staying at Messapth tonight and I would be returning the next day, if he would like to come. I said, "We need someone inside, should they agree to my proposition, and you and your wife would be ideal candidates to make sure they don't deviate back to their old ways."

"It's pretty austere there."

CHAPTER 37

WE ARRIVED BACK AT MESSAPTH around midday. They were all back in the fields and did not see us. The elders, Sheflin, Jojhinda and the pilot were in the men's house, gathered around a huge table. Sheflin saw us first and got up to kiss Pat and then introduced him as her husband. The elders were suitably impressed—he was a handsome man.

Sheflin's mother was one of the seven elders. She started to speak: "We will accept your offer and use our skills to do as you ask, providing Messapth is returned to its former glory."

"Agreed."

"Our possessions are returned to us."

"I cannot comply as they are either in museums or been sold and have new legitimate owners. However, you may be able to buy them back since you have the money. If all the houses give me a list of all the items they want back, I will trace them for you. That's the best I can do."

She continued, "We want freedom of movement."

"Agreed."

"We need to get our CPLs and helicopter licences renewed."

"Agreed."

"We want men to be able to come here."

"Agreed, providing they come by choice and can leave at will and not end up in the lime pit."

"We need to go shopping."

"Agreed. Why don't I organise a plane to pick you all up and take you to Paris? You can shop, and those that need the licences renewed can do it while there."

There were some other minor requests, which I agreed to. Our Sheflin said to Pat, "I would like to stay and help organise everything," and he could stay if he wanted to. He shook his head in agreement.

"While you are all away, we could get builders in to repair and restore all your homes. If you give Sheflin a list of what needs to be done, we will get it done. Once we have the list, we can see how many tradesmen we are going to need and fly them in."

I turned to Jojhinda. "How long will it take to get travel documents for them all?"

"At least six weeks."

"That's too long."

"The young daughters have theirs, and if you rented houses instead of hotels in their names, you would not need so many and would give me time to get them."

"We are looking this the wrong way," said Stephen. "All the women of Messapth have had identities when they were on station; they are just out of date and need to be renewed. They never had criminal records. In fact, the time they were here, they never put a foot wrong in the eyes of the authorities, so renewing should be no problem. We may just need birth certificates, which they must have, to get their passports."

The elders said they had birth certificates, so most of the other women should have theirs too.

I said, "The youngsters that have just returned have laptops that they could renew them from here and collect them from the relevant Paris embassy."

It turned out that all ninety-six women wanted to go shopping, but all had some form of old ID that would enable renewing and collection of documents. Jojhinda and the pilot helped in filling in the forms, and all were sent. Collection in Paris would be in three weeks. All were given temporary travel permits, acceptable to the French authorities. Our Sheflin gave me the list of requirements, and I spoke to the builder that had done all the work on Assington. He advised that sixty tradesmen would do but would need a cargo plane to bring in the equipment and furniture.

Stephen chartered an Airbus A320. The tradesmen

would fly in the Airbus, and the women would leave on it, then the cargo plane would arrive. We now needed the return of the helicopter. It duly appeared but with the inevitable changes. The pilot looked amazed. It was still a helicopter—it had rotors at the top and tail—but everything in between was different.

He said, "I don't know what the rental company is going to say when we return it...that's if I am able to fly it."

"We won't be returning it. We will buy it, and I am sure you will be able to fly it. Two fighter pilots thought the same when their aircraft were modified, but flying them was simple."

"Well, let's have a go." We walked over to the helicopter and got in. Horror appeared on the pilot's face as all the instrumentation had disappeared, leaving a solitary control stick. "I will not be able to fly this. The changes are amazing."

I said, "Put your helmet on." I put mine on and proceeded to ask, "What would you do first?"

"Prefight check."

"Next?"

"Start engines." The engines started.

"Next?"

"Check instruments." All the instruments on his visor turned green one by one. The pilot looked around for the throttle to increase rotor speed for take-off.

"Tell it what you want it to do next," I said.

"Increase rotor speed for take-off." The rotor speed increased, and the helicopter lifted off the ground. "Ascend to two thousand feet." The craft hovered two thousand feet above Messapth. "Now, fly south for fifty miles at maximum speed." The craft banked 180 degrees and went to maximum speed, which had improved by forty per cent, and it took just under eight minutes to do fifty miles. "Take us back to Messapth." Eight minutes later, we were back on the ground. The pilot looked around at the rest of the helicopter.

"What do think of the modifications?"

"Amazing!"

"Get in touch with the rental company and organise the purchase so they can keep it here. You or Jojhinda can phone them and say you need for it for a lot longer and need the price."

We returned to the men's house and told Elder Sheflin that they needed to buy the helicopter.

"But it's an old Bell 230. We want something newer," Elder Sheflin said.

The pilot said, "The changes made to this craft are incredible; I would say unique. I have flown many new ones, and none can do what this does. If you won't buy it we shall."

I handed Elder Sheflin a rather substantial list of all the artefacts taken from Messapth. Against each one was the price it made at auction and who had bought it. I told her, "I have no problem with you acquiring any of these items legally, but should you or any of the houses obtain items illegally, you will be returned here and back to the life you led over the last eight years."

"I do not think that's fair," said Elder Tewlin.

"I have personally given my word to the powers that

want to see you in prison or dead, that you can help rid this world of organised crime, so any deviation from that will result in your return here. The illegal proceeds from any crime, you can use to buy back your artefacts." I turned to our Sheflin. "You all had safe houses when you were on station. Do you know if they are still there as they would make a great base for each house to work from?" Once they had gotten their papers, they could flyout and check them.

Two days later, the Airbus arrived with the tradesmen who were shuttled into Messapth. The women were shuttled to the waiting aircraft—it took just over an hour, and the Airbus took off. An hour later a C-130 arrived, full of equipment. It took a day and a half to get all the into Messapth. What was thought to be a problem was the seven-tonne JCB, but the modified helicopter coped with it easily. Pat and Sheflin would oversee the refurbishment and liaise, should there be a problem.

CHAPTER 38

JON BRIDGES HAD BEEN IN CONTACT and wanted a meeting. The training of the seven houses had gone well, and they were all up to speed with new communications and weaponry. The shopping spree was more of an onslaught on the shops of Paris, much to the delight of the owners. With the right documentation and all the licenses renewed for those that wanted to fly, all houses were truly independent. Their safehouses were okay and ready, despite the need for a lick of paint and a good clean. As Messapth had always been the base, it would remain so, and everything would be organised from there.

I collected Jon from New York. Forty-five minutes later, we entered what was the men's house. It now looked like the reception to a posh hotel. We were taken to a conference room by a handsome young French man. I entered the young man's mind and could tell it was purely lust that kept him here with his other friends.

It had not taken long for the women to find several men in France that would make their life more enjoyable back at Messapth. The elders were already there. Jon put a flash drive into a laptop and several photos of men appeared on the screen. He went over and explained each one. "These men are responsible for most of the human trafficking in Europe—prostitution. The misery they cause women must stop. I want you to stop them, find evidence to incriminate them, and find the names of the police and judges that are in their pocket."

Elder Sheflin spoke, "I know some of these people." She turned to our Sheflin. "Ask the Senior Sheflin house members to attend our meeting." All the senior members of the House of Sheflin were now in attendance. Elder Sheflin pointed at one photograph. "I know this man, but he was a lot younger then."

Elder Sheflin's mother spoke. "I know all the men." She, too, pointed at a photograph. "This man is the head of the organisation—his brother should have been, but I killed him and his son for betraying us. Their organisation were the best smugglers from the East to the West. Our house were their principal customers. The son argued with his father that we could piggyback drugs along with our items. I never knew they were doing this until one of our special consignments were intercepted. Sniffer dogs had been employed and our and their shipments had been seized at customs. I only killed those that were involved in the drug shipment but it sent a message to the survivors never to use our shipments for any other purposes."

Our Sheflin said, "Why didn't you kill them all?"

"They were excellent smugglers; it was the only time they had failed us. We stopped using them when the wall came down. As we all now had pilots licences so we no longer needed them, we had our own customs people in our pockets."

Elder Sheflin said, "It looks like our house will have to clear up this mess."

The house of Sheflin elders worked out a plan to use the newly arrived youngsters as bait for the people traffickers. It was a simple plan, and to work better, we needed bracelets for all, so communication links would be secure and hidden. Monk got them and handed them to the team. The two mothers and youngsters would be Syrian refugees and put ashore on the border of Turkey and Syria and walk to the Turkish refugee camp. The traffickers had scouts in all the refugee camps, and seven beautiful young girls would soon have their attention.

It took nearly a day to walk to the camp, and they arrived just before nightfall. The camp was run by Christian Aid Charity. They took their names and showed them to a tent where they were given clean clothes. They showered them to the women's shower block and were each given a ticket for something to eat. After showering, the beauty of the youngsters became clearly visible. The mothers kept their full burkas on over the clean clothes.

The Mess hall was close to the shower block, and all made their way to it, queuing for a meal. There must have been over a thousand eating in the Mess hall. After collecting their simple meal, they looked for somewhere to sit, and two males started walking towards them. The men looked at a crowded table, and the people just got up and left with their. The men showed them to the now vacant table and introduced themselves. They told them the average wait for asylum was two years, but for a fee, they could be anywhere in Europe within a week.

A mother asked how much and the response that came was, "20,000 Turkish Lira each."

The mother said, "We cannot afford that. We have only 18,000 liras in total."

"That may be enough if you don't want to travel with paperwork. It's the costliest aspect of the journey."

"We will have to think about it, as it's all the money we possess." It was not the answer the men were looking for, but they knew how to get them to agree...or so they thought.

On their way back to the tent, several young men surrounded them and started to tease and torment them, trying to get intimate with the young girls, while the mothers looked on. A great deal of pushing and shoving took place until the two men turned up, having orchestrated the whole thing to get their new clients focused that this camp was not safe for them.

The mothers' pretend shock was plain to see, and the men felt they would be acquiring 18,000 Turkish lira. The mothers said they had reconsidered their offer and would give them all their money; they had hidden it just outside the camp as they were not sure how safe it would be. There was only one entrance to the camp, so the men had made their own gates to bypass the little security there was. The mothers took them about a ten-minute walk from camp, hopefully far enough so the screaming could not be heard. The mothers turned on the men so quickly. They were immediately bound extremely tightly with their own clothes in a peculiar manner, so any movement caused them pain.

"We have some questions. Are you the only people in the camp?" No answer. She went over and applied pressure to his bindings, and his eyes nearly popped from his head with the pain, but there was still no answer. "You're tough but be rest assured you will tell me everything I want to know. One of you will witness the excruciating agony of the other before his terribly slow bleeding to death." She went over to the other guy. "Is he a good friend?"

"No, he's my brother."

"Would you like to eat his genitals?" The look of sheer horror was plain to see. "Will you tell me what he won't?"

"Yes."

There were four other pairs in this camp looking out for primarily women or wealthy individuals, and he gave her their names. "When we have something of interest, we put a note into a dead letter box. We go back the following day, and there is a reply and a time we should bring the clients. We take them there and leave them. We are never there for a collection—it's death if we do. We just keep half the money."

Under normal circumstances, they would have killed them, but killing now was the last resort. The United Nations International Crime Agency now had assets in every corner of the globe and were to be summoned when prisoners had been taken. A helicopter was despatched to pick up these two, after they had written a letter that was then left at the dead letter box. The helicopter arrived, and a small elite force left the disembarked in search of the other eight traffickers, armed with their names and where to find them in the camp. It would not take them long to capture them and would now make this camp so much safer.

The mothers went back to the camp and joined the youngsters. "We will all be moving on tomorrow night with the next stage," they said. How many more stages, they did not know. The mothers slipped away to the dead letter box at midday, and a reply had been sent, telling them to be there at 21:00. It was a thirty-minute walk to the rendezvous point, and a fifteen-seater bus was waiting for them. Four well-armed men ushered them into the bus, and off they went. It was now pitch dark, and the only illumination was the coach headlights and the odd vehicle coming the other way. They were heading for Gaziantep, so it seemed. It had been over an hour when they reached the next leg of the journey. They left the coach and walked towards several truck containers.

One of the gunmen ducked under the fifth wheel and crouched along the trailer. Halfway along, he pulled a large trap door and pulled some steps down. The mothers realised this would be their next mode of transport—they had not learned much. It was time to find out what these men knew.

As the man crawled back from under the container, a mother smashed his head against the concrete road. The others were neutralised quickly and tied up in the trademark painful way. The interrogation started, it appeared that these guys were not as hard at the first ones. All told the same story—they collected and bought them here. They explained, "The trailer is always in the spot, and we put the people in the trailer and leave. We do not know what happens after that. If we hung around, we would be killed."

A mother told a youngster to get inside the container and check for cameras tracking the cargo. The youngster climbed up, and the step's lights came on. *Must be a motion sensor,* she thought. She had a good look but found nothing. If there had been cameras, they would be cheap and large, making them easy to find.

The accommodation left a lot to be desired. There were several mattresses on the floor, a porta potty in the corner, and a freezer box with food in it. The daughter reported back what she had seen. The two mothers listened, and one said, "I think we are going to be on this for some time." The other mother agreed. The mother touched her bracelet and summoned our Sheflin. While waiting for her, they broke into the office to see if there was any incriminating evidence on the CCTV footage. The coach was seen entering the gates and disappearing into a black spot. As far as they could see, there were no signs of their activity. Our Sheflin had arrived. The gunmen were bundled into the coach, and our Sheflin gave them a tracer to put in one of the trailers rear lights. Our Sheflin left in the coach to rendezvous with the UNICA. The mothers and youngsters climbed in, closed the flap and settled down. It was going to be a long night.

After 30 minutes a cacophony of noise could be heard, the tractor units were being attached to the trailers, they felt a slight bump as the fifth wheel engaged and heard air lines being connected, five minutes later they were on the road, there was nothing more they could do until it came to a stop. The truck came to a stop after four and a half hours. A mother asked one of the daughters to check outside, turned the lights out on opened the hatch and jumped down, keeping to the shadows, there were hundreds of trucks and what looked like a restaurant, it was a truck stop could be the only explanation when reporting back to the mothers. If the drivers break were 45 minutes, the mother knew that they were in for another long ride, as it happened the break was only 15 minutes his journey would be less than another four and a half hours. It stopped again after a further two and a half hours. The tractor unit was detached and left the trailer/container, before it drove off the driver made a call to say that the trailer had been left at the normal place and nothing unusual had occurred. The driver and tractor unit would be captured several miles away from the container so not to arouse any suspicion.

After twenty minutes, they heard other vehicles; not trucks. The flap opened, and they were told to leave the container and were loaded into two vehicles. It was just starting to get light, and the trailer had been left in a small compound as the vehicles got to a main road. The road signs showed they were heading for Aksaray. The vehicles were now being tracked by satellite. The vehicles stopped outside a two-star hostel, and they were ushered into it. They were shown straight to three rooms, and the doors locked behind them. The rooms were basic but had showers, which they all made use of. They were all trained to spot the bugs—which they did—but had to leave them in situ and use them for their advantage. The mothers still had their Niqab on so only the eyes could be seen, so when showering, two beautiful bodies were seen, and similarly the youngsters'. The three men watching the monitor were staggered by the beauty of the women. They realised they had hit the jackpot this time. The video was forwarded up the command chain, and the response was immediate. "Do not send them on. Keep them there, and we will collect them this evening. If you value your lives, do not touch them and give them food and drink."

The women got dressed, much to the disappointment of the viewers. A couple of hours later, Mother Sheflin went to the door. It was a yale type lock, and she easily opened it and looked along the empty corridor. She walked to the other bedrooms where the others were held. "It is now our turn to ask some questions. We need to secure the hostel and everyone in it."

The hostel was on four floors, ten rooms on each floor. It would be a lot quicker if they could get the room pass keys. At the far end of the corridor, there appeared to be a laundry room. They quietly made their way towards it. The smell of tobacco smoke told them that someone was inside. At lightning speed, the door opened, and two youngsters rushed in and secured two chambermaids. The youngsters slowly released their grip on their throats and mouths so they were able to talk. "Do your passkeys open all the rooms?"

"Yes," a chambermaid said.

"Give them to me." There was a reluctance soon overcome by tremendous nerve pain administered by a youngster. They took them back to their bedroom to interrogate them further.

They sat the chambermaids on the bed. "You have felt the pain we can induce. We are not going to kill you, but if you don't tell us truthfully what we want to know, then the pain you will encounter will make you wish you were dead. Do you understand?" They both nodded "How long have you worked here?"

"Eight and ten years."

"So, you must know a lot of what goes on here."

The chambermaid that had been there the longest nodded. "This is where the initial assessment happens. The refugees are assessed as to their usefulness, and videos are sent to what I assume is the halfway house."

"Do you know where that is?"

"No."

"Does anyone know here?"

"I am not sure the manager may know, but when a collection is imminent, we all leave, so we see no one. It's certain death, should we see someone or the vehicles. The manager is the only one that stays."

"How many staff does he have?"

"There are eight more; two in the kitchen, one on reception. The others are guards."

"Where can we find them?"

"They are normally playing cards in the breakfast room all day until some brute force may be needed by the manager."

"Have you any more guests staying at the moment?"

"We have twenty proper guests—mostly foreign pipeline workers and six similar guests to you, all female."

"Where are the other refugees?"

"All refugees are kept on the first floor just in case we are raided by the police. It's quicker for them to escape via the fire exit. We always get a warning when a raid is about to take place. The manager has someone in the police force to ensure they have time to escape."

"When do the pipeline workers return?"

"A coach drops them off at a bar, and they stay there until nine. They return here, have their dinner, and go to bed as it's an early start in the morning."

"What time does the halfway house collect?"

"As I told you, I don't know. We are never here for that, but generally, we are told to leave around six and come back after nine."

"We need to get hold of the manager; he is going to tell us more. We don't have to worry about the hotel guests but what to do about the other refugees," the other mother said.

"Surely, they will be facing the same fate as us," the other chambermaid spoke.

"I don't think so. They are old and certainly not beautiful, but wealthy. So, we won't be able to protect them. They will pay to get into Europe—we will report it to UNICA, and let them deal with it; we have much bigger fish to fry."

The neutralising of the guards was simple enough, and the kitchen staff were put with the chambermaids, but they could not find the manager. The guards were tied and left where they were found. Back at the bedroom, they asked where the manager was. The kitchen porter said that he would be having lunch and a game of back gammon in the bar round the corner from the hotel.

"What time does he come back?"

"About three."

"Tell me: the guards do not seem to be Turkish."

"They are Romanian, the same as the manager."

A chambermaid said, "All four of us were here when it was sold to them eight years ago. it was bought under duress, and we haven't seen the owner since. We were told he took the money and went to live on the coast. We all believe he was killed as he didn't want to sell."

"You realise that when we leave, there will be no more refugees coming here? We are going to put a stop to this trade."

"As far as we know, the hotel itself never got a penny, so it will be no loss. We could even take in more guests since the oil company is always asking for more rooms."

Our Sheflin was contacted and updated. There was a problem—of course they could get the manager to talk, but he would not be in a fit state to talk to the colleagues that were due to collect them that evening.

"I have an idea," our Sheflin said. "I will be in touch, do not harm the manager yet."

Our Sheflin contacted me and told me the problem. I told her Monk and I would be there in under thirty minutes, as we could solve the problem. By the time we got there, our Sheflin and the UNICA were interrogating the guards. The manager still had not returned from lunch but was expected any minute. It did not take long for us to turn the guards into telling the truth, and their answers certainly would see the manager into a long custodial sentence.

The kitchen porter advised that the manager was on his way. He came straight into the hotel and into his office. The mothers were about to go in, but I stopped them. Monk and I approached the office door, knocked, and walked in. There was surprise on his face but no alarm.

"We would like to ask you some questions about human trafficking." Alarm now started to show. He pressed a buzzer on his desk, expecting five guards to come storming in—we were already reading his mind. I told him that they would not be coming. "They have told us about your illegal operation, the murder of the owner of this hotel and his family...you are facing a death sentence here in Turkey unless you cooperate." His hand slowly opened his desk drawer and pulled out a gun.

"I don't think so," he said and pointed the gun at me. I took control of his arm and the gun was now pointing at his head.

"I shouldn't pull the trigger. You will make a terrible mess on the desk."

Absolute terror filled his eyes. Monk went round the desk and recovered the gun from his hand. Ten minutes later, we had all the information we needed, and now guards and manager were puppets to UNICA. They would continue tonight's work as if nothing had happened to them, and the mothers and youngsters would continue their journey. The information the manager gave us, there would be two more stops, Istanbul, then on to Bucharest. Their fate would be decided there by people close to the top of the chain—those people would certainly know who was in charge. The manager and guards played their part getting the women onto the transport as per normal. The next link in the chain had no idea that the guards and managers had been turned. As soon as they had left for Istanbul, they were marched off to jail to stand trial. The Turkish employees at the hotel were innocent of any involvement in the chain and were told that they would run the hostel since the owner and his family had been killed.

There were only two guards and a driver, and it was a sixteen-hour drive to Bucharest. The logical stopover was Istanbul, which they could do overnight and miss the intense heat of the day—there was no air conditioning in the load area where are team were put; just two ventilators in the roof which helped, otherwise it would have been intolerable. There was an adequate supply of bottled water in an ice box, but no food. The UNICA were following some ten miles behind. The van stopped twice for fuel on its journey and arrived in Istanbul just before dawn—another hostel type hotel, near an industrial area on the outskirts of Istanbul. The rear doors opened, and the mothers and daughters were shown to their rooms directly. All were hungry, so a mother asked for food, and was told breakfast was at seven, which was an hour away.

Breakfast was traditionally Turkish with different breads, cold meats with cheese, honey, butter and jams. They were told to take thirty minutes, and it would be another long journey that evening and the next meal would be in Bucharest. Obediently, they left and went to the rooms on the first floor, having devoured the breakfast and taken some food for the journey. The rooms on the first floor were at the end of the corridor either side of the fire exit. After half an hour, they easily picked the lock, and all joined into one room. It seemed that this stopover was going to be like the last one. The difference was that the guards knew the van guards, and the driver were Romanian. It, therefore, stood to reason that they would continue the journey in the van with the same crew. Our Sheflin agreed with her mother on their observations. "When they leave this evening, that is the time we will go in an arrest this link in the chain. All we have to do is wait."

It was just before dark when they came for them. Once

in the van, they took off to the next destination. Thirty minutes later, the hostel was raided, and two guards were killed in the process. The rest surrendered, knowing that strings would be pulled, and they would be free in the morning. They said nothing at the main police station. They could detain them for twenty-four hours without access to lawyers, but then the legal people would have them out. The Turkish police had no qualms about slapping them to get them to talk. They only had to put up with it for twenty-four hours, so they continued to say nothing. Our Sheflin asked for help again.

Monk and I arrived and met with the prisoners one at a time and got them to tell everything. Whereas at the last hotel nothing gave us any leads to the men at the top. However, this whole gang were related either by blood or marriage. The manager was a second cousin to one of the top men. We had all their names and the many houses they took their victims to. Jon Bridges was impressed by this intelligence, and he decided to fly them all out of the country to The Hague. Cars were ordered, and the prisoners were on their way. It happened so quickly; the police informants could not inform their masters. The leader of this link in the chain did not know which house they would be taken, but what he did say was that their beauty would be put to use and would become addictive to heroin to make them more compliant to the eventual owner and do his bidding.

The house that had been assigned to them was not in Bucharest but on the black seacoast of Mamaia. It still took over eight hours before they arrived at a heavily guarded villa just a few minutes from the beach. The gate guards recognised the van immediately, and the electric gates slowly opened. The van made its way up the long drive and went round the rear of this exceptionally large villa. The basement had been converted into bedrooms and each of the mothers and daughters were shown to their assigned room. The rooms were not palatial but nice. Each had their own bathroom, and the wardrobe was full of nice clothes, on the table fresh fruit and some food; breakfast would be at eight o'clock. All mothers and daughters found the cameras and microphones. The doors were locked from the outside, as each mother had noticed on the way to their rooms. The daughters were still not as wise but knew enough to find all the surveillance equipment in their rooms. It was now that the Utopian bracelets came in use. There was no problem of getting out of the rooms for the mothers, but it could be tricky for the daughters. All the daughters checked in with the mothers—Our Sheflin had told them what to expect. It was agreed that breakfast would be the ideal opportunity to take over the villa.

Everyone agreed that this villa or dacha, belonged to one of the top people in the chain; it could even be the top man's place. The intention here was to make them dependent on drugs. No one would allow that to happen without a struggle. Their captors had no knowledge of how dangerous their captives are. It could only be one way; at some time, they would be put to sleep and awaken as drug addicts. All would refrain from eating or drinking what was supplied in each room and would take over the villa at breakfast before eating or drinking anything. With that agreed, all showered and put another show on for those at the other end of the lens. They were all glad to get out of the clothes they had been wearing for nearly a week. Their beauty was highlighted even more in their new clothes.

They were ordered to follow up a short staircase, and one could only assume it was the entrance lobby. From there, a large winding staircase led to three other floors with no guards to be seen. Two large doors on the opposite side of the lobby greeted them. The guard opened them, and they entered the dining room where they found a large table with just nine place settings. They assumed they would not be joined by anyone. The guard closed the door, and they took their seats. Two servants came out and poured them all coffee. When they returned to what must have been the kitchen, the two mothers and young Deflin sprang from their chairs. In a moment, all three guards were knocked out and tied up painfully. The five people in the kitchen were ordered into the dining room. Two panicking servants faces were first to be interrogated. From that we had found out, twenty-seven were in the villa, eight friends of the villa's owner were in rooms upstairs.

Mother Sheflin turned to a servant, "Can you get the gardeners in, as we don't want to hurt them?"

"I will call them in for coffee." Five minutes later, two bewildered gardeners were now tied to the dinning room chairs with the other servants.

A daughter opened the gates and fetched the van to load

the guards in. The mothers started at the top and worked their way down. It turned out that there were eight couples, and all were easily subdued. The eight were walked down the stairs into the dining room and tied to the chairs. All the guards were now dragged into the dining room.

Mother Sheflin went to one of the servants and asked, "Is there a safe?"

"Yes." She was too frightened to lie.

"Where?"

"In the office opposite the dining room."

The other mother went to find the safe and did so easily. It was a combination safe. She returned to the dining room and asked, "Does anyone know the combination?"

A helpful servant looked directly at one of the guests. Quickly, the mother went to the guy, placed a hand at the back of his neck, and pressed hard. He screamed.

"What's the combination?" Silence. This time, she placed two hands at the base of his neck and pressed. His whole body quaked as he screamed. She eased the pressure when he screamed out the combination. She left to open the safe.

As the tortured guy slowly regained his senses, he shouted, "Do you know who you're dealing with?"

"Yes—scum of the Earth. I would really like to kill you all."

You did not have to be a rocket scientist to see that their female company had track marks on their arms and no doubt on their legs.

"We are obliged to turn you over to the UNICA in one

piece." A faint grin appeared—he, like the others yesterday, thought he would be back on the streets within a day. The mother returned with lots of cash, loads of documents, a laptop, and several memory sticks.

"Take the cash and close the safe."

"I will need some help." Two daughters followed her back to the office; they emptied the safe and put the cash in the van. It was timed to perfection. The UNICA arrived as the daughters and mother arrived back in the dining room. Looking at the dossier, Jon Bridges knew some of the captors and was sure these people would know who was in charge. He had to move rapidly, and once again called on Monk's and my services. We arrived and got them telling everything they knew. There was one man left—the top of the hierarchy, and he was in Bucharest. He would be heavily guarded. The safe had enough incriminating evidence to take them to The Hague.

CHAPTER 39

ILILYA ABESCU HAD JUST FINISHED his morning workout. He had a light breakfast and made his way to his office to catch up on the things his criminal empire had done. He got to the video link from the villa and watched the young girls. "These will make a fortune; even the old ones are worth a lot." He thought he recognised one of the old ones. He zoomed in on to her face—it was the face he would never forget. This woman killed his brother and the brother's son. It had to be a trap. He rushed to the phone and phoned the villa. It took a long time to answer, but eventually it was answered.

"Kill them! Kill them all! It's a trap!"

There was silence from the other end of the phone

before the Mother Sheflin spoke, "It's a bit late for that. They are now my prisoners, and I am coming for you."

Ililya slammed the phone down and called his head of security. "Get my plane ready. We are leaving. We have been compromised, and they're coming here to kill me."

"They will never get past the gates," the head of security said.

"You don't know these people. You, and all the security we have, are no match for them. They killed my brother and my nephew. They were protected too, but all that was left was bodies...lots of them. We have two hours, and I want to be a long way from here."

Mother Sheflin put the phone down. "Robin, how long would it take to get to Bucharest?"

I turned to Monk, we both looked surprised as neither of us knew where it was in relation to where we were.

Jon said, "We are about a two-hour car journey."

"Two minutes," Monk said.

"Can you take us? He will disappear if we give him that amount of time."

"Of course."

"I am coming too," demanded Jon.

"You will have to leave that gun behind." He handed it to one of his team. "Get them all to The Hague with the contents of the safe. Also get another team ready in Bucharest. Wait for my call."

We all walked towards the verticular, and the portal opened to let us in—sheer wonderment for our first timers in this transport. In under two minutes, we were on the grounds of Ililya's fortress home. Mother Sheflin told us to wait while they checked the grounds. CCTV was everywhere, but the women easily slipped past it. I thought I would give them a hand and asked the verticular if it could neutralise the CCTV and communications system. In seconds, their sophisticated security system was dead, but it put them on alert. Everything happened so quickly. With no communications, they ran around like headless chickens and were easily taken out. The grounds and gatehouse had been neutralised; it now only left the house, where five cars were parked. Mother Sheflin asked if we could do something about the cars, and twenty seconds later, no cars.

The nine females climbed the outside wall as if they were spiders. They would start at the top of the house and work their way down. They checked each floor—nothing. All must be on the ground floor. The women took stock of the situation and watched for at least five minutes. Signing their instructions, all knew what to do. The guards were disabled quickly, leaving just Ililya standing. He aimed his gun at her, and she leapt and kicked it out of his hand before he could get a shot off. He was in agony; the kick had broken his wrist and his bone was protruding from his skin.

"That looks painful," she said. "I told you I was coming for you."

"We have done nothing against you. It was my brother who offended you."

"Your whole business offends me. You turn desperate women and girls into drug addicts. I know drugs are freely available now in most countries, but you doctored them, so they are dependent on your drug only and whoever you sell them on to."

"If you let me go, there's over five million in those cases."

She pointed to the daughters. "Put them somewhere safe. No need for that to go to The Hague." She turned to Ililya. "Let you go? I would rather kill you so painfully you will be begging to die, but they want you to stand trial to be a lesson to all the other people traffickers." She then told us all was safe, and we entered. We put the cars back, and the Bucharest team was on their way. Monk and I got them all telling the truth, and we took our leave. Mission accomplished.

The debrief was held in New York and took two days much to the delight of the daughters. The information they had found together with the defendants' written statements...over another thousand arrest warrants had been served. Judges, police, and politicians had been arrested; it was the largest criminal case in the history of the world. The United Nations Secretary-General congratulated the team on behalf of a thankful world. The cash was never found, but no one was looking extremely hard, and Ililya five beach properties had been confiscated and auctioned, the proceeds going to the rehabilitation of those women violated by his organisation.

CHAPTER 40

IT WAS NOT QUITE NINE YEARS since Oblivion left our part of the universe. The newly developing worlds were full of terror, hatred, and evil, which he fed on and made him stronger. As long as Earth existed, he would never be strong enough to take on Infinity, so he alone could conjoin with Eternity. He had tried to destroy Earth from the inside, which was foiled by the Utopians. It was time to try something else. Summoning up a tremendous force, he pushed a comet out of its natural orbit to intercept a meteor in Earth's natural orbit, to crash into the planet with such force; it would turn Earth into dust. It would take over a year, but just a blink of an eye for an Immortal.

CHAPTER 41

THE WORLD WAS COOLING DOWN; freshwater was in abundance, and deserts were now inland seas. The refugee problem had long been sorted—food and work were plentiful. Political masters who abused their power were held responsible and had no escape from the power of the United Nations. Fossil fuels were nearly phased out, and renewable energy accounted for 95% of the Earth's energy requirements. Earth Corp were still investing in new ideas and funding those in the early stages.

The United Nations were the governing force of the world. The armed forces of every country in the world answered to the United Nations. The armed forces had a primary duty of defending their respective countries and not step outside their borders unless by UN mandate. Russia and China were still not full members, so America's armed forces had remained at the same level and would act if called upon by the UN.

Space exploration was proving expensive for individual nations, and early in the evolving new United Nations, all participants in the space programme agreed to cooperate, and massive leaps were made, despite no more manned missions taking place. Several more orbital telescopes were launched, sending tremendous amounts of data back to Earth for analysis.

The Xuntian Space Observatory in China were the first to see a new comet in our solar system. They informed the observatories around the world and now every telescope on Earth and in space allocated time to observe this new addition to our solar system. Its trajectory was deemed non-threatening to Earth—in fact, it seemed to move away from Earth, heading towards the asteroid belt. At its current speed, it would take two months to reach the asteroid belt.

Computer simulations were made of the comet, and if it came in contact with an asteroid, what would be the prognosis? The world's top astrological scientists came to a consensus that there was no threat to Earth, but they would track it 24/7. Governments were alerted and advised and would be kept updated.

John Henderson, an astrological fellow at Cambridge university, had taken a keen interest in the new comet. From its trajectory, he had calculated that it should be visible every 70 years, so why had it not been seen before? It was a puzzle. He put all the information he had into a computer model; it would take at least twenty-four hours for the computer to churn out the data. The following day, he studied various scenarios the computer came up with. All assured of no threat, except one where it would collide with Vesta, the second largest asteroid in our solar system at over five hundred kilometres in diameter. He needed more brain and computer power, so he contacted a friend at Jodrell Bank, who agreed that it was a possibility. He would put the information into his computer that the comet would hit Vesta and many variables, including impact speeds of up to a hundred thousand miles per hour. It would take a few hours on the larger computer, long enough for John to travel to Jodrell Bank.

It took over three hours to get to Jodrell Bank. His friend met him at security and signed him in. The computer churned away and would have several computations in about forty minutes. His friend took him to the director of Jodrell Bank and introduced him. Coffee came as they patiently waited for the computer to finish. Five computations showed that the impact of the comet on Vesta at maximum velocity would be equivalent to a five million megaton atom bomb. It would obliterate Vesta into so many pieces and would knock it out of the asteroid belt, and a piece could eventually end up in Earth's trajectory. It was truly a doomsday scenario. The information was shared immediately, and all eyes were now on the comet. It was not necessary that any of the ninety computations would happen.

"The percentages were in our favour," the director said.

John replied, "I am not so sure. The comet has just appeared. It should have been visible every seventy years, but it hasn't."

"We will know if you're right in a fortnights time," replied the director. "We must just sit tight and wait"

John could not take his eyes off it, and its speed had significantly increased. Now that it was in the sun's orbit, he had calculated that it would hit Vesta at ninety-three thousand miles per hour. Most of the scientific world were playing the odds and were not as concerned as John and the Jodrell Bank team were. The director was a friend of our Prime Minister and had advised him not to be complacent as the rest of the scientific world. He told the Prime Minister, "We feel that the Earth is in peril, and we need to take steps. If our scenario happens, we have just under a year to find a defence strategy to destroy it before it destroys us."

I was quite surprised when the Prime Minister contacted me and relayed the information. I had heard about this new comet, but everyone was playing it down. When he said this guy John Henderson reckoned the whole scenario could destroy Earth, I reckoned the sudden appearance had to have been orchestrated. It had all the hallmarks of an Oblivion threat. We could not look to Utopia for help as all the remarkable science was Earth-based. Earth was on its own.

Every space station was now fixed on the imminent

explosion on Vesta. Though the collision was being played down, some broadcasters would show it live around the world. I sat at home to watch the impact on television. We would not learn anything from the actual impact until sometime after. The impact happened; it was like a snooker break, but slowly, the clear void filled with debris and dust consumed vast areas of space. Visual examination was becoming impossible and infrared and ultraviolet had to be used. The explosion area was vast. Two thirds of the asteroid belt became a grey mass of enormity. Infrared signals showed asteroids colliding with each other, cannoning off one and propelling towards another. It would be some time before the asteroid belt would settle down, but no immediate threat was visible according to the scientists.

Three weeks later, the asteroid belt had settled—it was still a grey mass but movements within the belt had slowed down, and comparisons were being made before and after impact. Most of the activity was away from Earth, past Jupiter and beyond. Two new asteroids had appeared and had been pushed out of the asteroid belt, and all the scientific eyes were now on these two asteroids. It was too soon to work out a trajectory as the error in margin on so little information would be acute.

Jodrell Bank were working in real time, and the movement of both asteroids were fed into the computer minute by minute. It took a week for the computer to come from 'no problem' to 'probable collision with Earth'. This information was shared around the world, and all the scientists agreed with the prognosis. The details of the exact size and shape of both asteroids quickly came up, and the trajectories of both were calculated. One would miss Earth by half a million miles, our moon by two hundred thousand miles; the other would miss us by one hundred thousand miles and pass between Earth and the moon. Both asteroids were of similar size, three and a half kilometres in diameter. It was now deemed a positive threat to Earth.

The United Nations summoned the best scientific and military brains for the global problem that needed combined effort. They all agreed that the timescale to come up with a plan was just over a year. It was quickly decided that both asteroids needed to be taken out, and a plan would be made. Should it not be necessary for one of the asteroids, all resources would be directed at the other. The military said a hundred megaton thermal nuclear device would be needed for each asteroid.

The chairman of the committee asked, "Do we still have that ordnance since every country signed a treaty banning the use and development of such weapons?"

Representatives from America, Russia and China said they still had sufficient material to produce a bomb capable of a hundred-mega-tonne yield. The delivery system was next, converting an Intercontinental Ballistic Missile (ICBM) to deep space would take two years to design and build, so it had to be a manned mission.

The chairman asked, "Do we have the manpower and equipment to achieve this?"

A NASA spokesman said, "We have our manned Mars

mission rocket which could be ready in the timescale to be effective."

China and Russia said they had similar size rockets for a Mars expedition. All said they had trained crew ready to go.

"How long would it take to get up to speed on the deployment of the thermal devices?" the chairman asked.

"Two weeks intensive training," said the American military delegate.

"Let's do it," the chairman said.

Landing on Mars to landing on a piece of rock was going to be different. The pilots and co-pilots went through the procedure so many times they all could do it in their sleep. The other four members were shown how to arm and detonate the thermal device safely until they could do it blindfolded. The course to interception was circuitous to get the craft to match the speed of the asteroid so they would be able to land as if stationary. The journey would take three months. All three craft would be utilised—one would be back up. The launch of the crafts went without a hitch; the course plotted and regularly corrected to ensure arrival. It had been decided that the Russian rocket would attack the asteroid heading for Earth and the Chinese the other one. The crew of the American craft were to be back up and had two thermal devices should anything happen to the other crafts.

It took just over three months to intercept the asteroids. Both the Chinese and Russian craft were now alongside their targets. Two crew members entered the small landing vehicle that would detach from the mother craft. It detached and landed on the surface of the asteroid with a huge bump and they found a large-enough fissure to place and arm the device. It was only when the Russian crew tried to take off to join the mothership that the problem occurred, unlike on the Chinese drone—although the bump had been hard, it had not effected their take-off, so they joined the mothership. The Russian crew, however, were stuck on the asteroid. The Russian captain decided that it was foolish to attempt to land the mothership and that unless the drone crew could fix the drone, they would be sacrificed. The American backup crew monitored the radio conversation. The Chinese ship was too far for their drone to make a rescue. They told the Russian mothership they would rescue their comrades and asked how much air their suits had.

"Eighty minutes."

"That should be enough. Tell your men to climb on top of the drone and undo the magnets that help in docking and put them in their suit pockets. We won't land; we will come in low so they can cling onto the feet of our drone, and we can lift them to your space door. The magnets should keep them there until you can get an umbilical to them and bring them inside."

It all worked like clockwork. Mission accomplished. All were back on their mothership. The devices were to detonate in six hours, giving them plenty of time to get out of the way of the blast. Pleased with the mission, all would wait until the detonation before returning to Earth.

From Earth, two blips appeared and lasted about two minutes. The space crews returned home. Celebrations were round in the military and scientific world. Danger to Earth had averted. Or had it?

EPILOGUE

UNSEEN IN THE EXPLOSION by the three crew, a slither of asteroid, the shape of an aircraft wing, weighing seventy-five tonnes, four hundred metres in length and a hundred metres wide. The leading edge was five centimetres, and the rear edge was forty centimetres, making it invisible to all of Earth's telescopes. It had broken away from the asteroid after the explosion, which pushed the slither of the asteroid into a direct path towards Earth. The suns gravitational force would ensure that the asteroid would enter Earth's atmosphere at a hundred thousand miles per hour. It would take about five months to reach Earth and would only be visible after it had entered Earth's atmosphere, minutes from impact. It was too large to be burnt up in our atmosphere, and a large amount of it would hit the Earth. The impact of seventy-five tonnes hitting the Earth at hundred thousand miles per hour would be disastrous and equivalent to a hundred-million-megaton atomic bomb so powerful it could puncture a hole down to the Earth's core.

The United Nations had formed their own space agency, combining NASA and the European, Indian, and Japanese space agencies. Despite not being full members of the United Nations, Russia and China had allowed their agencies to work with the combined space agency. The UN agency had put four more space stations in differing orbits so to have Earth covered from every angle. The old but still functioning Russian, Chinese, and American space stations were still in a manned operation. The Chinese space station was by far the furthest out, and the crew were on the station for a year. The station was over twenty years old and needed constant repair, and its hull was continually being bombarded by meteor fragments—they had developed mechanical drones to replace the parts of the hull which were affected. The drones were operated remotely by the crew from inside the station. Several cameras were fixed to the drone, so the operator had a three sixty-degree view of the area he was working.

A drone was on its way to relace a panel when a camera picked up a momentary flash, it lasted not even a second, but the operator directed more cameras and started recording. It took just twenty seconds before it was too far away. Immediately, all the other space stations were asked to search for this object, and the film downloaded to

Chinese space agency, who immediately forwarded it to the UN space agency. Alarm bells sounded at the UN agency. Whatever the object was it would collide with Earth; when and where were the next tasks. All Earth's and space telescopes were now searching for the object, which was proving difficult because of its shape and speed. The object was found after adjusting the focus to its maximum. It would hit Earth's atmosphere in just over seven hours, but where?

The best brains determined that it would hit the Pacific or the Indian oceans. However, the dilemma was the shape and how the trajectory would change upon entering our atmosphere. There was no data for such a large object. The closest was the Russian space station that fell to Earth; most burnt up and the debris that hit Earth covered two continents. All concluded that the likelihood of the object breaking up was a long shot. If it hit land, the force could rip a hole to the Earth's core, and if it hit the ocean, the water would certainly slow it down, but it would still make a hole in the Earth's crust. Both scenarios were doomsday.

The military were put on a video link and asked if they could blow it up. The military said they could turn it into dust if they could hit it, but the speed would make it impossible. "We would need to intercept the meteor with so many drones that the object would fly into it. If all the drones have enough ordnance on them, that one hit will do the trick. No more meteor. Positioning the drones so they are in the exact path requires pinpoint targeting. Will we have that?"

"Yes, you will."

"How many drones will you need?"

"Assuming one drone's firepower should be enough to blow it to smithereens and putting additional safety margins in place, and contingency, twenty-one should do it. Three formations of seven will be enough." The confidence in which the military spoke diluted the major concern the Secretary-General. If the military missed their target, there was no failsafe.

The Secretary-General updated me on the crisis and that there was no failsafe, should the military fail.

"Okay, I will have word with my people and see what they come up with."

I put the question to the team, and they all came back with the same answers—it would be catastrophic if it hit earth or sea. We needed a backstop. Professor Dave Mac advised that it could almost destroy some or most of Utopia and if anyone could have a way out, it would be with their technology. I took the whole team down to the technical area of Utopia. The First Principal met us there and was bought up to speed. We had just under six hours before the meteorite would hit Earth. We had eventually learned to communicate with the droids effectively and told them the situation and the probability it could destroy Utopia. If alarm bells rang in the droids, it was the closet thing to it. The droid's sole purpose was to defend Utopia. But this was way outside their scope.

A verticular was sent to the surface to locate the meteorite and lock on to it, so exact measurements could be taken. It seemed that the concern was not the object itself but its speed. We were all watching the droids. All verticular were now in the technical area, and the droids were working on them. An hour had gone by, and the verticular were now on station, waiting for the arrival of the meteorite, having dropped the team off at Assington.

We had live feed from all the tracking stations. The trajectory of the meteorite was putting impact around the Indian Ocean. The military were in a bullish mood—the twenty-one drones with concrete busting warheads would easily do the trick. The first row would be enough to destroy the meteorite, the others were just in reserve. It was not until the UN team pointed out that the speed of the meteorite would be so fast that the split second at detonation would let the object pass. All the drones would have to be detonated together in a wall of explosive power that the meteorite would be destroyed within it. All was agreed. The drones would be detonated together.

The global press got hold of the story. The destruction would be filmed by the drones up to the point of detonation. The United Nations navy, which primarily was the US navy having been seconded to the UN, were on station in the Indian Ocean USS Lakenheath and Mildenhall both aircraft carriers. All their helicopters would be deployed to film after the detonation of the drones. The whole world were in front of their TV screens, and there was a countdown timer to impact at the top of the screens.

The timer reached zero. What happened next was over in seconds. The drones failed to stop it but altered its trajectory and slowed it down. It hit the foothills of the Himalayas and bounced off them and started to ascend. Everest was in the way, and the meteorite sliced through it like a hot knife through butter, shaving two thousand feet off.

What had happened at the point of impact was five verticular had superimposed their force shields into one. All five had sacrificed their existence to save Utopia. Number Six verticular was damaged but could still operate. Number Seven had slight damage, and Eight to Twenty-four: their force fields held and redirected the meteorite upwards. With the threat eliminated Six, Seven and Eight stayed to clean up the impact site. No remains of One to Five could be left for the world to see. Although mechanical, all the verticular were sentient, and there was sadness in all of them for their stricken comrades. When the impact site was inspected by the scientific community, they would find a perfectly round hole, over nine hundred metres in diameter and seven metres deep. The bottom was as smooth as a bowling green, and that was all they would find. It would be an unresolved mystery for a long time.

The meteorite was cooling and velocity was decreasing. Radar was the only way to keep up with its momentum. It travelled in a north-westerly direction and gaining height was slowing it down. By the time it got over Europe, it had lost speed but had reached the edge of the thermosphere and nearly made it back into space. With no more momentum, it started to fall back to Earth. It would make a thump as seventy-five tonnes would, but its shape would slow the descent as air pressure would build up underneath the meteorite, slowing it to half the gravitational pull of the Earth from 120 feet per second to half that. It would take about forty-five minutes to land. Everyone was working out where—so many variables to consider. First results estimated it would fall into the sea between Iceland and the North of Scotland. Two Typhoons were scrambled from RAF Lossiemouth to intercept the meteorite and follow it down to wherever. The science community were extremely interested in the meteorite's structure as the heat from entry had not reduced its size, the detonation of the drones had not harmed it.

The Typhoons used their targeting radar to lock onto the meteorite and followed its journey to the sea. It looked as if it would hit the sea about ten miles north of Cape Wrath. The meteorite was at thirty thousand feet. Both pilots went supersonic and flew under the meteorite, sucking the air from underneath it to guide it into following the wake of the aircraft. This manoeuvre made the meteorite land on the ground instead of the sea. It took another eight minutes to land in a middle of a potato field owned by a hippy commune—no one was hurt. The pilots radioed the co-ordinates back to Lossiemouth.

A detachment of special air service were at Cape Wrath training centre and were immediately ordered to secure the meteorite until it could be transported to safety. No one reckoned it was on private property, and the commune had no TV, so the locals were oblivious of what was about to take place. Five army vehicles sped across what was left of the potato field, ruining the rest of the crop. The troops leapt out of their vehicles and rushed to the meteorite, and were met by annoyed commune members who had gathered round the object. The members of the commune were mostly people that had become disillusioned with the drudgery of capitalism and sought life as far from it as possible. The leaders of the commune were a husband-and-wife barrister team and were Kings Council and nobody's fools. The curious communes had time to have a good look at the object. They had brought tools in a hope that could break it up into smaller pieces and hopefully save some or all of the crop. The tools were magnetically attracted to the object and those holding them had to let go. As hard as they tried, they could not remove their tools from the object.

The object was still warm, and they concluded it was a metallic and had a massive bubble at least three hundred metres in diameter in the middle. It looked like a giant drum cymbal with around twenty-one smaller bubble—more like blisters.

The lieutenant leapt from his vehicle, closely followed by his men, who quickly surrounded the meteorite. All their weapons were torn from their hands by the magnetism, and they watched in disbelief as each tried to recover their weapons from the meteorite with absolutely no success.

The leader of the commune spoke, "What right do you have in coming on private property?"

"I have orders to find and secure this object until further notice."

"You and this thing have decimated our potato crop, and it's going nowhere until we have been compensated fully."

The lieutenant told them that compensation would be paid in full, which took the heat out of the conversation. The commune now deemed no threat. The military started to live stream the meteorite info back to base to work out away to move it. The scientists back at base determined that it was all the same material and advised to cut it into smaller pieces for transport. The military vehicles on site had some industrial power tools which were rendered useless as they approached the meteorite and were and stuck to the meteorite. Four plasma lances and skilled operators were helicoptered to Cape Wrath to assist. On the flight in, the pilot radioed ahead and told them there was a cavalcade of TV vans and off-road vehicles heading for the site. the lieutenant told his troops to secure the roads and stop the press from entering the site until the plasma lances arrived.

Assington was in relief—a catastrophe had been averted. Monk excused himself and was back with bad news twenty minutes later. The verticular that was back on station at Assington had relayed to Monk that One to Five no longer existed and had a request to collect the meteorite and take it to Utopia for analysis. I knew the whole world would want a piece of it, but the sacrifice of the verticular...how could I say no to them? If it were not for them, it would have ripped through the earths crust and caused widespread devastation and maybe the end of Earth. It would never have been found, so I agreed that they could have it. It was not my call but then again it was not anybody else's. A couple of military satellites were continually targeting the small part of Cape Wrath and Stephen had linked up with them, so we were watching live footage. The military kept the press away while all in the commune were interviewed, so the meteorite was on its own. Four distinct shimmers appeared for a spilt second; four beams projected at the meteorite, and it slowly started to disappear. By the time the satellites could relay what was happening, it was gone. The plasma team got to the site and found a large indentation in a potato field, not one piece of the meteorite was left.

It did not take long for the Prime Minister to contact me—he knew that I had to be involved. I simply told him my reasons and would stand by them come what may. "I can promise you that when we know what it is, it will be shared with the world." I had two days of saying the same thing to those that knew about Utopia. The rest of the world's press, including Media Corp, believed a conspiracy theory that a secret weapon of the Chinese, Russians or Americans had stolen it.

Monk arrived with a report on the meteorite. It was a new element one thousand times harder than diamond, with tremendous magnetic abilities. Utopia technology had evolved beyond metal usage, so the magnetism of the meteorite proved not to be a problem for them. The droids were at a loss; nothing could assist them in finding out what the object was made of. Reluctantly, they would make it available to the surface population to identify the properties of the meteorite. Monk had asked where they should send it and who to. I threw the question out to the UN and received a list of countries and universities that would do the research. China and Russia were not included as they were still not full members.

The droids had easily managed to cut the meteorite up into pieces, but keeping them separate was the problem; the pieces had to be over three hundred metres apart to avoid the attraction force. Should two pieces come together, you really wouldn't want to be in the way.

Pieces of the meteorite were shared with all those countries that had asked for it. Special containment laboratories were hastily erected to contain parts of the meteorite as there had been some serious accidents with people getting in the way. The magnetic force it exerted could be of great value, if it could be harnessed. The cost of doing anything with it would outweigh any advantage with our current technology and most countries decided to hand back their samples and wait for the technology to catch up. Scientists had been studying what the meteorite was and why it had these properties. It was the University of Durham that determined that it was part of the core of an exploding sun. All asteroids in the asteroid belt could be pieces of the sun cores just far enough away not to join. The returned samples were released safely and reunited to the meteorite. Seven countries kept hold of their samples, trying to find ways of harnessing the magnetic energy. For them it was a long way to go. There were now more theories than answers, but the world was safe...for now.

Thanks for reading! Please leave a short review on Amazon, and let me know what you thought!

APPENDIX

United Nations Human Rights Charter

Article 1: All human beings are born free and equal in dignity and rights. They are endowed with reason and conscience and should act towards one another in a spirit of brotherhood.

Article 2: Everyone is entitled to all the rights and freedoms set forth in this Declaration, without distinction of any kind, such as race, colour, sex, language, religion, political or other opinion, national or social origin, property, birth, or other status. Furthermore, no distinction shall be made on the basis of the political, jurisdictional, or international status of the country or territory to which a person belongs, whether it be independent, trust, non-self-governing or under any other limitation of sovereignty.

Article 3: Everyone has the right to life, liberty, and security of a person.

Article 4: No one shall be held in slavery or servitude; slavery and the slave trade shall be prohibited in all their forms.

Article 5: No one shall be subjected to torture or to cruel, inhuman or degrading treatment or punishment.

Article 6: Everyone has the right to recognition everywhere as a person before the law.

Article 7: All are equal before the law and are entitled without any discrimination to equal protection of the law.

All are entitled to equal protection against any discrimination in violation of this Declaration and against any incitement to such discrimination.

Article 8: Everyone has the right to an effective remedy by the competent national tribunals for acts violating the fundamental rights granted him by the constitution or by law.

Article 9: No one shall be subjected to arbitrary arrest, detention, or exile.

Article 10: Everyone is entitled in full equality to a fair and public hearing by an independent and impartial tribunal, in the determination of his rights and obligations and of any criminal charge against him.

Article 11: (1) Everyone charged with a penal offence has the right to be presumed innocent until proved guilty according to law in a public trial at which he has had all the guarantees necessary for his defence. (2) No one shall be held guilty of any penal offence on account of any act or omission which did not constitute a penal offence, under national or international law, at the time when it was committed. Nor shall a heavier penalty be imposed than the one that was applicable at the time the penal offence was committed.

Article 12: No one shall be subjected to arbitrary interference with his privacy, family, home, or correspondence, nor to attacks upon his honour and reputation. Everyone has the right to the protection of the law against such interference or attacks.

Article 13: (1) Everyone has the right to freedom of

movement and residence within the borders of each state. (2) Everyone has the right to leave any country, including his own, and to return to his country.

Article 14: (1) Everyone has the right to seek and to enjoy in other countries asylum from persecution. (2) This right may not be invoked in the case of prosecutions genuinely arising from non-political crimes or from acts contrary to the purposes and principles of the United Nations.

Article 15: (1) Everyone has the right to a nationality. (2) No one shall be arbitrarily deprived of his nationality nor denied the right to change his nationality.

Article 16: (1) Men and women of full age, without any limitation due to race, nationality, or religion, have the right to marry and to find a family. They are entitled to equal rights as to marriage, during marriage and at its dissolution. (2) Marriage shall be entered into only with the free and full consent of the intending spouses. (3) The family is the natural and fundamental group unit of society and is entitled to protection by society and the State.

Article 17: (1) Everyone has the right to own property alone as well as in association with others. (2) No one shall be arbitrarily deprived of his property.

Article 18: Everyone has the right to freedom of thought, conscience, and religion; this right includes freedom to change his religion or belief, and freedom, either alone or in community with others and in public or private, to manifest his religion or belief in teaching, practice, worship and observance.

Article 19: Everyone has the right to freedom of opinion

and expression; this right includes freedom to hold opinions without interference and to seek, receive and impart information and ideas through any media and regardless of frontiers.

Article 20: (1) Everyone has the right to freedom of peaceful assembly and association. (2) No one may be compelled to belong to an association.

Article 21: (1) Everyone has the right to take part in the government of his country, directly or through freely chosen representatives. (2) Everyone has the right of equal access to public service in his country. (3) The will of the people shall be the basis of the authority of government; this will shall be expressed in periodic and genuine elections which shall be by universal and equal suffrage and shall be held by secret vote or by equivalent free voting procedures.

Article 22: Everyone, as a member of society, has the right to social security and is entitled to realisation, through national effort and international cooperation and in accordance with the organisation and resources of each state, of the economic, social, and cultural rights indispensable for his dignity and the free development of his personality.

Article 23: (1) Everyone has the right to work, to free choice of employment, to just and favourable conditions of work and to protection against unemployment. (2) Everyone, without any discrimination, has the right to equal pay for equal work. (3) Everyone who works has the right to just and favourable remuneration ensuring for himself and his family an existence worthy of human dignity, and supplemented, if necessary, by other means of social protection. (4) Everyone has the right to form and to join trade unions for the protection of his interests.

Article 24: Everyone has the right to rest and leisure, including reasonable limitation of working hours and periodic holidays with pay.

Article 25: (1) Everyone has the right to a standard of living adequate for the health and well-being of himself and of his family, including food, clothing, and housing and medical care and necessary social services, and the right to security in the event of unemployment, sickness, disability, widowhood, old age, or other lack of livelihood in circumstances beyond his control. (2) Motherhood and childhood are entitled to special care and assistance. All children, whether born in or out of wedlock, shall enjoy the same social protection.

Article 26: (1) Everyone has the right to education. Education shall be free, at least in the elementary and fundamental stages. Elementary education shall be compulsory. Technical and professional education shall be made generally available and higher education shall be equally accessible to all based on merit. (2) Education shall be directed to the full development of the human personality and to the strengthening of respect for human rights and fundamental freedoms. It shall promote understanding, tolerance, and friendship among all nations, racial or religious groups, and shall further the activities of the United Nations for the maintenance of peace. (3)

Parents have a prior right to choose the kind of education that shall be given to their children.

Article 27: (1) Everyone has the right freely to participate in the cultural life of the community, to enjoy the arts and to share in scientific advancement and its benefits. (2) Everyone has the right to the protection of the moral and material interests resulting from any scientific, literary, or artistic production of which he is the author.

Article 28: Everyone is entitled to a social and international order in which the rights and freedoms set forth in this Declaration can be fully realised.

Article 29: (1) Everyone has duties to the community in which alone the free and full development of his personality is possible. (2) In the exercise of his rights and freedoms, everyone shall be subject only to such limitations as are determined by law solely for the purpose of securing due recognition and respect for the rights and freedoms of others and of meeting the just requirements of morality, public order, and the general welfare in a democratic society. (3) These rights and freedoms may in no case be exercised contrary to the purposes and principles of the United Nations.

Article 30: Nothing in this Declaration may be interpreted as implying for any state, group, or person any right to engage in any activity or to perform any act aimed at the destruction of any of the rights and freedoms set forth herein.